Angel and the Ivory Tower

Don McAllister

authorHOUSE®

AuthorHouse™
1663 Liberty Drive
Bloomington, IN 47403
www.authorhouse.com
Phone: 1-800-839-8640

This book is a work of fiction. People, places, events, and situations are the product of the author's imagination. Any resemblance to actual persons, living or dead, or historical events, is purely coincidental.

© 2009 Don McAllister. All rights reserved.

No part of this book may be reproduced, stored in a retrieval system, or transmitted by any means without the written permission of the author.

First published by AuthorHouse 12/28/2009

ISBN: 978-1-4490-5221-8 (e)
ISBN: 978-1-4490-5219-5 (sc)
ISBN: 978-1-4490-5220-1 (hc)

Library of Congress Control Number: 2009913755

Printed in the United States of America
Bloomington, Indiana

This book is printed on acid-free paper.

In 1968 I was in my junior year of high school. My English teacher was Mr. Clyde Remo. I loved the colorful way he taught and how he led us to express ourselves through creative writing. I swore then that if I ever wrote a book I would dedicate it to him.

This is for you Mr. Remo.
Sorry it took so long.
I was sort of hoping for at least a C+

Table of Contents

Dedication		v
Acknowledgements		ix
Forward		xi
Chapter 1	The Summer Job	1
Chapter 2	The Soiled Virgin	5
Chapter 3	The Story Begins	9
Chapter 4	A Whirlwind of the Most Magnificent Sort	17
Chapter 5	Christmas in the White House	25
Chapter 6	Christmas Day	31
Chapter 7	Home to Saugerties	39
Chapter 8	Butterfly Days	47
Chapter 9	The Gadget Factory	53
Chapter 10	Down the Hudson to See the World	59
Chapter 11	Winter in France	65
Chapter 12	The Frozen Tears	75
Chapter 13	Orphan Girl	91
Chapter 14	Small Girl Big Town	97
Chapter 15	Mother Midge	105
Chapter 16	Fighting Back	115
Chapter 17	Bringing up Mother	125
Chapter 18	The Great Roscoe	135
Chapter 19	Newlyweds	147
Chapter 20	Vagabond Days	153
Chapter 21	Widow	161

Chapter 22	The Great In Between	167
Chapter 23	The Business Pilot	173
Chapter 24	We Did a Lot of Praying	191
Chapter 25	The Great Depression	201
Chapter 26	World War Alice	213
Chapter 27	Ethel	237
Chapter 28	The Enchanted Amish	245

Acknowledgements

I must first thank my brother Dave for the editing and encouragement as I fed him chapter after chapter. Dick Beamer was also very helpful with his many insights and challenges as he read over the work.

My sample readers Nancy Tatum and Debbie Holdzkom gave me a feel of the readability and general appeal of the work. The fact that Nancy stayed up all night reading the book straight through because she "wanted to know what Great Aunt Alice would do next" gave me some indication that I was on the right track with A&I.

My wife Sue, our son John, and our dog Jasper get the lion's share of credit for putting up with my loud typing late at night and early in the morning. I hope this pays off enough to make up for some of my long trips to Bauerhoff.

The encouragement of Cheryl Greene, Lori Ostrander, and Gary Clayton was greatly appreciated as they followed my crazy whim daily "publication" of the work on Facebook. With the limitation of 420 characters per post it took me 15 days just to post chapter 2.

My friend Hershel McCorkle has been plagued for years with my developing plans and schemes, so why should this be an exception? Thanks for listening to my many drafts.

My model for the character Rowe Montillo was the real Rowe Montillo, a combat Riverine in Vietnam. Everything about his look and personality fit the character so well. He really is a great man and a terrific friend. I hope his dear wife can forgive his near "affair" with Angel Burke. Great Aunt Alice assures me that he was a perfect gentleman at all times.

Frank and Nancy Mack are real people as well. Frank was a Marine Corpsman on Okinawa in World War II and a man who was magnificent beyond description. Nancy is just as kind in person as she is in the book. On December 2, 2008 I traveled with some friends to the Mack home. Frank was dying of cancer at the time. I left Nancy a copy of the chapter that highlighted them. I don't know if Frank was able to read it, but I can assure you that Frank was the greatest of men and we all miss him dearly.

I would like to thank the University for firing Great Nephew so he would be forced to capture Great Aunt Alice's story. Still I won't be sending my kids there as they were pretty heartless for letting Great Nephew go.

Many thanks to my friend Dick Whitaker for introducing me to his hometown of Saugerties, New York. It really is a beautiful part of our world.

Most of all I want to thank you for purchasing this work, and for keeping Great Aunt Alice's memory alive and Great Nephew better fed. I hope you will enjoy this story and be truly blessed in your own adventures.

Drawn by Karen Kovich (karenkovich.com)

Forward

As you can see by the caricature I love to ride my bike and there is no place I like to ride better than Southern Indiana's fall classic, the Hilly Hundred. There is one monster hill on the ride that has its own persona. As the saying goes, "All the rest are just hills, Mt. Tabor is personal." While it is not the longest hill on the ride it is a monster sight. Rounding the corner it rises like a wall for about two tenths of a mile. Many give up and walk its length. Others grind it out to the top where it gets steeper, and where one can sometimes feel the front tire lift off the pavement.

Approaching my 25th Hilly I had experienced some heart related problems and had not ridden very much. Still I was doing pretty well. I had climbed all of the hills non-stop on Saturday's ride and had completed all of the hills to that point on Sunday. As I approached Tabor I knew I would have to walk at least part of the hill, and I longed to be able to ride it to the top one more time and maybe even feel the tire lift from the pavement.

At the bottom of the hill my hopes were dashed as I threw the chain. To climb Tabor from a dead stop was beyond comprehension. I put the chain back on and put the bike into my granny gear, thinking I would ride up as far as I could.

As it is almost impossible to look up the hill at that angle and far too discouraging I kept my eyes just ahead of my handlebars. To my amazement I made it to the halfway point and was still in the saddle. The younger riders began to shout "Come on Don, you can do it!" It was hard to inhale, but my legs were still strong as I passed the three quarter mark, with the riders already at the top cheering on the old man. Finally reaching the top and steepest part of the hill I actually put a moment of pure air between the front tire and the pavement, and I didn't stop till I reached the next sag stop.

At the bottom of the hill everything told me to give up and walk. By staying with it and taking the challenge I was rewarded beyond my dreams.

I've said all of that to bring us down to this. In 2008, my job of over 29 years was cut, leaving my family to survive on a poverty income. While it's hard for a man over fifty to get a decent paying job, and even harder these days, I decided to fight back.

It is impossible for an unknown writer to break into the successful publishing game, and even harder during poor economic times. In taking a chance with a bit of our ever dwindling savings, I decided to do what "they" say can't be done. My risk may succeed beyond my wildest dreams or it may utterly fail, but by my act of writing a book, and your kind act of purchasing this work, we are both poking the eye of those forces of society and self that keep telling us that we can't possibly succeed.

I hope that you will enjoy reading the farfetched yet plausible tale of Great Aunt Alice. When you are finished I also hope that you will be inspired to begin that adventure that may have been restricted all of these years by your own lack of confidence. Whether you have the flair of Great Aunt Alice, or the insecurity of Great Nephew, the only way to guarantee failure is to never try.

Don McAllister

Chapter 1
The Summer Job

The greatest adventure of a person's life is usually the journey where they set out to discover who they are and where they are in life, and quite frankly I was not traveling well. There is a fine line between dying and never having lived, and I was standing on that line on one toe. It was the first summer after I had lost my job at the university. Times were tough, and it was hard to find work in the field of pre-Georgian literature. You'd be surprised how few people had an interest in the study of pre-Georgian at that time. I was excruciatingly single, so I didn't need much, but I couldn't very well eat my books.

Great Aunt Alice took pity on me and offered to let me stay with her in exchange for painting the house and barn. I'm quite sure she had a full awareness of my handyman prowess, but she invited me anyway. I was glad, for I wanted to learn more about my Great Aunt Alice to verify and document some of the stories my mother had shared with me about her. Mostly I just wanted to avoid having to live in the dumpster behind the student union.

The work schedule started too early, but the work itself was agreeable enough. She would supply me with lots of her good iced tea (refrigerated, no ice), and I'd hold the ladder while she painted anything I couldn't reach from the ground.

The truth is that we used more tea than paint and took copious breaks where she would tell me about her life while I took notes or tape recorded it for later compilation.

I begin with a general description of her incredible story. It is an American story, a woman's story, a pioneer's story, and a survivor's story.

Great Aunt Alice was no bigger than a bird, but she left giant footprints. I've often wondered if she actually was a bird in a previous life. The fact that she was born on December 17, 1900, just three years to the day before the Wright Brothers' first flight at Kitty Hawk, went a long way toward reinforcing that notion.

She loved the open sky and all that one could do with it. Hot air balloons, parasailing, gliders, skydiving -- they were all mother's milk to her. She could fly any aircraft available and had pretty much done so. I once asked her if she wished she could have gone into space. She replied, "Only if I could float around outside like some of those fellows do." I on the other hand grow faint and clammy on the first step of a household ladder.

She had a cluster of flying friends and acquaintances that included some of the all-time great aviators such as Lindberg, Cochran, Doolittle, and even some of the early astronauts, but she never sought fame or records. She was just "one of the boys" who flew for the peace and freedom that only a pilot could understand.

Great Aunt Alice was as fearless as anyone alive. Barring the physics of the thing, she would have no trouble at all walking the wingtip of a 747, or going to war, or scaling the outside of the Empire State Building. She did, however, have an unnatural fear of elevators, revolving doors, and ice water. She hadn't the slightest fear of death, and when the subject came up once I saw her light up and breathe . . . "Angel's wings! Wouldn't that be something?" She saw death and heaven as a great adventure and a chance to reunite with her many loved ones passed. Time was always her enemy. "So much to do and so few grains left," she would say. Still there were times when she may have lived too long and had borne too much.

I saw her as a distinguished lady tomboy, invincible, and as much a part of my life as the morning sun. Great Aunt Alice could be a sparkling beauty in elegant dress, or one of the boys, or the lone mechanic covered in oil. That was her public soul, but I was blessed with a special place. She loved me and I her as would a mother and son.

Had I known just how much she loved me I would have run for cover. A true "mother's" love does not so much protect the weak as it makes the weak strong enough to fend for itself. It's sort of like a young bird in the nest. The mother kicks it out not to be cruel but to make sure the chick can learn to fly; else the chick will die in the nest. Actually I wish I hadn't used that analogy. I get clammy enough thinking about the nest, let alone falling from it.

My nest was an ivory tower of books as far as the eye could see. It was a wall of security that kept me from the harsh realities of the outside world. While other children played, I read. While other boys learned firsthand of sports, and camaraderie, and love, I read about them. Safe in the womb of my room and the cleft of my books, I became an expert on everything and was experienced at nothing.

My real life education began at 5:00 the next morning.

Chapter 2
The Soiled Virgin

Great Aunt Alice gave me the upstairs bedroom on the southeast corner of the farmhouse. She did this for two reasons. First, it was the nicest room she had available. Second, the Indiana summer sun comes crashing through the southeast windows like a baseball no later than 4:55 AM between late May and early August.

It was within five minutes of that time, on the first morning after I had arrived that she first yelled, "BREAKFAST!" I soon found out that "BREAKFAST!" was a Hoosier word that meant, "Why aren't you down here, dressed, and ready for work?" It didn't matter if we worked all day or for five minutes and then quit -- Great Aunt Alice started most of her workdays at 5:00.

By 5:30 I was in the kitchen in time to see her washing the dishes and wrapping the leftovers. I hadn't been hungry, but the sight of this made my stomach growl. If I had disappointed her on my arrival time, at least I was dressed and ready to paint the house. I wore my brown tweed suit with my white shirt, brown bow tie, brown socks, and brown wingtip shoes. She took one look at me and asked, "Are those the only clothes you brought?" I assured her that I had also packed my blue suit, my blue bow tie, two more pairs of brown socks, three pairs of blue socks, four more white shirts, two of them short sleeved, and my black wingtip shoes, and of course a sufficient supply of underwear, and my pajamas.

"What was in the other suitcase?"

"Books."

She asked me if I had ever held a paint brush. I had to admit that when it came to manual labor I was a virgin. The fact that I was a virgin in everything else outside of books was not brought up. Besides I didn't like to get dirty, and as long as I stayed inside the house it didn't matter what the outside looked like.

"Take off your shoes and socks!" she demanded. "We're going to the barn."

I did as she commanded and left them neatly by the front door. The farm lot felt funny to my feet and they were getting terribly dirty in the process. The inside of the barn was still early morning cold. In one third of the barn there was a neatly arranged and elaborate workshop with a clean concrete floor. The other two thirds of the barn had a dirt floor, some of it covered with straw. In the center there were two airplanes facing two large sliding doors that opened to a grass airstrip. The far end of the barn held an old farm truck, and several livestock stalls with various farm tools hanging from the walls. This part of the barn was familiar to me as I had once read McCormick's "American Farm" 1869, Lerman House, Cincinnati, Ohio.

Great Aunt Alice told me to go into the middle stall and close the gate. She then turned her back to me and said, "Jacket."

I said, "Tweed."

"No, I mean hand me your jacket!"

I did, and then she asked me for my tie, my shirt, and my pants. I panicked, thinking this was how one dressed to paint and was relieved when she said I could wear the overalls on the peg. I didn't know what overalls were, but I understood the word peg. When I saw what was hanging from the peg I looked for another peg. There were none to be found so I dressed in the disgusting garment. It was filthy with stains I did not recognize, and it smelled like a combination of wet dirt and mold.

When I turned toward Great Aunt Alice she was gone. I walked back to the house, but she was nowhere to be seen. I searched for her in my room and found that both of my suitcases were missing along with all of my clothes except my underwear and pajamas.

Not finding her anywhere in the house, I walked back outside. There she stood in the barn lot with an open can of paint and a paintbrush. As I came near she swished it through the air and covered me from head to toe with white speckles. Then she placed the brush in my hand, bristles up. The paint ran down the brush handle all the way to my elbow. It was a sticky mess that made me cringe. I thought she was going to ask me to paint something, but instead she put the lid on the paint can and tapped it closed with a hammer and a short lecture on how important it was to close the paint can in this fashion whenever we stopped for any length of time.

Then she set down a bucket and poured in this awful stuff she called turpentine. She showed me how to clean the brush for the next day's work and how to use the turpentine to clean the paint off of me and handed me a rag to clean my glasses before the paint dried. The turpentine smelled odd and tingled on my skin. When the cleaning was over, she poured it back into the can through a funnel. I wondered if that was sanitary.

Great Aunt Alice then said sweetly, "I think that's enough for today. Go upstairs and take a bath." As requested I did so and handed my overalls through the semi-closed bathroom door. She in turn threw some clothes on the bathroom floor. She told me they had been my grandfather's and since I was about his size she thought they would fit. They did indeed fit, if one takes into account that Grandfather was six inches shorter and ten pounds heavier than me. They were faded, but clean. I had never owned a plaid shirt, and I had never dressed in a pair of blue jeans. Before putting them on, I turned them inside out for a complete precautionary inspection. When I turned down the cuffs small bits of ancient dried flora fell on the floor. The socks she gave me were heavy and white. I had never before worn another man's socks.

To my chagrin, I found the overalls in my closet, not washed as I had hoped, but dirty, smelly, and ready for another day's ordeal.

Chapter 3
The Story Begins

Much to my relief, when I came down the stairs, Great Aunt Alice had prepared an early lunch. She suggested that I had learned all that I possibly could about painting for one day, so we put that aside and began the work of recording her story. Depending on the situation, I would do this with either a tape recorder or a legal pad with two sharpened number two lead pencils. Later I would set aside some part of the day or night to compile the work into what you see here. For the most part, what you will read is her unedited telling of her history.

The first section of this story comes from both her words and my research of the family documents and photographs. I wanted to begin with a compilation of her ancestral history and later, as she progressed more into her own life, I wrote the story more directly as she told it to me in her own words. I began with "Where were you born?"

Great Aunt Alice was born in her parents' modest cabin in the coal country of West Virginia. When she was young I doubt she could have imagined that those humble beginnings could be shared by the same woman at the other end of her life. She had the good fortune of being brought into this world by mature loving parents who established that maturity through

The Story Begins

hardscrabble living. Their house was filled with love, laughter, and her father's lust for invention and discovery.

Her mother was the former Jane Ellen Mahafee. In polite society she preferred to be called Ellen, but most of the people who were close to her called her Ellie, while most of the folks in the hollow called her Jane Ellen. She was every bit an Irish coal miner's daughter from a deeply religious family. She had deep auburn hair, soft as a cloud, and perfect blue eyes. Her face was delicate and divine. She was taller than the average girl, but so perfectly proportioned that she could seduce any man without the slightest effort. Throughout her life she maintained as her strongest feature a kind heart.

Jane Ellen's father, Charlie Mahafee, was poorly educated, but wise in his standards. His hands were imbedded with the black from the mine and rough from the toilsome grind of his work, but his touch was gentle when he held his little girl. He had always wanted to play the fiddle, but his hands were too big. He had to make do by being the man who could clap with the music better than anyone else in the valley. Charlie Mahafee loved with all his Irish heart his wife Susie (Gwinn), who in turn ruled the home by making him feel all important. They were coal dust poor but faithful love rich.

Theirs was a life of "Survive the day and thank God for the morrow." A coal miner's life had a scant expectation of any more than the here and now. The company cemetery was far too fertile with husbands and fathers who had died much too young. The light of day was reserved for Sundays, and the rest of Charlie's life was spent in the dark of the pre-dawn, the dark of sunset, and the dark of the mine.

A miner in those days would usually marry in his mid-teens, father most of his children by his mid-twenties, and die by his mid-thirties. The lucky ones were crushed in one blow. The others filled their lungs till they drowned in the awful black dust. The remainder would lay in a cold dark breathing space where they would place on their body some memorial and wait for the sound of the pick and the shovel that would come only after the air had vanished.

Charlie's day came with the company whistle that stops the heart of every miner's bride. When they found Charlie's body, his stiff hand was holding a picture of his beloved Susie against his heart.

The years that followed took Jane Ellen and her mother from poverty to worse. There would be no monthly stipend to ease their plight. They were left to provide from their own hands all that was necessary for day-to-day life. The only rest from that point would be death, and they knew it.

The housing they could afford was deplorable, and they were often hollow and hungry. Susie would go days without food to feed her daughter, and sometimes there was nothing for either. However, they firmly maintained a clean home and a rightful character.

"There is no excuse for a dirty house or a dirty soul," her mother would say.

Both mother and daughter suffered from the various lung and other ailments that plagued so many in their impoverished situation. Jane Ellen would carry those scars for the rest of her life, but her mother was not strong enough. Susie Mahafee died when she was just thirty-one. Mrs. Maryanski was there as much as she could be the last few weeks and was holding her friend's hand when she passed. It was a sad ordeal for them all, for there was no medicine to speak of and no means to bring a dying woman to the nearest doctor. I doubt that anyone could have helped. The conditions had been too long term to overcome.

Susie died during a warm snap and there was no means to keep the body, so Jane Ellen and Mrs. Maryanski dug the grave in the company cemetery next to Jane Ellen's father. Mrs. Maryanski sent her son Billy to fetch the parson, and the four of them said a few words over Susie with only slightly more pomp than one would allow for today's family dog. It was not a coldness of the heart but the coldness of the times that called for her quick dispatch.

Mrs. Maryanski wanted to take Jane Ellen in, but she had lost her Karol in the same collapse that took Charlie Mahafee and had not the means to take in another mouth. Billy would be ten next year and old enough to work the mine, but that was next year and Jane Ellen was a full-grown woman of almost fifteen and could care for herself almost as well.

To keep her life sane, Jane Ellen kept a diary and recorded much of what we know of her from those impossible days. Because she was so old, she was also therefore marrying age, but there was no man she could bear to love. "No stomach is hungry enough to stomach that man," she would write. Her options were dwindling. She must marry, succumb to the sordid life as a few of her desperate girlfriends had, or die.

The thought of going to the roadhouse called to her on several occasions. "What would be the harm?" she wrote, "It is a natural thing, and I am pretty enough to draw a good dollar." Twice she gave in and dressed to go. Twice she stopped short of her own front door and commenced with a seizure of dry heaves of the heart and nerves. Each time she was glad the next morning that she had come to her senses, but a year later, desperately hungry and not a scrap of food in the house for four days, she stood in front of the mirror her daddy had made for her mother. There were tears on her cheeks as she made herself "available." With her heart pounding, she stepped through the front door - and then took another step. Despite her thin frame she was indeed "available" and would draw well that night.

The roadhouse was almost two miles away, and she wished it was farther. The cool late summer air braced her trembling steps as she walked past the shack where she was born. She dared not look at it, for she had "a job to do, nothing more." As she drew within sight of the roadhouse, she began to shake all over. The thought of some vile wife-cheating coal miner upon her made her sick. "It is a natural thing, no one would blame me, I may even enjoy it, and I need the food." She said it over and over, almost hyperventilating as she drew near the roadhouse and heard the music volume grow louder. There was one more path to cross before she entered the roadhouse grounds. It was the last crossing and the last chance to turn another way or to go home altogether.

Suddenly she was stopped dead in her tracks when out of the side path a tall shadow stepped in front of her progress. The shadow man had the light to his back, but even in the dark she recognized him. It was one of the miners, Frank Howard. She didn't have the courage to step around him, and he in turn just stood there like a stone. Neither one of them moved or spoke for what seemed like a minute or two. Frank had the full advantage of the light and without so much as an "evening ma'am" he blurted out "will you marry me?" Jane Ellen passed out dead cold to the ground.

She woke up in Frank's humble cabin. It was a man's place for sure. There were nesting chickens in the corner and mechanical drawings all over the table. There was the smell of scrambled eggs and bacon in the room. Jane Ellen was totally confused. Frank saw her stir and said, "I thought you might be hungry." Then Jane Ellen screamed hoarsely at the top of her fragile lungs "YES!"

"I hope you like bacon and eggs," Frank replied "It's the only thing I know how to make."

Then she shouted, "NO!"

"You don't like bacon and eggs?"

"NO! I mean YES! YES!"

Then it struck Frank what she was really trying to say. "YES?" he asked in return.

"YES! YES!" she affirmed, with joyful tears in her eyes. They were like an old deaf couple trying to out yell each other.

Then Frank knelt next to her and said softly, as if doubting his luck, "yes." As he nervously reached to kiss his fiancé for the first time, she stopped him with "The bacon is burning!" He replied with total abandonment, "I don't care." Then a ball of fire shot up from the skillet and she shoved him aside and smacked a lid on top to put it out.

"I'd have never thought of that," Frank said, as if bearing witness to a science project. Then with all of her Irish muster she looked him in the eye and said, "Well you'd better get used to my ways if you are going to live in my kitchen," and she jumped into his arms as if he were just returning from a war.

The Story Begins

The strange truth was that Frank was on his way to ask for Jane Ellen's hand when he met her on the dark path. It was one of those meetings of opposite forces that occur somewhat by plan, but mostly by fate. Frank had been working on his plan for weeks and had every intention of doing things the "right way," but he wasn't very skilled at the art of love. Frank was a playful lion among his fellows, but he was shy as sheep around women. He was a strong, independent man of about twenty who had worked in the mines since he was thirteen, when his parents died. He had every skill he needed except the skill he needed most, and he was completely dumbfounded at the task.

For weeks Frank had practiced his speech. After work he hurried home to clean up and paced the floor of his cabin at least a dozen times before he made it out the door. Even then he walked the path between the roadhouse and his cabin three times. Should he straight out ask her to marry him? No, that wouldn't do. Maybe he should just ask to call on her? Yes, that would be best, but doggone it he had already decided to marry her so why should he drag the thing out?

By that time it was getting late and he wondered if he should go that night at all. It was in the midst of that question that Frank suddenly stumbled across Jane Ellen on the path. He completely lost what little composure remained, and just blurted out his proposal.

Jane Ellen for her part never let on what she was up to that night on the path to the roadhouse. She wrote of it in her diary, but as he respected her privacy I doubt if he ever knew or would have dared to be curious.

Jane Ellen was now a woman of sixteen and very matured by her hard life. She had in all honesty previously cast an eye Frank's way. He was a good church-going man and a hard worker with fine lines and a melt-your-heart smile, but in his shyness he had never spoken a word to her and could barely look her in the eye. Jane Ellen had assumed that Frank just wasn't interested in her.

Frank was a kind man who took to heart the Lord's commission to care for the widows. He would fix their houses and they in turn kept him fed and full of the motherly advice he so dearly needed. Among his fellows, no one could beat him in a fair fight. He did an honest day's work for an often not-so-honest day's wage. Frank was a sharp fellow and had saved more than one miner when he spotted the occasional flaw in the shaft. He had an inventive mind and had plans in his soul that would someday take him and his family to another world.

That other world began in the pre-dawn hours when Jane Ellen said yes to his proposal. Being a practical man, Frank swept up his fiancé and rushed her to the parson's house. It wasn't 4:00 AM when he pounded on the door. The parson met them in his nightshirt and a sweater. Frank cut to the chase with, "we have to get married, RIGHT NOW!" The parson was a little confused and was still working on "hello." He looked at Jane Ellen out of habit to see if she looked pregnant. When his head cleared enough to recognize everyone, he realized the situation and, knowing Frank wasn't the kind to kid about a thing like that, went about looking for his book as though this scene was the most natural thing in the world. They had no license, and the only witness was the parson's cat, but that was not unnatural for those parts.

Frank kissed his bride and ran to the mine to start his shift. He hadn't packed his lunch and he hadn't slept for more than a day, but he was full of energy, and don't you think the other fellows didn't notice? It got around pretty fast that Frank had married Jane Ellen and the fellows started to plot some mischief, but Frank's best friend Big Carl Johnson made it clear what would happen if they interfered.

The friendship of Frank and Carl is a good story as well. They had hired into the mine about the same time and were nearly equal in size. One day they got into a fight over something that they soon couldn't recall, but at that time it must have been a pretty big issue. The two of them started to duke it out just outside of the number 7 shaft and a crowd of miners quickly gathered. It went on for almost twenty minutes before Frank caught Carl a good one and sent him to the floor of the mine. Carl was dazed and trying to get up when Gus Hachey leveled some hateful remark toward Carl. Frank turned on Gus and sent him flying several feet into the number 7 and everybody cheered, including Carl.

Nobody liked Gus. He was a self-centered hothead with a sense of judgment that usually made trouble for everyone. Hachey preferred to be called Augustus, but the miners labeled him "Jughead." Jughead was killed a few months later when he was carelessly whacking away at a shelf and it fell in on him. The only regret the others had was that it killed him instantly.

A few days after the fight Marty G (They called him that because no one could spell or pronounce his last name) made a snide remark about Frank. Carl picked up Marty G by the collar and made him apologize to Frank in a voice that sounded a lot like Donald Duck.

The day that Frank married Ellie he worked like a mad man to make the day go faster. That evening, as he climbed out of the earth, Frank ran to his cabin, where he found a fine meal, a tidy home, and a woman in love.

Chapter 4
A Whirlwind of the Most Magnificent Sort

Great Aunt Alice was born seven years after the marriage. Her mother's health was in need of quite a bit of repair from the damage of her extreme poverty before she would be strong enough to bear children, and there was a short break in the union while Frank went off to serve in the war. Those were hard months on the heart of his Ellie, as it is with all brides whose husbands are immersed in the uncertainty of war. Frank's loyal care had brought Ellie back to a more natural physical state. Still it was apparent that her health in general would never be as strong as it should be, and they weren't sure that they would ever be able to have children.

Their separation was aggravated by Frank's lengthy convalescence in a Florida Army hospital from war wounds he had suffered in Cuba. People just didn't travel then as they do now, so they had to give each other love and care through the mail that traveled so slowly between them. A letter from a dearly missed loved one is good for the soul, but it doesn't fix the hole in the roof and it doesn't present itself on the skin as does a real caress.

The day finally arrived when Ellie heard the dog bark and the thud of a strong step on her porch. Frank flung the door open and Ellie dropped the bucket of ashes she was taking out to dump. Her hair was a mess and she was covered in soot from cleaning the stove, but she was the most beautiful thing Frank had seen in a long time. She jumped into his arms and would not let go. Frank turned with his bride attached and closed the door, and the question of Ellie having children was soon and pleasantly resolved.

The birth of their baby Alice was more than a gift. She was a God-sent treasure. The pregnancy had been hard on Ellie, but she loved every minute of it. Frank helped her when he could, but there was no prenatal care as we think of it today-- just hard work and common sense. The delivery was almost tragic. The midwife later told Frank that Ellie had lost a lot of blood, but she was able to stop the bleeding enough for Ellie to survive.

Great Aunt Alice described her mother as having a beautiful voice, but not the air at times to sustain much more than a whisper.

"It's a good thing she and father loved each other so much, for she couldn't have scolded him in the proper volume if she tried. Still mother would sing so sweetly around the house as she did her chores."

She had her strong days and her weak ones. Her eyes sometimes showed the wear of her health, but her smile was always playful. Indeed Great Aunt Alice said there was a lot of soft humor and teasing in their home. I suspect it was the knife they used to cut through the tension of knowing that on any given day her mother could take a turn for the worse and slip away from the family circle. Many times they had gone through that cycle, and many times her mother had recovered, but each time it took a toll.

Great Aunt Alice's father, Benjamin Franklin Howard (he always went by Frank), as I said previously, was a coal miner, who started to work in the mines when he was just 13 years old. He enjoyed hard work and was a common friendly guy who stayed true to his fellows even after he became well to do. He was fairly tall and of medium build in general but very strong in his shoulders and arms, without appearing bulky. Indeed he was as well built and handsome as a fellow could be.

Great Aunt Alice told me that her father had a masterful mind for practical things, as well as an appreciation for the finer graces, and may have been the most perfectly balanced man God ever made. He loved all kinds of music and read voraciously. He studied the ins and outs of business as though he was a tycoon and was the only subscriber in McDowell County to a new publication called The Wall Street Journal.

On returning from the war Frank struggled a bit. Great Aunt Alice's mother wrote that on the outside he looked whole, but it was harder for him to work the mine and that she was always anxious for him to quit before he suffered the same fate as her father.

Frank continued to mine while he looked for some kind of work in the world above the ground, but the non-mining work in those parts was scarce, and in the summer of ought-one they moved to the booming river town of Saugerties, New York, where he found work at a saw mill. At nights he worked on his inventions.

By 1903 Frank Howard had perfected his first marketable invention and started the complicated work of bringing it to full manufacture. It was some sort of gadget for mining that I believe may be used, in some form, to this day, but the nature of it is lost to time, and I can't say for sure what it was or how it worked. Suffice it to say that the Howard "empire" began to raise its proud head. Frank patented the idea and incorporated his business.

There was an old railroad repair shop near the edge of town that hadn't been used since the regional facility was built in Albany. Most of the glass was broken and it was overgrown and in pretty sad shape, but it was structurally sound and had the right layout for the factory Frank envisioned. The floor was deep reinforced concrete, and there were great doors and winches and overhead tracks that would lend well to the operation. All he needed was money.

The town banker, Mr. Polo, was the answer. Mr. Polo had worked in the rail works as a young man and had a good mix of financial knowledge and practical life. As a result, his investments usually went very well. Frank's idea SEEMED like a good one, but Mr. Polo had no knowledge of mining and wanted to check it out first.

Through Frank's friend Big Carl Johnson, it was arranged that Frank would meet with the mine owners back in his West Virginia hometown. Frank was accompanied by Mr. Polo, and Mr. Donlon and Judge Harper representing the Saugerties town council. When they arrived the owners were impressed with Frank's idea and arranged for him to test it out in the mine. The other three men from Saugerties had never been in a mine and were a bit uncomfortable with the situation but not overwrought. Mr. Polo was a man who could look in the eye of any danger or problem without losing his head. His method was to work through the situation one step at a time. Mr. Donlon was the most intimidated. He was as brave a man as one could meet, but his delight was the world of the open forests and the river. Judge Harper maintained a closed mouth smile and quietly observed.

The test went as planned. Frank's device improved the cutter's performance while clearing the air for better visibility through less residual dust. Within thirty minutes the air in the shaft had improved significantly. While Big Carl worked the tool, Frank visited with some of his friends. He was taken aback at how many of the little boys he had watched grow up in church were now working the mine. He asked about his old friends and they told him that most of them were still there, but that "Pappy had retired and Bo and Dusty had been killed just before Christmas when the roof collapsed on the shelf they were digging."

Back in the mine office the owners offered to put up the ten percent Frank needed for the down payment in exchange for a one percent cut of the sales. Mr. Polo offered the loan for the rest at four percent with the factory as collateral and with all other fees waived. The papers were signed and hands were shaken all around, and the four men from Saugerties left for home.

Frank let the owners keep his prototype to thank them for their investment, and Big Carl showed the men how to use the new tool. In the months to follow some twenty of Frank's former co-workers would follow him to Saugerties. These would be replaced by young bucks ready to make an honest dime. Frank's greatest satisfaction was that the mine would be a safer place to work. Indeed, young Bill Maryanski was later saved by the tool as the rescuers were able to drill faster through to his collapsed shaft with Billy still alive.

Back in Saugerties the work began. The first step was to clear the trash out of the factory and get rid of the weeds inside and out. Frank hired several after school children to do this, with Ellie and even their little Alice at their side. Frank had to make several trips to purchase equipment and to generate advanced sales. While he was gone Ellie was in charge of the "crew."

A month later men were brought in to do what the children could not. Walls were scrubbed, bricks were tuck pointed, and rust was removed. Steel beams were painted and windows were replaced. The inside walls were painted white for greater light in the work areas. Heat, plumbing, and electricity were restored to the old shop, and in a few more months the first machine roared to life. Word spread like wildfire in the mining community and in two years the loan was repaid and Howard Industries was in full money-making mode.

The result was that the Howard's were able to move to a fine house on fashionable Jane Street, where they joined the lower upper crust of Saugerties, New York's fledgling middle class.

Before I say too much more about that, I found out through my research and her telling that Great Aunt Alice's grandfather had fought in the Civil War, and her father as I implied had fought in the Spanish American War. She would tell that story and then get real serious and shake her head. Then she'd say, "We just couldn't get along with anybody." It was the oldest joke in the world, but I laughed every time she told it.

Her Grandfather Howard actually spent an afternoon with Abraham Lincoln, escorting him through the camp when he

A Whirlwind of the Most Magnificent Sort

went to see General McClellan. Lincoln, despite his melancholy reputation, was described by her grandfather as an affable fellow and very interested in the stories and opinions of her grandfather and the other ordinary soldiers he met that day. After the war Great Aunt Alice's grandfather was in on the arrest of Jefferson Davis. He used to brag to his young Frank that he had rubbed shoulders with two Presidents. And then, being a Democrat, he would joke, "But they were both counterfeit."

I asked Great Aunt Alice if her father had come across Teddy Roosevelt in the Spanish American War. She responded with the grand story of how her father had shoved Col. Roosevelt to the ground and unloaded on a Spaniard who had snuck up on Roosevelt's blind side. Col. Roosevelt got up and plowed his hand into her father's and shouted over the noise of battle.

"Ted Roosevelt!" Great Aunt Alice's father retorted, "Frank Howard!" and Col. Roosevelt pulled her father to the ground to shoot the Spaniard who was on his back. It was nearly all in one motion and then they both went back to work.

In the heat of battle they were separated, and a few days later her father was wounded. When he came around, Frank was headed to Florida on a hospital ship. Col. Roosevelt tried to find Frank Howard after the battle, but they were hopelessly separated by events.

They didn't see each other for a proper thank you until 1904, when President Roosevelt made a campaign stop in Albany. Great Aunt Alice's father went to hear Roosevelt speak, with a dim hope that he might be able to finally express his thanks to him. When Roosevelt spotted father in the crowd, he stopped his speech and nearly jumped from the podium to meet his hero.

Roosevelt called him up, raised his hand in a champion's embrace, and shouted, "This is the man who saved my life on San Juan Hill!" In a rush of adrenalin, father shouted back, "And this is the man who saved MY life on San Juan Hill, and the man who will save our country!"

By this time Great Aunt Alice was so engaged in the interview that I asked no more questions for a while and let her take free reign of the conversation. This is the story in her own words.

"President Roosevelt was so energized that he nearly shoved the mayor off the stage so that my father could sit near him for the duration of the speech. Afterwards he drove my father all the way home to Saugerties to exchange contact information and to meet my father's family. I was just a small child at the time, but my mother said that father burst through the door and shouted, 'Honey, I'm home, and I've brought the President!'

"Mother nearly fainted and my father and the President helped her to a chair. The President rapidly briefed her on how her husband had saved him in Cuba, apologized for the unannounced intrusion, raved on her beauty and charm, held me high, smiled and kissed me, exchanged contact information, shook my father's hand, and raced on to his next appointment.

"My mother detailed this in her diary and described it as 'a whirlwind of the most magnificent sort.' My father's journal records that he washed dishes for some time after that."

Chapter 5
Christmas in the White House

We took a break for supper and after the dishes were washed (pronounced "worsht" if you are a Hoosier) Great Aunt Alice and I sat in the living room and she went on with her story.

"After the campaign incident, President Roosevelt and my father corresponded on a regular basis, and we were invited to the White House for Christmas that year. My mother was too ill to travel, so my father sent his regrets, and wished the Roosevelts a Merry Christmas. In his last year in office we were again invited, and that time mother was doing quite well.

"I was barely eight at the time, but I was a precocious and observant child and, thanks to my mother's tutoring, I could read at a fifth-grade level. I was young, but I remember it so well. It was the first time I had ridden on a train, and I was thrilled by the many things I saw out the window, and by how the world rushed past. I was in awe of the smartly uniformed crewmen with their gold-braided hats and shiny brass buttons.

"We made a new friend on board. He was smartly dressed in a white uniform. My father must have known him because he called him by his first name, George. Mr. George was what we used to call a 'colored' porter. I had never seen a 'colored' man before. My mother would apply rouge to give her cheeks color, so I assumed he must have put on some sort of makeup to get that beautiful brown skin. I brushed his face, and it felt just like my father's. I looked at my hand, and Mr. George laughed. 'That's just the way God made me young lady. I guess I'm so dark because I like to stay close to the light of the Lord.' My parents laughed at this and I giggled because no stranger had ever called me a lady.

"Sensing a good learning experience for me, my father asked Mr. George to sit a while and chat. Mr. George said that he wasn't allowed to, but my father insisted, citing that the customer is always right. It wasn't long before a white man in a black uniform came toward us and glared angrily at Mr. George. My father glared back with the most authority and ferocity that I had ever seen him muster. The white man melted before my father's glare and walked on by without saying a word. From then on, the conversation was as though Mr. George were a lifelong friend, and a natural part of our traveling party.

"My father properly introduced himself, and Mr. George said that his real name was Cornelius Jones. I was confused and said so. Mr. George explained that he was traveling incognito, and that 'Mr. George' was his train name. They all laughed, but I didn't know why.

"My father and Mr. George talked at length about life on the railroad, and Mr. George told about some wonderful innovations he would initiate if he owned his own railroad, which engaged my father's interest to no end.

"The conversation eventually turned to the holidays, and my father asked Mr. George about his plans for Christmas. He said he had to work Christmas day. 'But what about your family?' my father asked. Mr. George told my father that that was just the way of the world, and then he pulled a picture from his cap of his family. His wife was beautiful, though not as beautiful as my mother, and he had a little girl about my age. I pointed to her and asked her name. When Mr. George said, 'Alice,' my eyes got as big as dollars, and I told him that was my name too! I reached over to Mr. George and gave him a Christmas kiss and a Christmas hug to hold him until he could get one from his Alice.

"My mother was a tender-hearted sort and she too gave him a kiss on the cheek and told Mr. George it was to hold him until he could see his wife again. I could see a tear start to well in the corner of Mr. George's eye, but then my father broke the sad tension when he looked at Mr. George and said, 'I won't kiss you but you can borrow our dog.' It is due to that memory that I've never been the cause of an employee missing Christmas with his or her family.

"As we got off the train, my father collared the white man in the black uniform and informed him in no uncertain terms that if he heard from Mr. Herington that Mr. George had been punished for sitting with us, he would have his position. As we walked down the platform and out of earshot of the man, my mother asked my father who Mr. Herington was. My father responded that he was the owner of the railroad. She asked him how he knew such information, and my father said it was his habit to study such things' as they are often useful.

"Mother asked, 'Do you really know Mr. Herington.?'

'Not from Adam, but that fellow doesn't know it.'

With her poor health, it was rare to see my mother laugh like that. She was giggling like a schoolgirl without a care in the world. I've looked back on that moment, and thought I had just seen the young woman who had charmed my father into falling in love. I don't think he ever saw her any other way. There was never any doubt that they loved each other dearly to the end.

"For some time after, I thought about all I had seen that day, and the thing that stuck with me was the idea that black men wore white uniforms and white men wore black uniforms, so why should color matter? It's funny what goes through our minds when we are little."

I asked Great Aunt Alice if they had gone from the train to the White House.

She exclaimed, "Oh no, that was one of the best parts,--we stayed in a HOTEL! I had never been in a hotel, but first there was the taxi ride from the train station. I had never been in a taxi either. The nice man took us all over Washington D.C., our nation's capital. I marveled at all of the beautiful stark-white monuments and buildings and all of the wonderful Christmas decorations. Mother and I were thrilled, but my father insisted that the man had not taken the most direct route and refused to pay the full fare. It was the only bad incident in the whole trip, but still mother and I thought it a grand excursion so she slipped the taxi driver the rest of the fare plus a small tip. My father pretended not to notice, but I am sure he did. He was observant of all things, but he also had a tender love for mother and I never heard him scold her except in jest.

"The hotel was amazing. Outside there were guards in beautiful red uniforms. I was sure the king of England was staying in our hotel, and these were his escorts.

"The front door was one of those revolving doors, solid gold, I swear. I've always been afraid of revolving doors, so my father carried me through. I knew that little children could be lost in those things forever, or just plain cut to pieces.

"Inside the lobby was almost as large as our house. It had marble floors, so finely polished that you could see your face in them. I could hear my shoes click clock and echo as my feet walked toward the great ornate desk where they let little girls ring the bell over and over, as fathers autograph the book for the man behind the desk.

"A nice young man with blue eyes and blond hair in a short coat and a small round hat came to carry our luggage to our room. I wondered why he was dressed like the organ grinder's monkey. He took us up on an elevator. Elevators are dangerous you know. The door can snap you in half, and if the cable breaks you will fall and be smashed to pieces, unless you jump up at the last minute.

"When we arrived at the room, the nice young man showed us about and explained its wonders. Then he shook hands with my father and left us to devour the luxury. We had our own bathroom, a large closet, a writing desk with fancy stationery, and a telephone. My mother and father shared a high bed with a Christmas card and two pieces of candy on the pillows. I had a rollaway bed. I had slept on a rollaway bed only once before and I was excited to do it again.

"Through the window, high above the city, we could see the White House. My father said that the President knew Santa Clause very well and that he had made arrangements for my present to be delivered there and that I should not worry.

"It was toward evening and we were very tired, so my father thought it would be a grand treat to order from room service. But first I had to take a bath. The tub had real gold faucets, and the softest water I had ever experienced. My mother and father used the telephone to order the food, and my mother took her bath while we waited for its delivery.

"When the food came, it was rolled in on a fine cart with a long white tablecloth. Each dish was covered so that everything would be a surprise. I giggled while we ate the meal right there in the room in our pajamas, and when we finished we just put the dishes outside and didn't even wash them. The next morning I felt bad as someone had stolen them during the night.

"After dinner father took his bath, while mother sat at the desk and wrote in her diary. She had the most wonderful smile as she chronicled the events of the day.

"As for me, I just couldn't sleep. Tomorrow would be Christmas, today I had met Mr. George, and tonight I was sleeping on a rollaway bed."

Great Aunt Alice had such a pleasant look on her face after telling that part of the story. The mood of the house was peaceful as well. I forgot my troubles and slept well that night.

Chapter 6
Christmas Day

The next morning was a perfect day. It was raining cats and dogs, which kept us from doing any painting at all. We ate breakfast in our pajamas and robes and left the dishes for later so Great Aunt Alice could tell me her Christmas story.

"On Christmas morning I sprang to the window to see if Christmas had come. It had indeed. There was a bit of snow in the air, and the ground was covered with it. The White House nearly disappeared into nature's cold white blanket.

"I climbed onto Mother and Father's bed, plopped between them, and gave them each a Christmas kiss. 'Wake up, wake up, it's Christmas!' Mother and Father pretended not to be as excited as I was, but after passing around the usual Christmas greetings, we were soon up and about the room in search of our clothes. Father's Sunday suit was freshly cleaned, and he had purchased a fine hat for the occasion.

"Father had also purchased two beautiful dresses, one for my mother and one for me. After we were properly festooned--do you like that word, festooned?" Great Aunt Alice gave me a wink and laughed. I responded to her in kind and she went on with her story.

"My father looked my mother over and swore that she looked like a Christmas angel. Mother blushed and curtseyed. 'And you are my prince,' Mother said, 'a fitting beau for such a fine lady,' and then she laughed. 'What about me?' I said. Mother bent down to give me a hug and told me that I was a Christmas cherub. I had no idea what a cherub was, but it sounded nice.

"With the experience of Mr. George fresh in their minds, my mother and father decided to forego breakfast so they would not be the cause of someone working on Christmas. They had saved me a piece of bread and an orange to eat for my breakfast.

"After I ate we brushed our teeth and set out of the room to walk to the White House. We took the stairs this time because we didn't want the elevator operator to work for us on Christmas. I was much happier for this, but we still had to go through that scary revolving door.

"The snow was two or three inches deep, so Father tramped the snow in front of Mother and me to make it easier for us to walk. When we got to the White House, two Marines met us sternly and asked our business. When my father told them who we were and that the President had invited us, the one Marine said to the other, 'That must be him.' They both wished us a Merry Christmas and sent us through.

"My father was always one to recognize the contributions of the working man, so he made sure the President knew of the fine job the guards had done. The President was pleased and ordered replacements long enough for the guards to eat some Christmas dinner in the warm White House kitchen. My father later received a nice thank you letter from one of the guards and the President's military aide.

"As we walked up the drive, the house seemed to grow in size. I had never seen such a thing and could not imagine that this was someone's home. We were met at the door by a stately butler who led us to a magnificent room. It was a wide tall room, larger than our entire house. It had a deep red carpet and an enormous chandelier. The centerpiece was a wide white marble staircase. The butler asked us to wait where we were, and he gracefully ascended the stairs to alert the President to our presence.

"Shortly President Roosevelt raced down the staircase and went straight to my father. He gave my father a two-handed handshake, and the two launched into conversations about the war. Mrs. Roosevelt followed him down and came straight to my mother to welcome us to the White House. 'You must call me Edith,' she said to my mother, and then Mrs. Roosevelt commented on how beautiful we each looked, and told us to feel at home.

"After introducing herself to my mother Mrs. Roosevelt knelt down to wish me a Merry Christmas and told me I looked like a Christmas cherub. My eyes grew wide -- how did she know? One could tell she was a woman of high class, but not snooty. Mrs. Roosevelt reminded me a great deal, both physically and socially, of my own mother, and I remember thinking that I would have enjoyed being one of her children. In her later years we remained close and somewhat adopted each other.

"Mrs. Roosevelt told me that Santa had left me a present under the White House Christmas tree and that the children were eager to meet me. I didn't know they had children, and I was ready to run up the stairs to meet them.

"President Roosevelt broke away from my father long enough to wish Mother and me welcome and Merry Christmas. He kissed my mother on the cheek, and then he picked me up and groaned as though I weighed a ton. 'My, my young lady, you are half grown, and as pretty as your mother. Let's go see the children.' The President grabbed my hand, and we raced up the stairs with a laugh. We walked down a wide hallway to two large white doors.

"Inside was a great room, larger than any I had ever seen. It had a gigantic Christmas tree, so beautifully decorated. There were guests, and children, and servants scattered all about the room. The room itself seemed more like a living thing rather than just a room sheltering the life within.

"The President-Elect, William Howard Taft, was in one corner, on the floor playing with Quentin and a steam locomotive that Quentin had received for Christmas. He was the most enormous man I had ever seen, but he had an agility and grace about him that few smaller men have. His voice sounded just like that grandfather on the original 'Parent Trap' movie.

"The other man who stood out was Major Archibald Butt. He too had served with my father in the war, and the three Veterans spent quite a bit of time that day reminiscing.

"Mrs. Roosevelt introduced us to her children. Alice was the oldest. I excitedly told her that my name too was Alice, but she was completely unimpressed. Alice was much too old to be troubled with an eight year old. She spent most of the day with the women. At one point Mrs. Roosevelt leaned over to my mother and whispered, 'There are times when she is too high-classed for me.' My mother chuckled lightly and returned, 'That will only last until she becomes a mother.'

"I can't say that I was ever fond of Alice, even in our old age. She was much too socially contrary and always at odds with her father, a man I dearly loved. I understand that the trouble came from her father's depression over the death of Alice's mother, his first wife. I can sympathize with some of it, but to let it linger so long and to not allow some room for the cause of his sorrow was her own self-inflicted albatross.

"She should have taken into account that the bitter sorrow was the result of his deep love for her mother, and he should have taken a stronger hand in making her a part of his new love and family, but those were different times, and people valued not the same graces we do today. Alice was a beautiful woman. However my father always said that a beautiful woman without a smile wasn't much to admire.

"The child nearest my age was Quentin. I liked him, but he was a boy and interested in boy things. There was also Theodore Jr., Archie, Kermit, and Ethel. All of the children were polite and friendly, but the only one I really took to was Ethel. My dear Ethel -- at seventeen she was twice my age, but that day began a lifelong friendship.

"Ethel was somewhat shy but a willing worker. She treated me as the little sister she had always wanted, and the two of us would later spend most of that day off from the others.

"Not long after we arrived, a servant came into the center of the room and announced that dinner was ready to serve. There was a table that looked as long as a train car. It had a beautiful lace tablecloth, elegant china, and hundreds of fine silver forks. A large chandler lit the room, and the smell of fresh pine floated from the Christmas greenery that decorated the room for the occasion.

"Mrs. Roosevelt sat between Mrs. Taft and my mother. Mrs. Taft and Mrs. Roosevelt had long been social rivals, but neither showed any animosity at this event. The fact that Mrs. Roosevelt seated Mrs. Taft next to her showed a good deal of class on her part. Alice sat across from Mrs. Taft, and next to Alice was her Aunt Corinne, who was the President's sister. Aunt Corinne was an unusual woman, somewhat bohemian, and as colorful a woman as there was. Her husband, Uncle Doug, was a polite but solemn man who seemed her polar opposite. He did, however, carry on an interesting conversation in response to my father, who was across from him. My mother would say that my father could 'open any tomb' when it came to making new friends. President Roosevelt was next to Uncle Doug, and Mr. Taft was directly across from the President and next to my father. Major Butt was on the President's left and across from Ted Jr. The rest of the table was lined by the boys, with Ethel and me at the end.

"President-Elect Taft led us in grace, and the parade of food began. There was turkey from Pennsylvania, sweet corn from Indiana, cheese from Wisconsin, cut-up oranges from Florida, potatoes from Idaho, oyster dressing from Maine oysters, and cranberries from Michigan. It seemed like the whole United States had organized a pitch-in for the President's table. My favorite was the date pudding. I didn't know which state had dates, but I wanted to live there.

"I could see my mother watching me to check on my manners, and I was doing pretty well, except for the turkey. I couldn't get the hang of eating a turkey leg with a fork. President Roosevelt must have seen the look on my mother's face. He looked my way, and seeing my dilemma, he took a turkey leg by his fingers, gave me a wink, and launched into it like a hungry cowboy. Mrs. Taft was not amused, but Mrs. Roosevelt recognized what he was doing and gave him a quick scowl followed by a wink and a smile. My mother leaned over to her and whispered, 'I can see why you love that man.'

"Ethel and I had the grandest conversation and were nearly in our own world. After the feast we all adjourned to the Christmas room. The adults sat about drinking coffee while we children opened presents. True to his word, Santa had come and left me two beautiful hair combs, just like the ones I had admired in Mr. Apgar's store window. Mrs. Roosevelt gave my mother a plate that had been hand painted by First Lady Caroline Harrison.

"My father was embarrassed and protested as we had not brought presents for the Roosevelts. Mrs. Roosevelt patted her husband's leg and said that my father's actions had given them her Ted, and that was more than she could repay. The President joked that we had better check see that Edith hadn't given us one of the cracked plates.

"Around 3 p.m. Alice excused herself to go skating with some friends, and shortly thereafter the Tafts and Aunt Corinne and Uncle Doug left the party. The men adjourned to the President's study for cigars and a lot of men talk.

"According to my father, Major Butt talked of his boyhood in Georgia, my father talked of coal mining, and President Roosevelt gloried in his cowboy days in the Wild West. My mother and Mrs. Roosevelt went to her sewing room to look over Mrs. Roosevelt's needlepoint. My mother showed her a stitch that her mother had taught her, and Mrs. Roosevelt pushed her to tell my mother's stories of growing up as a coal miner's daughter. The boys went their ways, and Ethel and I set about to explore the White House.

"First Ethel took me to the Oval Office and showed me how to spin till you were dizzy in the President's chair. Then we saw the Blue Room, and the Red Room, and all of the unusual places that the average visitor would see.

"Finally Ethel took me to the basement, and the attic, and through the secret passages that had been the source of great adventure for the Roosevelt children.

"We settled in Ethel's room where we played a board game, and she gave me one of her dolls to keep. In a way she was much older than me, but in other ways Ethel was still a child. She was caught at the threshold of being an adult and was quite comfortable with both older people and younger people, but uncomfortable with her peers. A part of that came from her schooling where she attended with the children of the robber barons, who had in turn been cut down to size by her father's trust-busting moves. They would often speak ill of her father and treat Ethel like an outcast.

"Ethel didn't wallow in self pity. She had a clear idea of what she wanted. She had her heart set on becoming a nurse, or maybe even a doctor. Ethel wasn't so sure about her true love future, but I had no doubt. Her soft blond hair and sparkling blue eyes made her a sure bet to attract any man she wanted. Ethel smiled when I said that, and she said that I was a good listener. I laughed and said that I had never been accused of being a good listener, but my father said I was a good talker. Finally Ethel showed me some of the needlepoint she was learning from her mother, and I decided that I would have my mother begin to teach me when we returned home.

"By now the daylight was fading, and my father suggested that we go back to the hotel before it became too dark and cold. The next afternoon we were to return home so Father could go back to work. Ethel popped up and asked her mother to let us stay the night in the White House. Mrs. Roosevelt thought it a splendid idea. My mother insisted that it would be too much of an imposition, but Mrs. Roosevelt leaned to her and said, 'Believe me, Dear, we have the room.' The President told my father that it was an executive order and that there was no way around it -- we would stay! He called for someone to handle the task of having our hotel arrangements withdrawn and our luggage delivered to the White House. I can only now imagine the commotion that made at the hotel!

"That night I slept in Ethel's room, and my parents in the Lincoln bedroom. I say slept, but we did more talking and giggling than sleep. We spoke of favorite dolls and special play adventures. We gossiped about Alice's dreamy boyfriends, a discussion that both repulsed me and made me tingle. Ethel even revealed that she had once been kissed by a boy, almost on the lips. She swore me not to tell anyone, especially her father, and I never did, but I don't suppose it matters much now.

"In Ethel I was the little girl looking into the eyes of my own adolescence, and through me she had the chance to be the adult taking one last look at her childhood."

Great Aunt Alice paused a moment and began to weep. "I loved her so. I was seven days short of my seventy-seventh birthday when she passed. She was my very best friend."

The spell was broken. She was no longer in the mood to talk. The rain had stopped, but it was too wet to work. Great Aunt Alice walked to some distant part of the farm for solitude. I picked up the only book I could find and was very nearly through Deuteronomy before bedtime.

Chapter 7
Home to Saugerties

The next morning I was eager to continue with Great Aunt Alice's story, but so far we hadn't painted anything but me and there was work to do. This time I was at the table before 5 a.m. dressed in my overalls and ready to paint.

After breakfast we went out and she surprised me again. I was expecting her to hand me a paintbrush and a can of paint. Instead she told me that we would have to scrape the old paint off before we could apply the new, and she handed me a flat metal tool with a handle. I was totally confused. She showed me what to scrape and how to remove the old paint without digging the wood off the house.

This was work for the insane. The smallest imperfections in the old paint turned into major breaks. The chips were in my hair and creeping down my back. The chips that flew at my glasses seemed to fly through the lenses and stick to the back side. To ease the situation, Great Aunt Alice found an old fedora hat in the barn. It helped a great deal, but the hat smelled worse than the overalls.

By lunchtime it was evident that we were going to have an afternoon storm, so we quit for the day and continued with Great Aunt Alice's tale of her return trip from the White House Christmas.

"I haven't mentioned much about my hometown, Saugerties, New York on the Hudson River. It was close enough to the capital in Albany to satisfy my father's political interests, and close enough to New York City to satisfy his business interests. It had enough hills and forests to make my mother feel at home, and I loved the Hudson River that flowed past the town, especially the sandy shoreline near the lighthouse. I often imagined that I could build a raft and travel that river to any place in the world.

"I loved our White House visit, but it was great to be going home. Early the next morning the Roosevelts rode with us to the train station in the Presidential limousine. These days you wouldn't hear of such a thing, but in those days the President still had time to enjoy some personal life. The President shook my father's hand, slapped him on the shoulder, and asked him to keep in touch. My father promised that he would and wished his old war buddy Godspeed. Mrs. Roosevelt hugged my mother, and they kissed each other on the cheek. Ethel and I did the same, and we promised to write.

"It was only as we turned from the Roosevelts that I realized what was going on around us. Everyone at the train station had their eyes on the President's family and us. Their eyes were wide open, and their mouths open as they couldn't believe what they were seeing. The President took off his hat and waved to the crowd. He went over to shake the hands of the people nearest and wished them all a Merry Christmas. As they drove off they turned for one last goodbye wave, and then our hosts were gone.

"Following the President's departure, the crowd turned their attention squarely on us. I could hear them ask who we were, and whisper that we must be important whoever we were. Porters raced to collect our luggage, and my mother and father played along, holding their heads as if they were first class. Best of all, as we boarded the train, we saw the man in the black uniform. He just stood there with his eyes and mouth open, unable to speak or move.

"A few feet away, completely unnoticed, stood Mr. Herrington, the owner of the railroad, and Mrs. Herrington. Mr. Herrington loudly cleared his throat, which broke the porters' trance and sent men scurrying in all directions. My father, who notices everything, saw what was happening. He didn't know Mr. Herrington, but he could read the reactions of the railroad workers and suspected it might be him. Mr. Herrington looked right at my father with a business look in his eye, and appeared to be asking the porters who we were. Of course they didn't know either, but they must have assumed that we were very important friends of Mr. Roosevelt, and probably said as much to their boss.

"As we settled in, we saw Mr. George, -- or I should say Mr. Cornelius Jones. I had so much to tell him about our Washington adventure. My father asked Mr. Jones to meet us later for an update.

"As we were speaking to Mr. George, oh there I go again -- his real name is Mr. Jones. Well anyway, the white man in black came up to us. He shot a disapproving glance to Mr. Jones and then groveled to my mother and father something about Mr. Herrington wishing to meet with us in his personal car. My father sensed that there was good sport to be had. My mother took his cue and, being in a playful attitude herself that day, we proceeded to the 'palace' car, as I called it. It was the most ornate thing I had ever seen. Even the hotel lobby and the White House paled in comparison. There was red velvet and ornate gold everywhere. My father later said that it looked like a rolling brothel, but of course I wasn't sure what he meant by that.

"Mr. Herrington introduced himself and his wife, Magnolia. Mrs. Herrington was obviously of Southern aristocracy and a high strung belle as well. She was one of those high society types that are always looking down their noses to find as much dirt as possible. My mother later referred to her as 'Queenie.' Mr. Herrington was one of those men who wanted to own everything, and as such kept looking at my mother in a fashion that none of us appreciated. It was obvious that the Herringtons were the type of people who would easily trip over their own greed and that my mother and father could make perfect fools of them without anyone suspecting their ruse.

"The first interrogation came from Mr. Herrington, who said that they had seen us with the President and asked how we had come to know the Roosevelts. My father told him that he and the President had spent some time working out a problem with Spain (he didn't tell Mr. Herrington that it was the Spanish-American War). Mr. and Mrs. Herrington were certain now that my father was an important diplomat. When pressed for details, my father told them that his service to Mr. Roosevelt was a past debt and that he was not free to discuss the particulars, but that he was currently too busy with his mining and manufacturing operations to do much more than spend a few nights in the White House.

"Father told Mr. Herrington, 'We did get a chance to get to know Mr. and Mrs. Taft a little better yesterday. I'm certain now that we will work well together when he is President. He is a fine man, you know.' 'Yes, of course, a fine man,' replied Mr. Herrington.

"By now their heads were spinning. Father knew that Mr. Herrington had never met nor would he ever meet President Taft.

"Mrs. Herrington decided to take her shot. She asked my mother where they were from, and she replied, 'Why, New York of course.' "Mrs. Herrington instantly related the answer to New York City society, never suspecting that a place like Saugerties existed or that New York was also a state. She asked my mother if they had been to the Vanderbilt party last July. My mother responded that she had taken ill and was so disappointed, as it had also spoiled their plans to travel to London to spend time with King George the following week. She turned to Father and implored him to forgive her. My father assured her that he had always found George to be an understanding man and that he had probably not given it a thought. Father assured Mother that they would make it up to him soon, 'Perhaps Ascot?'

"The Herringtons were practically slobbering at this point. Mrs. Herrington pressed my mother for dirt on Mrs. Roosevelt, but of course there wasn't any to be had.

"She asked my mother where we got our 'start,' her nose inching ever closer to the trap. My mother told her that her father received most of his wealth from mining. Of course she didn't come right out and say that Grandpa was a poor coal miner. She did say that her husband also was into mining and that their marriage was a 'mining merger.' There was a general chuckle at her comment, and then Mr. Herrington asked what kind of mining. My father responded, 'Mostly coal in the East -- plenty of money there of course -- but the real glamour is in the Western mines, gold, silver, if you know what I mean.' My father had never been west of Chicago, and he had never seen a western gold or silver mine, but the statement in general was true.

"Then my father hooked them good with, 'By the way, you mentioned the Vanderbilts. Did you know there was one on this very train?'

"Their eyes got as big as dollars, as my mother used to say. 'By all means, we must invite him to our car,' Mr. Herrington stuttered. He started to call for the man in the black uniform to ask that he get this Vanderbilt, but my father said that he knew where he was and insisted that he needed to get something from his room anyway.

"When my father went to look for 'the Vanderbilt,' mother excused the two of us to 'freshen up.' Mrs. Herrington insisted that we use the facilities in their car. A gold toilet seat is a thing to behold, but it sure is cold.

"Racing back to our stateroom, my father grabbed Mr. Cornelius Jones and pulled him in. Mr. George was my father's size, and he hurriedly worked Mr. George into his extra suit. My father asked Mr. George -- "oh there I go again -- Mr. Jones," what his middle name was. He told my father that he had no middle name, and my father said, 'Well it's Vanderbilt now!'

"When they returned to the Herringtons' car, my father came into the room first and announced, 'Ladies and gentleman, please welcome Mr. Cornelius Vanderbilt Jones!' We were all standing at that point. When Mr. George entered, the Herringtons nearly fainted. Mrs. Herrington sat down with an audible thud. Mr. George held out his hand to Mr. Herington, who did not return the favor, but meekly asked Mr. George to sit down.

"Mr. George turned to Mrs. Herrington and said 'Not what you expected? I get that a lot. You see, my great grandmother was a servant for THE Mr. Vanderbilt. She was a beautiful lady, if you know what I mean.' (We found out later that the statement was technically true.) 'We seldom attend the family gatherings, but the Vanderbilts have shown us quiet respect' (which only means that the Vanderbilts had never spoken to the Joneses except as servants).

"Mrs. Herrington's demeanor went from horror to that of a cat ready to pounce on a mouse now that she thought she had some dirt on the Vanderbilts. 'An illegitimate child,' she thought, 'and a Negro at that -- what would Mrs. Wetherspoon say?'

"My father slapped the table and said, 'Cornelius and I were talking the other day about an ingenious plan he had for your railroad. Did you ever stop to think about all of those people who swelter every hot summer in places like Philadelphia and New York? More and more of those people are willing to pay top dollar for some relief for their families. How about special trains that take them to places like Atlantic City, where they can enjoy the ocean?'

"Mr. Herrington responded that he already had some of this in place. My father said, 'Yes, but what if your cars were as cool as an autumn day?' 'I could double the fare,' Mr. Herrington said. My father, sounding like a corporate big-wig added, 'C.V. here told me that it could be done using an ice car with an air flow to the passenger cars.'

"When Mr. Herrington asked if he was certain of this Mr. George nonchalantly assured him that he had already engineered a design and could easily build a working model if he had the investment backing for materials and a suitable laboratory.

"Mr. George gave Mr. Herrington that man-to-man look and appealed to his fragile intelligence as he dramatically bemoaned, 'It's so hard to find a man with both money and foresight. I've approached the Vanderbilts but they don't have a grasp of advanced technologies -- they have no vision.'

"Mr. Herrington took the bait -- hook line and sinker. He of course wanted to be known as a man of vision, and even more so to humble the Vanderbilts, so he immediately hired Mr. George to an executive position to oversee the project. Mr. George was not to work in the home office, of course, but he offered Mr. George a salary that nearly choked my father and gave him wide authority to do his tasks.

"Mr. Herrington called in the man in the black uniform. When he entered the car, his faced turned beet red as he glared at his missing porter. He was about to throw Mr. George off the train when Mr. Herrington introduced Mr. George as his new vice-president of innovation, and ordered the man in the black uniform to spend the rest of the trip as Mr. George's personal porter.

"My mother, with all of the grace and sobriety she could muster at that point, thanked the Herrington's for their entertainment, which was an even more enormous burden for my father, who was trying to keep from laughing out loud. Mother cited that her little girl must be tired as we bade the Herringtons goodbye. I of course sported my most weary look for emphasis.

"Mr. Herrington was slobbering with thanks to my father for connecting him with this profound advantage. My father told him not to mention it as it was of little use to his own path to fortune. He was just glad that he could help a fellow captain of industry. 'Besides, one can only spend so much,' he said with a good old boy laugh. I doubt that my father had two bits in his pocket at that point.

"A few steps outside of the door we heard Mrs. Herrington screech, 'YOU HIRED A NEGRO?!?!?' Mr. Herrington defended himself with, 'No one will know, Precious, no one will know.'

"In fact Mr. Cornelius Vanderbilt Jones did remain in an obscure part of the company, cranking out new patents and bringing in new wealth to the railroad and himself years after the board of directors fired Mr. Herrington for incompetence.

"Mr. George went with us to our room, where we managed to retain our laughter until we closed the door. My father told

Mr. George that he could keep the suit and buy him a better one with his new found riches, which he did that summer. There were hugs, handshakes, and kisses all around.

"As Mr. George left the room, he called out to the man in the black uniform 'Porter!' If laughter were fatal we could have died on the spot.

Chapter 8
Butterfly Days

We broke for supper, and after washing the dishes Great Aunt Alice was eager to get on with her story:

"My experiences in Washington had changed me forever. For the first time I had experienced an exciting world outside of my quiet little village and in a sense had taken my first trip on that raft down the Hudson.

"Barely realizing it was so, I was also beginning to make that transition from my safe cocoon of childhood. I had seen elegant ladies and had been involved in taboo conversations about boys with Ethel. This girl child was beginning to look to her future as a lady and was less satisfied to remain a little girl. My model was my dear Ethel, and I began to trace the steps I suspected she had taken to come this far.

"I studied my mother and wanted to know what it was that made my father fall in love with her. I wanted to learn her ways and the things her mother had taught her. I still had no use for boys, but I now felt funny, sort of 'different' when I was near them in school or at neighborhood play. I was confused. I was afraid. I was excited. These were my butterfly days.

"During the winter and spring quarters, I did well in school. Academics of any kind were easy for me due to my upbringing at home, but socially things were still awkward. For one thing I found myself giggling more, as were the other girls in my class. One would have thought we had all caught the 'silly' virus. The boys were insufferable. They chased and teased us as never before. Outwardly I couldn't stand it, but in my heart, I liked it a lot.

"Each afternoon I raced home to learn more from my mother of a woman's ways. I never told her what was in my heart, but I don't suppose I had to. It was a wonderful time for both of us, and we drew even closer than ever. I suppose that's because every day we developed more in common. My father never suspected that I was growing up. I was and would always be his little girl."

Great Aunt Alice paused for a moment and wept softly for the memory of her father. When she had sufficiently recovered her composure, she continued.

"But that was all right, for I still needed to be a little girl, if only in my father's arms."

She began to weep again, so I sat down next to her and held her and just let her cry. It had been another long day, and we were both very tired. I suggested that we get a good night's sleep and return to her butterfly days after breakfast and a bit of painting.

In the morning we ate a hearty breakfast, did a little painting, for only an hour to be exact, and spent the rest of the day sipping tea and continuing with her story.

"As the end of the school year neared, I had an intense desire to live this summer doing all of the things I had done, and all of the things I had promised myself I would do. Strangely, somehow I sensed this could be my last summer in Saugerties. Had I known then what the next few years would bring, I would have raced back to my mother's womb.

"All summer I was gone from morning to night. It was almost like going to work. My playmates consisted of a mixed group. There was Molly and the other Alice, Tommy and George, and Bud and Eileen. We would play baseball and tag to be sure, but we had serious interests as well. In the morning we worked on our raft, which we were determined to sail on the Hudson by August. In the heat of the day we would swim in the Hudson.

"The raft was a thing of grand design. We found four barrels behind one of the stores on Jane Street. The decking consisted of any boards we could find, mostly from the dump. Tommy and George carved a mast from a downed tree near the lighthouse. Bud came up with a sheet to use for a sail. He never would say from where. We girls wove the ropes we would need from the hemp plants that grew wild in the field behind the Kiersted House.

"In early July, Bud found an old collapsed shack in the tangled woods above the lighthouse. It was buried deep from sight and sometimes hard to find, but the timbers were perfect for the raft, with very little wood rot compared to those we had found in the dump.

"Shortly thereafter, some of us went up to drag the timbers out to our 'shipyard.' Tommy found the site first and began to fight a long board through the tangle of trees and brush. I found Tommy before the others and took the end of the board to help. We had to move the board up and down and twist it every which way to move it through the woods. Finally Tommy decided I needed a break, so we stopped to catch our breath and I sat on the board.

"As I sat, Tommy stood there with his arms dropped to his side. He had been carrying the board a little longer, and I'm sure his arms ached even more than mine.

"Then he did something strange. He looked at me and without asking my permission, sat down very close to me. We both nervously looked straight forward into the woods, and Tommy thanked me for helping him. His voice shook as he said the words, and I shook hearing them. Then he let his shoulder touch mine and my heart almost jumped out of my chest.

"We heard a snap in the woods, and Tommy shot to his feet. It was the other Alice, the youngest in our group in both age and nature. She had gotten lost in the woods and was tearfully glad to find us. I was relieved as well, and also somewhat sorry. That night at supper my mother asked me if I were ill.

"It was August 30th when we finally decided to test our raft out. We would be going back to school in a few days and were not about to let the summer go by without attempting a cruise. We launched the raft in the quiet bay near the lighthouse. All seven of us had an oar of our own fashion to get us up to where we could set the sail, but none of us had thought to include a rudder. We drifted peacefully for a little while and congratulated each other for our accomplishment of finally conquering the great river.

"Suddenly things took a turn for the worse. A passing barge pulled us into the channel and we began to twist and turn with the whim of the river. We rowed with all of our might to get out of the strong current, but it was to no avail.

"Our entire summer's labor started to unravel as one barrel broke off and drifted away and another began to take on water. We were in big trouble now, and all of us screamed at the top of our lungs. The boys were just as loud as us girls, but they later denied that they were afraid.

"Molly fell into the river and began to founder. Tommy jumped in to save her, but he too was in over his head. We threw Tommy the one end of the sail sheet and he finally managed to catch up to it, but we couldn't pull him in. Tommy held onto both Molly and the sheet for dear life, and then things turned to total disaster. The raft broke apart with two loud cracks and we all spilled into the swirling river. I immediately went under and fought to the surface for a quick gulp of air before going down again. Once more I broke the surface and grasped for a piece of the splintered raft, but I couldn't reach it and another piece came from behind and struck me in the head. I went down again, this time dazed and deeper.

"I was losing strength and was certain that I would drown but was still determined to live, breaking the surface for only half a breath. As I sank once more, I felt a giant hand on my collar. It was Flood!

"Flood was the hermit who lived in the flood plain of the river in a vile shack that he had to rebuild each spring. No woman in her right mind would want to go near him. He was the dirtiest, smelliest man alive. Flood would sift through the town dump at nights looking for things he needed. He was feared by every child and was the butt of jokes and scorn from all of the townsfolk. My mother had felt sorry for him, but still my father warned me not to go near him. At that moment Flood was an angel in white.

"Flood had heard our screams and rowed his boat out to rescue us. It would have been a hard task for an average man, but Flood was as strong as the river.

"Bud and Eileen clung to Flood's boat as he hauled me in. Next he pulled Eileen and then Bud into the boat. George, Alice, Tommy, and Molly were nowhere to be seen.

"For an hour or more we shouted their names in vain until our voices collapsed. Flood said nothing but kept rowing, and rowing, and rowing. A small flotilla of boaters began to gather as word got out in the town. Every man, woman, and child scoured the river till dark.

"The tears flowed that night in Saugerties, and knees were raw from praying for the missing children and for the return of the morning sun.

"The next morning around 10 a.m., Mr. Donlon found Alice and George on the opposite side of the river. Somehow they had made it to the bank and were hidden from sight by a stand of reeds. They had heard the shouts from the day before but were too weak to respond. George and Alice were cold, hungry, and covered with mosquito bites, but they were alive. A shout went up that swept both banks with wild celebration from everyone except Molly's and Tommy's parents.

"A melancholy and fresh determination fell back on the townsfolk as the search plodded on for the missing two. Men in boats drug the river but none of us dared to look their way. It was nearing 4 p.m. when Mr. Whispell, the telegraph operator, raced his bicycle down to the river, shouting and gasping 'Albany! Albany!' A cluster of the old men stopped him and calmed him down for the rest of the news.

"Molly's and Tommy's exhausted bodies had been snared by a sloppily laid cargo net dragging in the water over the edge of a passing barge. They fell unconscious from the ordeal and were drug limp several miles upriver. By some miracle their heads were tipped back and remained above water until a crewman spotted the children. They were pulled in and taken to Albany, where they were treated and identified, and arrangements were made to send them home.

"There was a prayer service that night in the street near the courthouse. Everyone in town was there to give thanks for the children's safe return. Even people who had never been to church before or since were praying and shouting their thanks to God.

"The only one who wasn't there was Flood. In the days and weeks after the adventure, people came to see Flood. They brought food and gifts to show their thanks. Strong men just stood there shaking his hand unable to speak as they openly wept. Women in fine dresses who would not otherwise think of doing so buried their tears in his massive dirty chest. Flood in response said nothing, but gave only a slight nod of appreciation and forgiveness.

"As for us kids, Flood became our best friend. We made things for him in school. We brought him cookies. We fished with him on Saturdays -- always upwind. He never said a word to any of us, but then he didn't have to.

"It had been a summer of butterfly days. I had learned and grown so much that summer.

"Flood died that winter."

Chapter 9

The Gadget Factory

It would be a week before Great Aunt Alice would say anything more. I don't know the reason for sure, but it was her way to do what she chose to do and when she chose to do it. So I didn't push the issue.

We finished painting as far as I could reach from the ground, so we worked together to build a scaffold. It was her idea that the high places would seem less intimidating if I stood on something more stable. It didn't help much. I was scared witless and made the scaffold shake so much that she couldn't paint straight. She finally said something to the effect that it was getting hot and we should quit for the day.

As we continued our conversation, I wanted to know about her father's business.

"I was very proud of my father. He was a self-made man. I used to go to his factory as often as he would let me, and I suppose you could say I was sort of a company mascot. Most of the men who worked for my father had been his friends from his coal mining days. They were fiercely loyal to him, as he was to them.

"Big Carl Johnson was my father's right-hand man. They had worked together in the West Virginia mines and were the best of friends. When my father was away, Mr. Johnson was in charge of the day-to-day shop work. All of my father's workers were loyal and hard working. Never once did I hear him complain about any of his employees.

"There were men of all sizes and skills. Some worked with small hand tools, while others ran huge presses. Still others kept the place swept and clean. It was my father's contention that if his factory was clean and well ventilated he could get half again as much work, while keeping the men safe and happy. My father always said that the most important wealth the owner of a company could earn was the respect of his men.

"I remember the time when Bill Maryanski had to return to West Virginia to be with his dying mother. This was the same Billy who was at my grandmother's burial. By then Billy was in his late twenties, and his mother had encouraged him to seek his fortune with my father. My father was of course more than happy to help our old family friend. Billy had stayed with us on Jane Street until he could get a place of his own.

"Well anyway, Bill got word that his mother was dying. My mother insisted on going back home with Bill and taking me. She wasn't very well herself, but death itself would not keep my mother from returning the kindness Mrs. Maryanski had shown her own mother.

"When Mrs. Maryanski passed, it was with my mother holding her hand. I had never seen someone die before, but I was not frightened. The overpowering love in the room pushed away the fear. I did cry a lot, for there was a great deal of that as well. My mother cried as I had never seen her cry. Two of Billy's sisters were there, and they kept sobbing 'Mama, Mama.' The other siblings were either dead by then or living too far from home to make it back in time. Billy himself buried his head in his mother's chest and sobbed so hard that the whole bed shook.

"Before we left Saugerties, my father had given my mother enough money to pay for a proper funeral and had arranged for an undertaker and a bronze coffin to be on standby in Charlestown. The parson arranged for the wake to be at the Baptist church, and almost all of the families from the community came to pay their respects. As a sign of added respect for the Maryanski family, the parson offered the church to be used as a Catholic facility for the funeral. With Frank Howard's help, a priest was brought in to perform the burial mass, something Mrs. Maryanski was not able to do for her Karol. Billy left for Saugerties the next day, but my mother stayed for two more days so she could show me where she was born and the other places she had lived. She showed me the cabin where she and my father first lived, and the family who lived there now was nice enough to let us inside.

"Finally my mother showed me the point in the path where my father proposed, and she told me the whole story of the meeting, without mentioning the roadhouse part of it. I would learn that later from her diary after she passed. The roadhouse had burned to the ground two years before. I couldn't then explain the look in her eyes or the smile as she looked into the ashes, but I shall never forget it.

"I know that was a long side story. The thing I originally wanted to convey was that the whole time Bill was gone my father worked his shift, and Bill didn't lose a dime of his wages. That's just the type of businessman my father was.

"There was only one man on my father's staff who was a rotten apple -- Roland Self, an appropriate name as ever there was. Mr. Self was the business manager for my father, who called him a necessary evil. He was a wizard at purchasing and finance, but he had ambitions to run the company his way.

"Mr. Self always thought that he was of a better class than my father, and he hated the way my father fraternized with the general workers. He hated that there were too many electric lights in the place, and too many windows, and two fifteen-minute breaks in every ten-hour day, and BOTH days off on the weekend. He thought my father was an incompetent fool for paying the exorbitant sum of $1.50 every day to his workers. Most of all, he was jealous of my father's success and popularity.

"Roland Self was rolling in himself. After all, he was the one with the business degree. He was the man who kept the books

The Gadget Factory

and finances straight. He even had a better office than my father, which may have been the only flaw in my father's judgment.

"My father was glad to give up the executive office in the old factory. He didn't need a fancy place to hang his hat. He saw his 'office' as being out among his customers and his workers, with the company being itself foremost and not any one man. On the other hand, Mr. Self's office was like the powder puff palace of some two-bit king.

"My father was constantly coming up with new ideas for products to manufacture in his factory. He would often take his ideas to some worker that he knew would have some special insight into their worth and practical production. Some would fail to get off the ground, while others were impractical to manufacture with the technology of that day.

"From time to time he would get a chance to talk shop with and learn from some of the giants of his day. There were men like Henry Ford and Wilbur Wright, whom he counted as his friends and thought starters, but most of his ideas came from conversations with butchers, or barbers, or housewives. It was my father's mindset to find out what the ordinary customers needed in their lives and to invent a solution to meet those needs.

"While the mining tools remained his mainstay, he also made several thousand dollars from products like an advanced cutting blade for commercial meat cutters. He made an improvement for barber shears that netted the company over $100,000. He invented an improvement in automobile suspensions and manufactured a lighter and more efficient gear system for aeroplane controls.

"My father loved 'aeroplanes,' as he always called them. They were the reflection of his inventive spirit. When I was ten, we visited Wilbur Wright and he took my father for a ride. When they returned, to my surprise, Mr. Wright took me up. I was thrilled and hooked on flying for life.

"The pictures we see of Mr. Wright seem so sullen and serious. I suppose in the general public he was somewhat self-conscious. That was not the man I met. Mr. Wilbur Wright was so much like my father. When it came to the physical world around him, he was like a child with a Christmas toy. There were so many things to be done that had not yet been tried. Worlds to conquer you might say, and it all began with the smallest parts. No detail passed his attention.

"That afternoon we shared lunch with Mr. Wilbur and Mr. Orville. The three men spoke of how the aeroplane would improve and how it might shape the world. They even spoke of one day flying to the moon, and they made it sound so possible.

"As father became more involved in growing the business through invention, Mr. Self became more involved in the contract and bylaws end of the business. Mr. Self pointed out the growth and insisted that the company be regulated by a board of directors, as was the case with all companies of that size so that they would be protected from increasing government regulations and such.

"My father reluctantly agreed but was too busy to organize it. Mr. Self was glad to take on the burden to free up my father for expanding the business. My father was never truly happy with the 'business' end of the company. He understood business as well as any man, but his love was for the lathe and the laboratory, and Mr. Self was a spider who was more than happy to spin his front office webs.

"By 1911 my father had amassed a larger fortune than he could ever have hoped to build. We were set for life financially -- but blissfully unaware of the dreaded course that life would soon take."

Chapter 10
Down the Hudson to See the World

As Great Aunt Alice went on with her story, I noticed a hesitation. It was like someone trying to decide how to run past a machine gun.

"In the late fall of 1911, my mother took a turn for the worse. We had seen this before, but this time it held an unshakable dread. Her smile was so frail and her breathing so labored. With her tender instruction, I did all of the housework and was tired from it but glad for the education. I would not be a little girl forever, and I might become the lady of the home all too soon.

"The doctor told Father that our only hope was to winter in a warm place far away from Saugerties. He was sure that the healing powers of a hot sun would dry out her lungs and stimulate her pale skin.

"At that time there were only two places to winter. One was Florida and the other southern France. My father was worried that Florida was too primitive and that there would be no adequate hospitals nearby if mother should take a turn for the worse. He also balked at France, but only because he had never considered foreign travel possible with his humble roots.

"As was his habit, he discussed all of the major upheavals of his life with his lifetime friend Big Carl Johnson. Mr. Johnson assured my father that he could run the production end of the place and that 'old fat hat' (what the workers called Mr. Self), could manage the office. 'Besides,' Mr. Johnson said, 'what are you going to do with all of those gold coins -- line your coffin to make us pallbearers sweat more? Ellie needs you more now than we boys do. Give her a thrill, go first class, lie on the beach all day. You and I both know, Frank, those coins are gonna last you a lot longer than Ellie may. You'll never forgive yourself, Frank.'

"I was going to Whistler's grocery when I saw my father and Mr. Johnson having this conversation in the park. My father hung his head and slightly nodded in the affirmative. He shook his friend's hand and went for a solitary walk by the river.

"My father had a way of hiding his fears with rabid enthusiasm. When he returned from his walk, he burst through the door and boldly announced that we were going to winter in France. Mother did her best to respond with happy surprise, and I was beside myself.

"When I told my friends and teacher they were all abuzz. After class Miss Wilson took me aside and told me that she would miss her 'Best Student,' and that I must promise to keep a diary of the experience so I could give a full report in the spring.

"Outside little Alice was waiting for me with a tear in her eye. Ever since the rafting disaster she had developed a morbid fear of the water. She was certain that I wouldn't return from two trips across the deep Atlantic. I assured her that I would see her in the spring and that I would think of her every day. We hugged and I went home to pack.

"In the morning Mr. Donlon put us in his boat and rowed us out to meet the Albany ferry. He refused to take anything for his service except our thanks. He wished us a safe voyage and rowed back to the lighthouse dock, where I spotted Alice and Bud playing hooky, to wave goodbye. I waved back, but I don't know if they saw me amongst the crowded ferry.

"At last I was on my way down the Hudson to the great world beyond. Each turn of the river was an adventure of fall's splendid colors and nature's wonders. There were little streams that fed the great wide Hudson. I saw deer, raccoons, and even a red fox.

I watched fish leap and turtles lumber along, and snakes slither through the water. I saw colorful towns of all sizes, with horses and people moving about. Men and boys fished and worked on the river in all sorts of small craft. Some waved, while others were oblivious to the big ferry that rocked them with her wake. We passed a small cove where I could swear that I saw Flood fishing on the bank, but I knew that couldn't be true.

"With each bend we drew closer to the massive city of New York. We could see the smoke of the city first then the water grew turbulent and dirty. As we approached our berth, we found ourselves dwarfed by mason towers, some of them ten stories high. We were all fascinated by the size and the noise and bustle of it, but I think even my father was uncomfortable and a little frightened of it. The city seemed like some unnatural giant that would step on us without the slightest notice. In my much later life I would learn to enjoy and even love New York, but it was never to me what one would call a home.

"Fortunately we had little time to see the city as we had only two hours to arrive at Pier 54 to board R.M.S. Carpathia, bound for the Mediterranean. It was an enormous one stacker that belonged to the Cunard Line. She made the Albany ferry look like a rowboat. It was only eight years old and had added a first class section just two years before, so much of it was brand new. Standing at the rail and looking down at the people below was almost like the flight I had made with Mr. Wright. The giant buildings of the city were much less intimidating than from the pier level.

"Father got us settled in our stateroom and Mother rested while he took me to the rail to wave goodbye to the people on the dock. My heart nearly stopped when the ship's whistle blew, but it was a good surprise, and then we began to move from the pier.

"We moved so slowly at first. I told father that we were moving as slow as . . . but I couldn't think of how to finish it. Father chimed in with 'As slow as Bud on a school day,' and we both laughed out loud. I thought of that last sight of Bud and Alice on the Saugerties lighthouse dock and how easy it was to see them, and how they would have been nearly invisible in the New York City crowd below.

"Soon the tugboats came alongside and moved Carpathia toward the open water. Father took me up to see them operate, as he always approved of my curiosity for machines and used that excuse to observe them himself. As we watched them maneuver, he murmured to himself, 'Hmm, side thrusters,' as though he were making a mental note for some future invention. We passed the Statue of Liberty, and I was amazed at the size and beauty of her. A boy stood in the torch and waved to our ship. I waved back but I don't know if he saw me.

"Soon we were out to sea. The air smelled fresher than anything I had ever inhaled. The land drifted farther and farther until there was nothing but ocean everywhere. I remembered what Alice had said and was a little uneasy. It was for sure that we could no longer swim to shore and that even Flood would not be able to row to us in the event that we would sink.

"The uneasiness passed quickly, and I began to enjoy the passage. The enormity of the sea, the endless sky, the curve of the earth, the fish that played along the bow -- all of these things were new and wonderful.

"The ship itself was full of curiosities. There were great funnels sticking out of the deck that looked like tubas, and chains with huge links. There were lifeboats and cranes and the towering masts. I studied the crew and the tasks they performed. I met the captain on deck and had a nice chat with him.

"I don't remember the captain's name anymore, but I can picture him now. He was of medium build and height with a ruddy complexion. He was a man who seemed comfortable in both his position and attire. The captain had a friendly face and casual stance that lacked the authority one would associate with a ship's captain, but the vessel was clean and well run. He told me that he had a daughter back in England who was now grown and soon to be married. I told the captain of my mother's circumstances and why we were on this trip. He wished her well and thanked me for the pleasure of our chat. Then he tipped his worn hat and moved on to his other duties.

"The next day was rough and we were asked to refrain from going on deck. My poor mother was deathly seasick and my father to a lesser extent. I was still enough of a child to enjoy the unusual sensation. I sat on the floor with my legs spread and watched a ball roll from one foot to the other without my doing anything to move it. It didn't occur to me to be afraid until I looked out the porthole. One moment it looked like we would capsize into the ocean, and the next the sea would disappear altogether. I didn't have much time to be frightened though, as I had to help clean up after my mother.

"That was the only day of bad weather -- the rest of the trip was pleasant and warm. On the fourth day my mother and father sat on the deck and enjoyed the sun in their faces and some good conversation with a couple from Minnesota who had been wintering in France going on seventeen years.

"Meanwhile, I was free to explore the ship with a boy I had met on deck the first day. His name was William Buckley Longino, but his friends and family had always called him Billy Buck. He was on his way to Italy to visit with his ancestors and to study the Roman wonders before he began his full-time studies at the Citadel. His grandfather had been the governor of Mississippi, and it was his invitation to Teddy Roosevelt to join him in a delta bear hunt that led to the phrase 'Teddy Bear.'

"The thing I liked about Billy Buck was that he didn't put on airs, unlike so many of the other children in first class. He also liked to study mechanical things, and of course we had the connections with President Roosevelt. The fact that he was a year older and quite handsome didn't hurt either.

"We followed our plan to explore each deck from bow to stern. When we tried to enter the bridge, the captain gave us a warning scowl that told us not to enter, but he followed it with a wink and a shake of the head that told us to scoot. The ordinary seamen could have cared less where we went as long as we were not in their way. We took advantage of this to explore the galley, the immense hold, and the loud inferno of the engine room.

"Several years later Carpathia was sunk by a Germen U-boat, and five of the men in the engine room were killed. I've often wondered if any of the men we saw down there were among the ones killed in 1918.

"Our favorite stop was a visit to Mr. Cottam in the wireless shack. It was a place of fear and wonder. As I watched the sparks flash I felt quite sure that one could easily get electrocuted in such a job. The wonderful part was the fact that Mr. Cottam was speaking to people all over the ocean through dots and dits and thin air. He showed us how it worked and even let us send one message each to his counterpart and friend on R.M.S. Mauretania.

"When we were safely alone, Billy Buck would hold my hand. I liked that. When we were deep in the hold one day he kissed me. I liked that even better. In fact he kissed me with a passion that made my heart pound even more strongly than when I had been with Tommy. My skin was tight and I was feeling faint. I wanted to run and I wanted him to touch me more at the same time. Fortunately a large rat ran across our feet and broke the mood at once."

Chapter 11
Winter in France

"As we drew near to the Mediterranean Sea, we could begin to see its door, Gibraltar. My father and I stood at the bow as the great rock first rose over the horizon. Growing closer, we could make out the strait that divided Europe from Africa. To that point I had only seen one continent, my own, and now I was looking at two additional continents at the same time.

"The water going into the Mediterranean was so rough that day that it seemed that she was unwilling to let our ship enter. I found out later that the roughness sometimes occurs as a natural combination of the fact that the sea bed rises in the straits along with the narrowness of the passage. Still I was very uneasy as the violent nature of the water reminded me of the raft being torn apart in the Hudson. I thought of what Alice had feared, and wondered if her intuition would be right.

"Once we passed through the rough water, the Mediterranean opened up to a world of deep blue sea, crystal blue skies and warm sun on our faces. Carpathia seemed to float higher on the water, as though it was relaxing from its long Atlantic passage.

"Father brought mother out to the deck to enjoy the beauty and to feel the sun. She seemed truly happy with the glorious warmth and the inspiring sights. Her eyes were more like the eyes

I had remembered and she smiled as I had not seen her smile for some time. They walked the decks like a couple of newlyweds.

"Our destination was Marseille where we would secure land transportation to a seaside cottage in Rayol-Canadel-sur-Mer. Billy Buck came to see me off as we left the ship. He touched my hand, and I gave him a kiss on the cheek. My mother asked me what that was all about, but I just smiled and she let it pass. I was a transforming girl of eleven now. I would never be as tall as my parents, and I would always be thin as a rail, but let's just say that I was maturing nicely for my age. My mother knew that I might not see Billy Buck again, but there would be other boys to draw her concern.

"Rayol-Canadel-sur-Mer is a place of steep cliffs and overlooks where one can look straight down to the bottom of the sea. There was a massive stone staircase that led to the wide sandy beaches. It was not the center of tourism, and a good quiet place to relax and enjoy life. We had a Frenchwoman who would cook a meal for us each day in her nearby home and bring it to us in the evening. My father and I fixed any other meals we chose to eat, and did the cleaning as needed. All of this was to allow my mother to rest and enjoy our vacation.

"My parents preferred to stay near the cottage where they could look out to the sea from their balcony and sit in the sunshine. Sometimes they would go to the beach, but not as often as I would have cared to go.

"I wanted to live outside every minute I could. I would explore the hills, and what there was of the town, but of course the beach was my main course. I loved the sand. I loved the water. I loved the boats and the fish of the sea. I loved to study the people who came to enjoy it as well.

"After a week or so we settled into a routine. Father and I would fix breakfast and do any morning chores that were needed. Father would then set me down for some schoolwork. My mother taught me to read at an early age, so I had been ahead in my school. I was proficient in grammar and I loved history. My best subject was geography, which fed my interest in world travel. I was above most in the mechanical sciences, but only fair in the biological sciences. My weakest subject was mathematics, so my father concentrated on that alone and left the other subjects for Miss Wilson when we would return in the spring. By noon my schooling was over for the day, and I would fix a light lunch. Then I would go off for three or four hours of exploring and play. In the evenings I would often write to my dear friend Ethel Roosevelt, and was always glad to hear from her.

"The rest of this daily routine came from my parent's journals. It seems that they took quite an advantage of my time away. At first my father was hesitant. He was afraid that he would tax Mother at a time when she needed rest. She let him know that it would make no difference to her remaining span, and that she wanted more than anything to feel again like a woman, and not an invalid. My mother wrote that it was like their newlywed days when they were both inexperienced and father was so cautious to not hurt his bride. She did now as she had in those days. She pulled his strong hands to her and whispered in his ear, 'Touch me.' He nervously complied and was so tender. She took pleasure in his gentle ways, but as he gained confidence that he wasn't hurting her she urged him to give her the full force of his strength as a man would give a roadhouse girl. With her long bouts of poor health she had lost confidence in her ability to inspire Frank. Her general health was no better or worse, but her spirits were made strong by the knowledge that she could still create and feed her good husband's passions.

"My afternoons were spent in adventure. I met some interesting people in the town and on the beach. Madame Furnet sold music boxes to the tourists, and by their word of mouth had developed a clientele all over the world. The boxes were made by craftsmen in Switzerland, Germany, and Southern France. There were very large boxes that would play various disks. There were very tiny boxes with ornate designs that played single tunes.

"Once a week I would work for her by dusting the merchandise. In turn she paid me by letting me listen to their pretty tunes, and by teaching me a little French. Madame Furnet knew enough English in order to get along with her international customers, so the communication between us wasn't perfect but adequate and quite fun at times. By the end of our stay I had learned enough to enjoy the language and eventually became quite good at it if not fully fluent.

"Monsieur Charcuterie couldn't speak a word of English. He appeared as being gruff with children, but I believe that was his way of play, and not so much a genuine dislike of children. He was the town butcher, and a good one. It was fun to watch him work, and one could tell that butchering was not a job to him but his proud profession.

"What drew me most to Monsieur Charcuterie was the fact that he was using one of my father's machines. When I pointed this out to my father he was eager to come to the shop. Neither could speak the other's language, so my father introduced himself by placing one of his cards next to the label on the machine. Monsieur Charcuterie lit up and indicated that he was proud to have such a fine machine.

"As he went back to work, my father listened and detected an odd sound. Through sign language he asked Monsieur Charcuterie for a screwdriver which father used to make the slightest adjustment. After the adjustment father indicated that Monsieur Charcuterie should try it again. There was a broad smile on Monsieur Charcuterie's face as he tested my father's work. Obviously the machine had been working well or Monsieur Charcuterie would have raked my father over the coals when they first met, but now his good machine was working to perfection. Above all Monsieur Charcuterie was a professional, and anything that took him from better to best was important to his pride.

"Monsieur Charcuterie said with great enthusiasm, 'Merci! Merci!' He then cut a fine piece of beef and gave it to my father. My father reached for his wallet to pay for the beef and Monsieur Charcuterie staunchly said, 'Non, Non!'

"My father held out his hand to thank his new friend, but Monsieur Charcuterie hesitated. His hand was sticky with blood, and he didn't want to offend my father. My father had always told me that no man's hand is too dirty to shake, and would cite his own initial poor judgment of Flood. Without hesitation he pushed his hand into Monsieur Charcuterie's. As they shook hands my father said, 'Blood brothers.' I don't know if Monsieur Charcuterie understood, but from that time on they were the best of friends. That was the way my father was with people, and I have always been most proud of him for it.

"Another interesting character about the place was Mr. McKinzie, a retired Scottish school teacher. Mr. McKinzie was an artist. I could expect to see him just about anywhere. One day I would see him on the cliffs, and another I would see him painting on the beach. He would paint interesting people he had observed, or he would paint from the beautiful vistas the area offered. Mr. McKinzie was as nice a man as one could meet. He was gentle and friendly. He didn't mind my watching him paint. In fact I think he enjoyed my company. I marveled at his skill, but I can't say I learned anything from it, for I have never been able to paint more than a barn."

"Which is more than I can say for you great nephew." I blushed when Great Aunt Alice told me that, but I couldn't argue against it. She continued with her story.

"As a rule I would spend the first hour of two of my play time with the adults, as the children were still in school. I would then play by myself, or with Jean Louis and Günter.

"It was hard to find friends at first. The society girls who were wintering with their parents, were tutored in the mornings, and spent their afternoons at social events, or sitting like china dolls near the beach. They would have nothing to do with me. I'm sure they thought me a local urchin. There they were in their expensive clothes that couldn't be soiled, while I played carefree in outfits that could serve equally in climbing the cliffs or swimming in the sea.

"I could do both activities in a day's time and could care less how I looked. Perhaps I was a little too casual as I came out of the water. I was blissfully unaware of how my wet clothes drew attention to my emerging body, but I'm quite sure now that the boys noticed.

"I first met Jean Louis on the beach. I was making a sand castle, and without the slightest introduction he came over and began to work with me. Jean Louis was thirteen and still small as boys often are at that age. He spoke very little English and I spoke only a little French so we mainly communicated through gestures and smiles. He did have an awfully impressive smile. He had coal dark hair and perfect brown eyes, which he didn't hesitate to use on me. He wasn't shy about looking at me all over, especially when we came in from swimming. I didn't encourage him though I wasn't about to tell him off either.

"Günter was a blue-eye German blond of fourteen whose father was apparently involved with the German government. His father was still in Berlin working while his mother and grandmother were wintering in Rayol-Canadel-sur-Mer with Günter and five servants.

"Günter was always better dressed than we were but he was not afraid to get his clothes dirty. Günter was just the opposite of Jean Louis. While Jean Louis preferred the beach, Günter preferred the hills. Günter was shy around me, and would look the other way when I emerged from the water.

"I met Günter while I was exploring the cliffs. I had just left Mr. McKinzie, who had been studying an ocean liner through a telescope for some future painting. Günter and I surprised each other on the path and he could only say 'Guten Tag, Fraulein.'

"I said, 'Hello'

"In return and he said, 'English?'

"I told him I was an American and he lit up. Like me Günter had dreamed of sailing to a great foreign land, and America was his goal as Europe had been one of mine. Günter spoke excellent English and fluent French so it was easy to talk to him. He did not speak fluent 'girl' so it was harder for him to talk to me.

"I was pleasantly surprised to find that Günter and Jean Louis were already friends. Being small, Jean Louis had always been picked on by the boys in his class, so he admired the strength and protection of Günter's friendship. Günter on the other hand, being so shy, enjoyed the outgoing adventurous nature of

Jean Louis. They both seemed to enjoy me as I was not like the other girls. I was just enough of a tomboy to make them feel comfortable.

"We played well together, but there was some love interest on both of their parts, and at times I noticed some tension. Still I did not experience the passion of my shipboard relationship with Billy Buck.

"Our winter friendship was fun, we swam, we explored the caves in the hills, we wondered through the town and interacted with the shopkeepers, and sometimes we would go to the beach at night and marvel at the stars and the lights of the ships in the distance.

"Life was wonderful and winter was summer, but on two occasions it almost became tragic. The three of us were swimming one afternoon when Günter suddenly found himself caught in a riptide. He was only a fair swimmer and was soon in terrible trouble. Jean Louis was a very experienced swimmer and knew the sea well. Somehow Jean Louis made it out to Günter before he went under and pulled him along the grain of the riptide until they could find a way back into the beach. I had been closer to the beach and swam back to it as fast as I could. I kept my eyes on the struggling boys, running parallel to their swimming, and screaming for help.

"Mr. McKinzie was working on the beach that day and saw the boys in peril. We found a rope and waded into the water as far as we could. He threw the rope four times. It fell short each time. Finally in desperation I took an end of the rope, and swam for the boys. I too was now in the riptide, but the boys had fought to where I could just reach Jean Louis's hand. With one hand in Jean Louis' and the other on the rope we shouted for Mr. McKinzie to pull us in. The sand was shifting below Mr. McKinzie's feet and he too was nearly swept out to sea. An Ethiopian couple on their honeymoon saw his plight and ran to help Mr. McKinzie. Finally we were close enough to the shore that Günter's feet began to touch and Mr. McKinzie and the Ethiopian honeymooners were in a better position to pull. With an almost dying effort the three of us finally made it to the beach.

"When the boys were safely ashore they were both too exhausted to celebrate. They lay on the beach flat on their backs, gave each other a pat and told each other 'Mon Ami,' 'Mon Ami.'

"The other near tragedy took place on Günter's home turf. We were playing along the steep cliffs when the ground gave way. It was by near superhuman ability that Günter was able to grab both Jean Louis with one hand and a stable rock with the other. It was a straight drop to the rocks below, and it was up to Günter to hold on to save them both. With the strength of an ox Günter pulled Jean Louis up to where he could grasp Günter's shoulders. Jean Louis climbed the big German boy like a rock climber to the point where I could lend a hand to pull him to safety. Now it was up to us to pull Günter to his own safety, but he was too big for the two of us. Once again Günter summoned his strength, this time to save himself. We did what we could, but it was mostly his will that defied the inevitable. Finally his foot caught a hole in the cliff, and he was able to coax his body to safer ground.

"This time all three of us were flat on our backs and exhausted. I was shaking like a scared rabbit out of fear and relief. When I regained the strength I gave Günter a kiss smack on the lips and buried my face in his chest. I was crying like a baby, and thoroughly overcome with emotion. Günter grew red as a beet, and looked at me as though it was the most wonderful thing anyone had done for him. Jean Louis just lay there huffing and puffing, 'Merci, merci, merci, mon ami.'

"By comparison the rest of the winter was uneventful. We swam in the sea and played on the beach. We explored the hills and found a cave where I stepped on the skull of a rat in the dark. We convinced one of the 'China Dolls' to build a sand castle with us, and the boys buried us both in the sand, and ran off. I'm sure it was the only fun she had that winter, but we made a mess of her 'doll' clothes, and we never saw her again.

"On the day for our return to America, the boys and I parted with kisses, and hugs, and a few tears. We had made and survived the perils of our diverse friendship, and I knew I would not likely see them again.

"Sadder still was the end of this episode. Years later, near the end of the Great War, both boys were conscripted into their opposing armies. In a battle late in the war they came upon each other. Unable to identify their foe in the smoke of battle, they both fired on each other. As Jean Louis drew near he recognized the boy who had saved his life on the cliffs in 1912. Günter raised his hand to the boy who had saved him from the riptide, but he could not speak as the blood choked in his mouth. Jean Louis fell across Günter's chest in grief as he passed out from his own wounds.

"At the time my friend Ethel was a nurse at a field hospital along the front. She recognized Jean Louis by matching his ramblings with my letters of that winter in France.

"Poor Günter lost his life to his friend, and poor Jean Louis recovered from his wounds but he lost his mind, and perhaps his soul."

Chapter 12
The Frozen Tears

Once again several days passed before Great Aunt Alice would tell me more of her story. I couldn't tell if she was recovering from that last bit of sadness or avoiding a burden to come. There was something very dark and violent in her mind, as if she were protecting herself, and maybe me, from some satanic force.

We worked on the ornate porch railings. They were loaded with gingerbread -- and hard as the dickens to scrape and prepare for painting. That seemed to suit Great Aunt Alice. It was solitary work, and she needed solitude. I watched her scrape and scrub on that gingerbread as if she were scrubbing away the house's sins. All the while, she said not a word to me.

Days passed, and finally she just stopped what she was doing, and said, "It's time." Great Aunt Alice went into the house and brought out the recorder. She wouldn't look at me, but she began her telling with a deliberate effort, as if she were riding a bicycle into a head wind and not worrying about the results, just turning the crank until the task was finished:

"It was time for us to come home. After I said my goodbyes to the boys, we stopped in to say farewell to Madame Furnet, and my father purchased a music box from her for my mother. I noticed that it was one that I had been eyeing for myself, and I wondered if he was buying it for me to enjoy as well. We then took a moment to say goodbye to my father's friend Monsieur Charcuterie, who wished us well and gave us some cheese for the trip.

"I had looked everywhere for Mr. McKinzie. He was apt to be anywhere, so it was difficult at times to cross paths with him. As luck would have it, he was at the bridge, where there was a good view of both the Mediterranean and the town. Father was kind enough to make the side trip so I could say goodbye. Mr. McKinzie was surprised to see us, as he thought we would be leaving a week or so later. We hugged each other like father and daughter, and I began to cry. To my surprise he did too. Before we parted, he reached into the bottom of his box and pulled out a small painting of me swimming in the Mediterranean. I was immensely pleased and thanked him profusely. We exchanged addresses and promised to write, but I never heard from him again.

"I don't remember where we boarded the train for Paris, but I remember the French countryside and how much it seemed like rural New York State.

"Mother had only held her own that winter and she tired easily, so when we reached Paris we didn't do much sightseeing. What we did see was magnificent, and of course one is always impressed by the Eiffel Tower.

"From Paris we traveled to Roscoff, where we stayed a few days to rest before taking the ferry to Ireland. Father had decided that since we were so close, and may never get the opportunity again, we should visit my mother's ancestral home in Cullenagh.

At this point Great Aunt Alice began to soften and relax a bit in her storytelling.

"My mother had always wanted to see her father's home. Her mother, as a dying wish, had asked Mother to take some dirt from Grandfather Mahafee's grave, and sprinkle it on the home place if she would ever have the chance. Mother never dreamed that she would have the opportunity, especially in those days of her impoverished and orphaned youth, but she wore a small locket with a few grains of dirt from Grandfather's grave for years for this express purpose, and to keep him near to her heart.

"When we arrived in Cullenagh, we stopped at a local pub, where my father asked for information that might link us with some family members. A fellow named Dorsey knew exactly where to look, and he took us to the farm of Robert Mahafee, who was a first cousin to my Grandfather Mahafee.

"Cousin Robert had not seen his cousin Charlie since he had departed from Queenstown, but he had a letter from my Grandfather Mahafee telling about the birth of my mother. He gave the letter to my mother, who was very happy to accept the priceless note in her father's own hand. She put it in her diary, and I have it to this day.

"Cousin Robert took us to meet my Grandfather's elderly Aunt Molly. Aunt Molly was 103 years old and was so happy to see us. She studied my mother and told her over and over how much she looked just like her sister, my grandfather's mother. My mother had never seen her grandmother, and she was more than a little excited to know that Aunt Molly had a tintype of her. It took a little bit of searching, but we found it, and my mother wept at the sight of it. Here she was looking at her grandmother's face for the first time.

"Aunt Molly let us stay with her that night. Cousin Robert went home after supper. Mother was very tired, so she and Father went to bed while I helped Aunt Molly do the dishes. We talked for some time before Aunt Molly interrupted with, 'Bless my soul, now I know who you favor. You are the spitting image of my mother, your Great-Grandmother Riley Mahafee. She was small like you and she was a real tomboy, and had those same beautiful eyes.' Aunt Molly was the sweetest thing. She was more like a close girlfriend than an elderly aunt. The age between us just melted as we spoke.

"She asked me if the boys had noticed me yet. I told her about Tommy, Billy Buck, Jean Louis, and Günter. She in turn talked about the beaus she had to fight off when she was my age, and we both admitted that we hadn't fought very hard to discourage them. We talked and giggled like two schoolgirls. Like I said, one couldn't have guessed that there were ninety-two years between us. We kissed goodnight, and she tucked me in like she had her own girls, one of whom she had already outlived. I was too old to be tucked in, but I wouldn't have missed it for the world that night.

"In the morning Cousin Robert took us to the cabin where my Grandfather Mahafee was born. It was no longer in use, and was worse for the years. In somber exploration, my mother found a post in the home where the initials 'C. M.' were carved at about the height of a little boy's reach. There were also some marks on the north wall that looked like a growth chart, and Mother wondered if those too were related to her father. Father held us back so she could 'visit' with her father and weep in privacy. She wrote that night of how much she wished she could hold his rough hands, and bury her head in his loving chest.

"We stood in a circle on the front lawn and Mother sprinkled the dirt from Grandfather's grave. Father said a general prayer for Grandfather Charles, Grandmother Susie, and Mother. Then we all joined in the 'Our Father.'

"A mile down the road was the graveyard where my great-grandparents were buried. We paid our respects, and then Father took out his pocket knife and loosened the soil so that Mother could place some of it in her locket. It was her intention to sprinkle the dirt on her father's grave to join him once again with his parents.

"We stayed that night with Aunt Molly, and the next day we were off to Queenstown, where we would catch our ship for home. I wanted to stay, and I now wish we had forever remained in Ireland. Aunt Molly's tears mingled with mine as we hugged for the last time. I know that those few days in Ireland have remained in me all of these years and were perhaps the best days of my life.

"To our great surprise, Father had booked us second class tickets on the newest and grandest ocean liner of the day, White Star's R.M.S. Titanic. To say the least, we were thrilled. It was so large that it made Carpathia look like a rowboat. It was too large to come all the way into the port, so we had to take a small ferry out to the ship to board her. There were a good number of

Irish immigrants who were ferried out with us, making us feel at home. Despite my father's wealth, we were always more at home with the common classes.

"As we pulled alongside the great ship, we were struck with the overpowering size of her, and the shine of her paint. By boarding from the ferry, we were able to see more of the ship as the stewards led us through the ship and up the many decks to our cabin. To either a child or an adult, it would have been the greatest playhouse if we had it all to ourselves. The wood was new, the doorknobs were new, the carpets were new deep and luxurious. It had a smell about it that I can't describe, except to say it smelled new. Our stateroom was wonderful, even better than the first class cabin we had on Carpathia.

"My mother was tired, so we stayed in our stateroom the rest of the day, and we ordered our supper in. In the morning we strolled the deck in wonder, and we met the nicest people. There was a couple from Menlo Park, New Jersey, who had just taken their son to attend school in Oxford that fall. The gentleman was a bulldozer operator, and since the bulk of his work ran from spring to fall they had stayed in Europe to sightsee before returning to work. They were very proud of their son, who apparently was some sort of prodigy in the field of physics, and he could play the harp 'like an angel.'

"An Irish shopkeeper was traveling to America with his wife to see their first grandchild. It seems his daughter had fallen in love with an American pharmaceutical chemist who worked for the Eli Lilly Company. The chemist was traveling in Ireland just because he had the means and the desire to do so. While he was there the young American went into the shop, and he was smitten with the shopkeeper's daughter. One thing led to another and they were wed in Ireland before he took her to a place called Greenfield, Indiana.

"The shopkeeper was proud enough of his son-in-law and sure of his financial ability to care for his daughter, and certainly he was anxious to see his first grandchild, but he was deeply concerned for their safety. He asked my father if he knew anything of the Indian situation in Greenfield, Indiana, and if there were any hostile tribes. My father had never heard of Greenfield, Indiana, but he assured the shopkeeper that the Indians there were most noble and lived by a code that would not think of harming a woman or child. My mother, as was her custom, drew very close to my father, and when she was sure the shopkeeper could not see, she poked him in the ribs with her sharp elbow."

Great Aunt Alice had relaxed a little more. She was in the part of the story that was pleasant to her memory. She turned to face me with her back to the opposite porch post. Her smile had returned a bit with a slight dream accent to her looks. She asked me if I wanted some tea and I said, "No," not wanting to disturb the momentum we had gained.

She returned to her story with her family still enjoying their second class deck stroll.

"We heard a shout from above -- 'Frank, Frank Howard, is that you?' It was Major Archie Butt, whom we had met at the Roosevelt Christmas party, calling down from the first class deck.

"'Archie!' my father replied, 'What are you doing here?'

"'I work for Taft now. For heaven's sake man, why are we standing here shouting like a couple of fools? Come up and join me for lunch.'

"My father replied that we couldn't, as we were second class on this voyage

"'What the blazes man, you saved the President's life. You've spent Christmas with two Presidents at the table. Next to that, these people are steerage.'

"We went back to our stateroom to dress for lunch and walked up to the first class gate, where we were stopped in our tracks by a vigilant steward. 'I'm sorry sir, first class only.' Major Butt anticipated the problem and was there to greet us. He pressed his hand on the steward's shoulder and with his best military demeanor explained the situation. 'Sir, I work for the President of the United States. Last week I had tea with your King George, and I consider this man to be their equal and one of my dearest friends.'

"'But sir, this is first class and I have my orders.'

"'Then let me pose this situation to you. How fast do you think you will have to swim to catch up to this ship after I forcibly throw you overboard?'

"On the walk to the dining room, my father gave Major Butt a brief synopsis of our winter and mother's condition. He shared with his friend how he had found a butcher by the name of Charcuterie who owned one of his machines and how he had fixed it on the spot.

"Major Butt remarked on the good service, and offered his view that someday U.S. companies would be manufacturing, servicing, and selling goods all over this world. My father doubted that, as it was hard enough running a company in one small town.

"We had a lovely lunch that day. The first class dining room was beyond description. First Officer Murdock joined us at the table, along with a man and wife of some high social order. I can't tell you their names, as I vowed to forget them about a minute after I met them. They were two stuffed shirts, out to impress everyone they met. The man spoke little, as if he were too high in the pantheon to speak to mere mortals. The woman was simply horrid. She impressed me as a high class golddigger who lacked nothing, and complained about everything. Her corset was so tight she could hardly breathe, but it didn't restrict her snide remarks.

"She was at our table to rub elbows with Major Butt, as he was an important aide to President William Howard Taft of the United States of America, if you get my drift. She hung on Major Butt's every word in order to gloat about her close association with the President's right-hand man. Mr. and Mrs. High Hat were miffed that Mr. Murdock, and not Captain Smith, was the crew's representative. They ignored us like we were servants.

"Major Butt sized up the situation and decided to have a little fun with these pretenders. He introduced Father as the man who had saved President Roosevelt's life on San Juan Hill, and went on about the Christmas in the White House, and how the three of them had sat for hours after dinner smoking cigars and sharing war stories.

The Frozen Tears

"The High Hats sat up and took notice at those words, and they began to look at us as possibly someone important. My mother joined their fun with a remark about how gracious Edith Roosevelt was, and what a good friend she had been over the years. There was some truth to that statement, as Mrs. Roosevelt and my mother continued to swap letters every month or so since our Christmas visit. Then she added, 'How are Bill and Nellie these days? I bet we haven't seen them in over two months.' Major Butt assured her that they were both in good health and that he would make sure to tell Mrs. Taft to call Mother when he got back to Washington.

"The High Hats were now fully engaged and ready to swallow anything we were scoundrel enough to feed them. Major Butt finished them off by asking my father if he had been involved with any of those 'foreign assignments.' He said that phrase as if it were something so diabolical as to be left unsaid in front of polite company.

"The two men kept casually eating their steaks as they conversed, and between bites my father said, 'Well there was that problem in southern France with that Monsieur Charcuterie. You know about him don't you?'

"'Oh yes, a real butcher -- how did you make out?'

"'I FIXED the problem.'

"'You FIXED the problem?'

"Both men said the word FIXED as though it were a terminal word.

"'I was the better butcher,' my father replied, and both men laughed.

"Mr. High Hat choked on his wine. He had heard of such 'special government assignments,' but he had never dreamed that they were true, or that he would be sitting at the same table with a cold-blooded killer. Mother finished off Mrs. High Hat by imploring Mr. Murdock to ask his chef, to share with her chef, the recipe for the delicious red sauce. At the mention of the red sauce, Mrs. High Hat turned quite green.

"By this point the High Hats seemed confused as to whether they wanted to know us or not. They appeared quite anxious not to make Father angry.

"Just when I thought things couldn't get better, I saw my mother waving to another table, where a woman jumped up and walked briskly across the room.

"Mrs. High hat said, 'Oh goodie, it's Molly.' She said 'Molly' like it was some sort of disease.

"'Ellie! Frank!' she shouted.

"It was Mrs. Brown. She and her husband had once visited with us in Saugerties. Mr. Brown had come to my father's factory to order some mining machinery, and my mother insisted that they stay with us for a few days of rest before they traveled on. Mr. and Mrs. Brown were very much like my parents. They had made their wealth by the sweat of their brow, as my parents had, and Mrs. Brown enjoyed playing a little social poker with the society crowd.

"Mr. Murdock and Major Butt smiled when they saw Mrs. Brown coming over. Most of the men enjoyed her playful relaxed demeanor. Most of the first class women looked down on her as classless.

"Mrs. Brown looked at me and said, 'Oh my little Alice, you are now a full grown lady.'

"I smiled from ear to ear and gave her a big hug. Mrs. Brown chatted with Mother for a few minutes, and she made us promise to dine with her that evening. Mr. and Mrs. High Hat avoided us for the rest of the meal, and the rest of the trip.

"When we were finished, Mother suggested that Father spend the afternoon with Major Butt, as she was growing tired and would like a nap before supper. When Father returned to the cabin, Mother was still asleep. He sent his regrets to Mrs. Brown and suggested we meet the next evening, and then he ordered room service. We all slept very well that night.

"The next morning after breakfast in the second class dining room, I asked my father if I could spend the day exploring the ship. My father replied with great emphasis that it would be a wonderful education for me to see firsthand the acres of engineering marvels that abounded throughout and on each deck of this, the mightiest vessel that had ever sailed. It would be a grave dereliction of his fatherly duties to not sanction his daughter's only chance to learn from the majesty of this moment. He didn't fool Mother for a second. 'Oh get on, you two, I'll be fine.' Father kissed her quickly and we raced off to explore the ship. 'And make sure you come back on time to clean up for supper!'

"There was so much to see. We didn't know where to start. A voice behind us spoke up, 'I'd start from the bridge.' It was First Officer Murdock, and he was quite willing to show us around, as he was just going on watch. The bridge was a wonder of shining brass and technology. Mr. Murdock showed us the telegraph device that they used to communicate with the engine room and the tubes for exchanging verbal commands with various parts of the ship. He showed us the electric board from where he could throw a switch and close all of the watertight doors. He showed us how to plot and maintain a course in the unrecognizable expanse of the sea. He even let me steer the ship for a minute or two.

"The bridge itself was a sort of office for the ship. There were many crewmen attending to their specific duties. The view of the ship and the wide flat endless sea gave one the feeling of standing on the throne of God to survey the universe. Mr. Murdock told us that the only better view of the world was from the crow's nest, but he could not allow us up there.

"My father thanked Mr. Murdock for his time and we pressed on to the next logical step, the wireless shack. Titanic had two wireless operators, Mr. Phillips and Mr. Bride. When we reached the door we found Mr. Bride pounding out a huge stack of messages from the passengers to their friends. My father asked if we could watch, and Mr. Bride had no objection.

"Father was like a kid in a candy store as he looked over the equipment. With a look of wonder he said, 'Alice, there is a potential in wireless that we have yet to realize. The day will come when we will hear music, or the voice of our President sent over the air to all parts of our country. Oh, I know it's all a bunch of Morse dits and dots for now, but someday that will be a voice. Mark my word, Alice, there is great potential. Take that chair, for example. If it were adjustable for height, the operator would be much more comfortable and could do half again as much work without fatigue.' My father always had a way of bypassing the beautiful curtains and looking at the rod.

"During a break I told Mr. Bride about meeting Mr. Cottam and using Carpathia's wireless. He said that he knew Cottam well but that he hadn't heard from him on this trip, and didn't know the whereabouts of Carpathia. As we turned to leave the shack, Mr. Bride invited me to come back after 8:00 that night and we would see who was out there. My father made me very happy by saying yes.

"As we explored we found a gymnasium, an elevator, and even a swimming pool. There was a whole car in the hold, with room for a hundred more.

"The last stop was the engine room. It was like descending into the depths of Hell. Loud and hot, it was a world of giant pistons, huge gears and wheels, and boilers as big as a house. Men with muscles the size of trees fed coal to the insatiable appetites of the fires. My father saw in their labor the toil of his fellow miners, and wished for them a better life. That night my father worked on a sketch of a great auger system that could feed all of the boilers or just one at the pull of a lever, thus eliminating the back breaking work of the firemen."

The tone of Great Aunt Alice's voice grew very serious.

"There was the electrical generation room, where they made all of the electricity for the ship, with its roar and spark."

Great Aunt Alice stopped and turned from me. It was several minutes before she could speak again, and when she eventually resumed she could not look at me as she spoke.

"I remember the faces of those men, every one of them. They stayed on duty till the ship went under, just to give us a little more light. They stayed on duty. They died in that room. I can still see their faces."

The strain was beginning to tell on Great Aunt Alice. I didn't know the details to come, but I knew enough about Titanic's story to know there was tragedy very near and could see that she was not strong enough to tell it yet.

I suggested that we stop for the day. Great Aunt Alice went to her room and didn't wake up until the next morning. She spent all of that day alone. She walked down by the creek, and later she went up for a midday flight. She passed me on her way from the barn to the house and gave me a melancholy hug. It would be another week before she would say any more about Titanic. Then one day we were scraping the east side of the house and she just started talking.

"Sunday was very cold. The sun was shining, but it was cold. The ocean was so smooth it looked like one could walk on it. Mother was not doing well at all that day, but she accompanied Father and me to church. After the service she went to her cabin to rest and fell asleep until after 4 p.m. Father and I went to the point of the bow and counted the steps to the stern. I wish I could remember how many we counted, but I can't."

We put down our scraping tools and sat on the porch floor. She pulled her legs up and put her arms around them as if she was trying to make herself very small. Great Aunt Alice was usually so "take charge" in her demeanor, but she spoke now in a tone that was somber and detached -- not hateful, just like a bewildered lost child.

"Father and I stopped to study one of the lifeboats. He showed me how they worked, and he talked of an idea he was formulating for a pulley and winch system that would have worked better. Then he stopped and surveyed the whole line of the lifeboats. He had a look of deep concern as he surveyed them. Father had saved many a worker when he spotted safety problems in the mine. He said nothing to me, but I knew he was unhappy with whatever he saw.

"I don't remember much more about that day. He held my hand. He had big hands, miner's hands, and yet he held mine so gently. I don't know why, but I remember stopping on the deck, turning to him, and asking, 'Do you love me?' He told me that he loved me more than anyone in the world except Mother. I asked if he still loved her as much, now that she was older and in such poor health. 'Is she still beautiful to you?' 'Your mother is more beautiful to me than she ever was. I love her twice as much as yesterday, and that has doubled with every day before. I would give anything for you and your mother. I would give my wealth, my inventions, my friendships, even my life. I know you are worried about your mother, and you know that I am too. Alice, someday death will part us all. That is the way of life. We also know that God will bring us together in a wonderful place where we will never part. Alice, no matter what separates us in life our love for each other will always be here.'

"Father took his massive hand and placed it on my heart. Then he took my small hand and pressed it to his heart. I don't know why he said all of that. Was it a general sentiment directed at my inquiry, or did he have a premonition?"

Great Aunt Alice's eyes were now fixed forward toward the barn. Great streams of tears flowed down her cheeks. My first impulse was to give her a hug, but something told me not to disturb her trance. I thought she would stop for the day, but she pressed on.

"You know what happened. Father had been visiting with Major Butt earlier in the evening and was on deck when Titanic hit the iceberg. He scanned the looks on the faces of the officers and he overheard the word 'lifebelts.'

"Father burst into our stateroom and explained what he had seen, and that we were to immediately dress very warm and put on our lifebelts. With Father all the time shouting for us to hurry, we dressed quickly according to his instructions. Mother grabbed the satchel with their valuables and threw in a change of clothes for each of us. With one sweep she gathered our toothbrushes and such into the bag, slightly nicking her hand on Father's razor.

"Father almost carried us to the boat deck where some of the protesting women were just beginning to be loaded. The ship's funnels roared as the steam was let off. There was confusion in the eyes of everyone on deck, and yet nothing seemed wrong. My father shoved us toward one of the lifeboats and tried to put us in. At that point my mother became frightened and screamed, 'NO!' My father shouted with great force, 'GET IN THE BOAT!' Then he physically grabbed my mother and me and threw us into the boat. I was shocked, I had never heard my father speak so roughly to my mother, and he had never laid a hand on her in a crude fashion. As we were lowered, Mother screamed, 'FRANK! FRANK!'

"He shouted back twice, 'I LOVE YOU!' Then he shouted, 'ALICE, ALWAYS REMEMBER!' and he placed his hand on his heart.

"I never saw my father again."

This time Great Aunt Alice rolled against me and I held her like a ball, like a lost child. She cried and cried. I told her it was OK. We should stop for now. She jerked up and shouted angrily, "No, I want to get this behind me!" She paused . . . . and then she spoke.

"When we touched the water and the lines were cut loose, I began to grasp the gravity of the situation. I didn't have a feel of it from the deck, but in the water I could see that Titanic was not nearly as tall as she had been when we boarded her from the Queenstown ferry. As we pulled away from the ship, I could see that the bow was most definitely lower in the water. Still there was so little that told me to be alarmed. The ship was indeed sinking, but so gracefully, so slowly. Mr. Hartley's band played so cheerfully. The lights were full ablaze, most people not realizing the agonizing fear among the engineering crew, who would work till the end to keep them lit. The noise of the people was like that of a large party. The rockets lit the sky as if in celebration.

"My mother's condition was made all the worse by the extreme wet cold. She looked at the ship once and then turned away and shivered uncontrollably. Her breathing began that raspy sound that Father and I had often feared.

"As the end of the ship drew near, and the boats were gone, the party noise of the crowd turned to a roar of panic. The lights were on. The band played on. Then the front half of the ship disappeared. I heard an awful scream of metal and a roaring, crashing, tearing sound. The stern rose like a skyscraper. The lights flashed once, then twice, and then it grew dark. The stern floated for a while and some thought she might remain afloat until the people clinging to her could be rescued, but then it began to slide like a playground child into the sea. The water boiled for a bit and the great lady was gone, with all of those souls.

"A roar rose up from the sea, over a thousand people begging for salvation and rescue. It was like the roar of Hell. Then I realized that my father was drowning, as I had been when the raft broke apart on the Hudson. 'DADDY, DADDY!' I screamed and I tried to jump out of the boat to save him. Mother was too weak to stop me, but several of the other women held me down till I was too weak to fight.

"The night was so cold. Throughout our boat, women softly wept in turns and fits. The crewmen alternately rowed and rested on the oars.

"My mother held me for warmth and solace. Her tears fell on my ears and ran down my cheeks and neck, where they crystallized from the cold night air. It was the night that would change us all forever, the night of the frozen tears."

Chapter 13

Orphan Girl

It was now dark and a bit cold for a summer night. The night sky was without clouds or moon. The cold and the stars that filled the rural Hoosier sky were ominously reminiscent of the night of Great Aunt Alice's frozen tears. Exhausted but desperately anxious to get past this part of her story, she continued:

"As the dawn drew near, we saw rockets in the distance. We would soon be saved, but no one on our boat cheered. During the night, Fifth Officer Lowe had tied our boat to two others and had brought some order to our situation. We drifted near enough to see one boat that was actually upside down with men standing on its capsized hull almost up to their knees in the frigid water. They looked like they were walking on the water, and they were trying to shift in unison to keep from losing the boat altogether. I recognized one of the men at the back as Mr. Bride, the wireless operator.

"The scene around us was otherworldly, but our emotions were weak and catatonic and we took it in as though it was the most natural of situations. Whereby the pervious day I had seen only smooth water from Titanic's deck, I now saw a maze of towering icebergs. They had been all but invisible during the night. One could hear the lap of waves against their sides, and once in a while one of them would block out the stars. But to see them blinding white and in such clear numbers was a shock.

"A one stacker was threading its way through the ice field, seen only by her rockets at first and now growing larger. It was a most welcome godsend, as my mother had been growing weaker by the hour, and I was anxious to get her to a warm place. To my surprise I realized that the one stacker was the same Carpathia that we had sailed on to France.

"Mother and I were lifted to the deck in some kind of a swing. She collapsed like a rag doll and was taken to the hospital immediately. I was not allowed to follow her there. A very kind lady wrapped me in a blanket, and gave me a cup of hot tea, which I held to my chest for warmth until it was cool enough to drink. Once she felt that I was secure, she left me to assist the others that were coming aboard. I will never forget her. She had the face of an angel, and a tender spirit that gave me no doubt she was indeed an angel.

"Once I had recovered, I did what I could to help. There was a small girl of about six who was wandering about on her own. She was crying and calling for her 'Mama and Papa.' I took her aside and wrapped the both of us in my blanket to get her warm, and to restore some sense of security I sang to her very slowly as a lullaby, the popular hymn 'Jesus Lover of My Soul.'

"The little girl fell asleep in my arms for about thirty minutes. When she awoke she said in a little voice, 'I'm hungry.' I found a lady who was passing out tea and biscuits and gave the girl something to eat. Like me she held the cup to her chest while it cooled. I told her that I was Alice, and she replied that her name was Elizabeth, but that her papa called her 'Little Bit.'

"When she had recovered sufficiently, I told her that we would go about the ship to find her parents, and that I knew the ship well. If they were anywhere on this ship we would find them, and my father as well. I had seen male survivors, and I still had some dim hope that Father was alive.

"We started at the bow and worked our way to the stern on each deck. Wherever we found a cluster of people I announced in a loud voice that I had a little girl who was looking for her parents. Her name was Elizabeth, and would they please spread the word that she is on the ship. I also asked them to look for Frank Howard.

"We stopped at the wireless shack, where Mr. Cottam was working away on a high stack of messages. Mr. Bride was alternating the work with him. His feet were badly frostbitten from standing all night in the water, but he could sit in the chair and help his beleaguered friend. I asked about Mr. Phillips, and Mr. Bride told me that he had been right behind him on the overturned lifeboat. 'We spoke to each other all during the night to keep each other's spirits up. When he grew silent, I dared not to turn and look lest the boat tip. He must have succumbed to the cold and slipped off in that last hour.'

"It was sad to hear of Mr. Phillips' demise, but I was glad to see my friend Mr. Cottam. To ease the tension he said, 'Bride, we must put this girl to work. She is a natural at the wireless.' Mr. Bride replied that I had helped him immensely the other night, but I knew they were both being nice, as I had barely learned a dit from a dot. I asked if they would send out a message to the other ships to look for Little Bit's parents and my father.

"Mr. Bride grew silent and turned his head for a minute. Then he took me aside and said, 'Alice, there were no other ships. Do you understand? I last saw your father heading for the stern with a child in his arms.' His words pulled the breath right out of my hope. I already knew the truth, but until that moment I refused to believe it. My lip began to quiver and a tear formed in my eye, but I held it in, not wanting to frighten Little Bit. The tiny girl and I continued our search, but I no longer asked the people we met to look for my father.

"As evening drew near, I began to look for a place for Little Bit and myself to spend the night. Near the ship's hospital I again saw the angel lady who had given me the blanket and tea. She realized our situation and found us a room just off of the clinic where she and her husband were sleeping that night. They had given up their stateroom to four Titanic survivors.

"I found out that her name was Nancy Mack, and that her husband Frank was a doctor who had been pressed into service for this emergency. Dr. Mack was a large man with a deep bass voice that could have scared a child to death if he were not also the kindest of men. In light of that fact, his voice had a most comforting sound.

"I asked Dr. Mack if I could see my mother, and he took me to her. She was unconscious and her breathing was much labored. I speculated that she had pneumonia and the doctor seemed surprised that I knew her diagnosis. Dr. Mack asked if she had experienced pneumonia before, and I told him that she had, many times.

"Then I asked him, 'Do you believe in Heaven?'

"'I do very much,' he replied.

"'Then my father is in Heaven and he needs my mother, but I need her too. How should I pray?'

"Dr. Mack knelt down on the hospital floor next to my mother's bed. He put his large hand on my heart, just as my father had, and he prayed 'Our Father, which art in Heaven, hallowed be thy name. Thy kingdom come, thy will be done.'

"That was all he said of the prayer, and then he rose to his feet. He held me close to him and said, 'Cry Alice.' It was then that I realized I had barely shed a tear from the time I had last seen my father's face. So I cried, and cried, and cried. I have always believed that Dr. and Mrs. Mack were angels sent from God for that moment.

"When the doctor took me back to the room where we were to sleep that night, Mrs. Mack had made up a bed for Little Bit and me on the floor. She was brushing Little Bit's hair as she chewed on a slice of cheese that Mrs. Mack had given her. I knew in my heart that Little Bit was now an orphan girl, and I wondered who would care for her when the Macks moved on.

"I was restless and walked the decks as bedtime drew near. A few others were doing the same. Titanic's survivors were weary and bewildered. Our emotions and fears were raw and devoid of any skin.

"I should have slept the deep sleep of exhaustion that night, but all I did was dream. I dreamed that my father was bursting into the room. I dreamed of him at the rail as we were lowered. I dreamed of that last prophetic talk I had with little Alice as we planned to leave Saugerties. I was worried sick for my mother, and wondered if I too would soon be an orphan girl."

Chapter 14
Small Girl Big Town

It was nearing midnight, but Great Aunt Alice pressed on with her story:

"In the days to follow, the survivors had a little time to let the tragedy sink in. The mood seemed to be one of wanting to go home as soon as possible, and yet one of wanting to stay at sea to avoid returning to the world and its harsh realities. We were leaving our loved ones in the icy water, and turning our backs on any hope for their rescue. Reality had laid out the facts to us, but reality took on the sound of babble in our hearts and minds. Had it not been for the kindness of Carpathia's passengers and crew, I don't know if we could have stood the strain.

"I continued to search for Little Bit's family, to no avail. It was during one of these searches that I met Captain Rostron. He was new to Carpathia, having joined her as captain earlier that same year. He was nothing like the old captain that I had met on the voyage over. Captain Rostron was much more of an officer than the casual former captain, but his predecessor's equal in good nature and kind heart. He will always be a hero to me for so rapidly threading the same ice field that had doomed Titanic.

"Each night Little Bit and I slept with Dr. and Mrs. Mack. At the end of the day we would swap the news, which never changed. Little Bit was still an orphan, and mother was still gravely ill.

"On the morning of the day we were to dock in New York, I was grabbed with great uncertainty. I asked Mrs. Mack what was to become of Little Bit and me. Would we be placed in an orphanage? Mrs. Mack smiled and said, 'Dr. Mack and I have grown very fond of you two. We have spoken to the captain and have wired the social services people in New York. The arrangements are all set. Little Bit will live with us until we find her parents.'

"Little Bit was concerned that they would have to travel across the big water to get to her new home. Mrs. Mack calmed her and assured Little Bit that the only water she would see again was the old lazy river that grazed the firm banks of their Illinois home.

"Dr. Mack came into the room as I asked what was to become of me. He assured me that I would stay with my mother, and that she would get the best care in New York. I was still uncertain about my fate, but I thanked the good doctor and his wife for their care. They in turn thanked me for taking such good care of Little Bit.

"Years later I managed to find the Macks, and I asked them for an update of their situation. They reported that when Little Bit had turned eighteen, she married a fine local farm boy. She was very happy, when near the end of their first year together she became pregnant. Sadly, the Macks reported that she had died giving birth to a little girl they named Alice, but everyone called their granddaughter Little Bit.

"We hugged and kissed goodbye, and I went on the deck to watch the city come into view. As we entered New York harbor, boats of every size swarmed around us with reporters shouting questions, and supporters simply applauding or waving their blessings. When we passed the Statue of Liberty I looked for the boy I had seen when we left, but of course he wasn't there.

"We survivors took time to thank our saviors on Carpathia, and many hugs and prayers were exchanged on both sides. The next ordeal was to offload the survivors and any Carpathia passengers who did not wish to resume their Atlantic crossing. The poor people were swarmed with pushy reporters and well wishers. Some of them were offered great sums for their story. All this mayhem boiled, while most of them just wanted to be left alone to mourn their loss. Some of them, to avoid the crush, lied to the reporters that they were Carpathia passengers and had been asleep when Titanic's passengers were boarded.

"The sick were taken off last to let the crowd do their mischief on those more able to defend themselves. I was allowed to stay with my mother. Mrs. Mack had already taken Little Bit off, but Dr. Mack stayed on board to help organize those who had to be carried. I saw Mr. Bride one last time and thanked him for his friendship. He told me to brush up on my Morse code so that we might try to find each other over the wireless some night.

"Poor Mr. Bride was mobbed as he reached the dock, but I was just a little girl, and my mother was unconscious, so they left us alone.

"An ambulance was waiting to take my mother and two others who were able to sit up but had suffered from the exposure. At first the driver would not allow me to go in the ambulance, but Dr. Mack was there, and with his commanding bass voice explained that the two of us were all that each other had in this world, and that I was to remain with my mother, 'DOCTOR'S ORDERS!'

"The driver backed down and I was allowed to ride up front. At first he was cold to me, stinging from Dr. Mack's admonition. Then the driver warmed up to me and asked for the detail of my ordeal. I told him everything from the moment my father burst into the room until I sat down in his ambulance. He was quite sympathetic, but I found out later that he immediately ran to the newspapers to sell my story. They were not interested as I was just a little girl, and not very important, and as the story was second hand. The hospital later learned of his misdeeds and fired him on the spot.

"Mother was taken to a city hospital, where she was placed in a ward. I was told to go to a waiting room, where I stayed for several days. I was so unimportant that nobody noticed I was there. When I asked to see my mother, I was told to go to the waiting room. To be quite blunt I was caught in a system that had no eyes. I was invisible in plain view. I wasn't about to leave my mother, and I wouldn't have known where to go if I did.

"It was simply a matter of perseverance, and I am proud to say that I fended for myself quite well. To survive, I began to take food from the finished patient trays as they waited for pick-up, and I bathed during the early morning hours in the patient bathrooms. I would find a shared bath between one patient who was bedfast and another who was ambulatory. By going in past the bedfast patient, I wouldn't be noticed. If the nurses heard a noise, they would assume it was the ambulatory patient going to the bathroom. If the ambulatory patient needed to go, he would assume that the nurse was helping the bedfast patient. It was especially helpful to learn the habits of those nurses who were more likely to fall asleep at the nurse's stations.

"Thank goodness my mother had thrown in a change of clothes as we left our Titanic stateroom. It gave me a chance to wash out one set of clothes after hours in the laundry room sink while I wore the other. All of my worldly possessions consisted of what I wore and what I carried in mother's satchel. It seemed to me that I could go anywhere in the hospital except my mother's ward, and that was how I lived for the better part of a month.

"Eventually I was discovered by a suspicious housekeeper who turned me in to one of the nurses, who in turn took me to the head nurse for the ward. She was shocked to hear my story and quite embarrassed. She told the other nurse that she would see ALL of the nurses in her office in fifteen minutes. She scolded me for what I had done and asked where my parents were. I told her that my father had died in the sinking, and that my mother was deathly ill in her ward. I had no one else. Then she asked me to describe my mother and when I told her she grew faint and grim. 'Oh, my dear child. We didn't know. Your mother died last week.'

"'Where is she? Where is my mother?'

"'We thought she was a pauper. The city took her. I don't know where she is buried.'

"I fell to the floor and screamed and sobbed. The head nurse knelt down and took me in her arms. The other nurses arrived to the curious scene, and the head nurse told them, 'This is the daughter of that Jane Doe. Do you remember her calling for 'Alice' in her delirium? This girl has been living like a shadow in our hospital, alone -- not knowing her mother was dead!'

"A look of horror spread across the other nurses' faces, and they fell on me with their hands saying, 'I didn't know, I didn't know.' I had fallen into a crack that no one had noticed. I was now, as I had feared, an orphan. I never found my mother's grave.

"The head nurse called for Miss Quinn, the social worker. Miss Quinn was a well-meaning do-gooder who was never braver than the rules allowed. She was pathetically sympathetic in the words she used, and I'm sure she slept well at night knowing how much she intended to love and serve the children in her care, but her actions fell short of the results needed. In her own heart she was a saint, and I'm sure her colleagues praised her work. In reality she was no better than one of those slave masters who thought himself generous because he didn't beat his slaves as often as the other masters.

"She had a phrase that she used over and over again to facilitate her own absolution, 'Oh you poor child.' She grilled me for an hour on who I was, and if I had any family, and where I lived before taking to the street. I told her that I wasn't an urchin girl, and that we had just returned from Europe on Titanic, and that I lived in Saugerties. She told me that was ridiculous, that according to the records, my mother was a pauper and could not have traveled to Europe, and that I had better tell the truth. 'Oh, you poor child. Please me the truth so I can help you.'

"Finally tiring of my persistence, she decided to call my bluff. She asked if there was anyone in Saugerties that she might call to confirm my story, and I told her to call my father's factory and ask for Big Carl Johnson. She didn't believe me for a minute and thought me delusional, 'Oh, you poor child.' Finally she placed the call to prove me wrong. A secretary answered the phone and transferred the call to Roland Self, who told Miss Quinn that there had never been a Carl Johnson at that company. He didn't deny that a Mr. Howard 'had worked for him once,' but that he had died in a tragic accident three years ago. He told Miss Quinn that Mr. Howard's wife had gone berserk and had, he heard, gone off to a life of drinking and prostitution in New York City, but to please keep that confidential, as he was too much a gentleman to besmirch her reputation in public. When asked about the child before her, Mr. Self told Miss Quinn that the Howards had no children and that the girl before her must be an imposter or insane.

"The truth was that Mr. Self's hand-picked board had made him the company owner upon hearing of father's death. He had fired Carl Johnson, and Bill Maryanski, and anyone else who was more loyal to my father. He cut back on the lighting and increased the work week to seven days, and cut the workers' pay to 50 cents a day. By rights it was my company, but Roland Self had stolen it from our family.

"Miss Quinn was so furious with my 'lie' that she no longer called me a poor child and railed at me for the long distance phone call charges that I had wasted the city.

"Out of desperation, I thought of my best friend. 'Call Ethel Roosevelt -- she is my dearest friend and can vouch for me!'

"'Who?'

"Ethel Roosevelt, the President's daughter. We met at the White House Christmas in 1908.'

"With that Miss Quinn thought me completely mad, and had me thrown into a padded cell in Bellevue hospital.

"For two days I beat at the walls and refused to eat. Then I realized that my rebellion only confirmed my insanity, so I began to eat normally and behaved like a perfect lady. Within a few more days I was taken to a psychiatrist, to whom I apologized profusely for my behavior. I told him that was in shock from my mother's untimely death. He agreed, and after another week of observation he declared me sane enough to go to an orphanage.

"The city orphanage was no more than a warehouse for children. We had a place to sleep and two meals a day. We had a laundry and were expected to keep up our two sets of clothes and to care for the younger girls' laundry as well. The dormitory was to be spic and span every day if we wished to play in the drab courtyard.

"We had little schooling, for we were orphans and would have no need of schooling past the ability to read and do simple arithmetic. The boys my age were forced to work in the local factories but were not paid. Their wages were paid to the orphanage for their upkeep. Some of the older girls were let out to do light domestic work, again with payment to the orphanage and not to the girls who did the work. It was a place of survival and no more.

"When I first arrived, they took my clothes and my satchel and locked them in a storeroom for the day that I might be adopted, become emancipated at age eighteen, or die. I was completely cut off from the girl I had been and the mementos of the parents who had loved me so much.

"At night, as I lay in bed, I would put my hand on my heart and wish upon the mice on the rafters that my father would come to save me."

It was now past dawn. Great Aunt Alice had pounded out a painful story, and we were both exhausted. I put my hand on Great Aunt Alice's heart. She buried her head on my chest. We would sleep this day and paint some more tomorrow -- or maybe not.

Chapter 15
Mother Midge

We slept all day, and into the night. By the following morning Great Aunt Alice seemed almost relieved to have survived the telling of that part of her story, and she was in a happier, almost defiant mood.

After a hearty breakfast, she decided to try again on the side of the house with the scaffold. The finished painting on that side was far above what I could reach, and climbing on anything higher than the soles of my feet was out of the question, so Great Aunt Alice came up with a plan to hang sheets across the outside of the scaffold so I would feel more secure.

I had to admit that her idea worked well. It placed me just above the first floor windows and allowed me to scrape, in relative security, the part of the windows we hadn't painted, and about four sections of the siding the width of the house.

My biggest problem was climbing the ladder to the scaffold. On the third rung I looked down and began to grow clammy. Great Aunt Alice gave me a shove and threatened to pull the ladder out from under me if I wasn't on the scaffold in three seconds. I complied with her suggestion immediately and we began the process of dividing the paint and tools so she could do her part of the house. Then she took half a gallon of paint, a rag, a scraper, and a brush in one hand and shinnied up the scaffold

Mother Midge

like a monkey to the peak of the roof where she casually sat on the planking kicking her feet, thirty-two feet off the ground, as she scraped and painted the peak of the roofline.

Things went fine for about an hour. I had finished scraping one section of siding and both windows, and Great Aunt Alice had finished scraping and painting the peak down to the next section of the scaffold. Then I messed up royally by dropping my scraper between the scaffold and the house. When I looked for it I realized that I was eight feet off the ground. I fainted dead away and collapsed to the planking. Great Aunt Alice paid no mind to me and continued to scrape and paint her way down the side of the house for another hour. The sound of her paint chips falling to the ground made me sick.

Finally she used a rope to rappel down the scaffold and drove her old flatbed Ford up to where she could dump my limp body into the back. The next thing I knew, I was a mile in the air in Great Aunt Alice's airplane, not her primary plane but her old open-cockpit Curtis Jenny. I was absolutely terrified. Then she flipped the plane over and I fell out like a sack of flour. Twenty feet later I felt a sharp tug. She had put me in a parachute and had attached a static line to the seat (See "The History of Silk" 1954 Webster & Porch).

I was now floating gently to the ground and screaming like a girl in a cheap horror movie. Halfway down I was overcome with a sense of flying. The world below was beautiful, and the sound of the air was like heaven.

Then I came to my senses and screamed like a fool until I landed with a thud. The parachute came down on me and I fought to get free from it. When I did, I ran to the house, zipped to the top of the scaffold and scraped and painted until most of that side was finished.

Great Aunt Alice buzzed the house, did a couple of loops, and parked the Jenny in the barn. She walked spryly to the house and shouted, "Good work Great Nephew. Wasn't that fun? I'll fix supper and then we'll talk about my mother Midge (pronounced Mid Gee)."

After supper and the dishes, we sat in the living room and she continued with her story.

"If you can imagine holding your breath for two years that was what it was like living in that orphanage. Every day was the same. Our clothes were the same, our routine was the same, our friendships were stilted, and no one really wanted to dare to love again. We had either lost our parents or had been abandoned by them. We were wards, not children or human beings. The girls who did outside domestic work were buckets and scrub brushes, not people. I had done some of the floor scrubbing for those rich enough to hire our services. They thought that they were being kind to us, but they were only trying to relieve their own guilt, or impress their peers with their false Christian virtue.

"The boys who were let out were in even worse shape. They would come back dead tired and often injured. I remember one poor boy whose arm was burned badly. We girls did what we could to clean him and dress the wound. One of the girls had stolen a sheet from one of the rich households we served. We cut it up for bandages and used some Ludwig's solution on the boy's burns.

"The next day the injured boy jumped off the back of the truck that was used to transport the boys to the factories. They said the fall dazed him and he ran right in front of a streetcar. None of us cried. He was better off. The days of hiring children were passing but there will always be ways of taking advantage of cheap laborers who can't otherwise fend for themselves.

"Personally I had passed the point of hope when a miracle began to work in the heart of a twenty-five-year-old uptown woman by the name of Midge Meyer. Midge Meyer was like Carol Channing on speed."

I was a little shocked to hear that my Great Aunt Alice knew what speed was.

"She had been a show girl only a few years prior when she met Charles Stanley Meyer Jr., son of the aging 'Baron of Beer' as he was known. Like so many spoiled rich boys, he was a pedigreed prodigal who had set his mind to squandering his father's business and inherited wealth.

"Midge was a woman with absolutely no inhibitions, and not the slightest hint of normal Christian virtue. But I've never met any woman with a greater sense of moral justice. Oh, she believed in God all right, but she was such a whirlwind of here and now that God could have run out of breath trying to chase her down.

"She was born in a brothel and was nursed by the various girls who were 'off duty.' Her father was completely unknown -- the only 'father' she had was her mother's 'manager.' He was a vile man who let Midge stay in the house for future working stock and was killed by Midge's mother the first time he tried to lay a hand on Midge.

"Her mother died in jail, and the then-thirteen year old went to work at the cheap show houses for her keep. Her 'performances' as a showgirl were not of the kind my father would have attended, and her private performances were even worse.

"We could not have been more different in our upbringing or character, but my father did say that no man's hand is too dirty to shake, and his faith in basic humanity proved to be true in Midge's case. When God sent me an angel he sent me a wild one, but an angel still the same.

"Stanley, as she called her husband, was a drunk and a playboy, but he was a RICH drunk playboy and 'awfully fun.' He was just a few blocks shy of being disinherited when his father collapsed from a massive heart attack on his way to his attorney to change his will.

"Stanley inherited a large apartment suite on Park Avenue along with a housekeeper named Mrs. Kinsey, who was always addressed as just Kinsey. Kinsey was an excellent cook with her best quality being that she was brutally truthful. She didn't approve of Stanley or Midge one bit and let them know it often. They in turn were well aware and unafraid of the truth and quite glad to have her tell it. It was a mutual degradation society in which Kinsey had the freedom of being able to tell her employer to stuff it, and in turn the Meyers could tell Kinsey what she could do with her moral compass. The truth was that Stanley and Midge needed that moral compass to keep from falling over the edge.

"They had a daily routine. Stanley would get out of bed in the morning around 9:30. By 10:30 he was at his favorite bar getting as drunk as he could. At 11:30 Stanley would shuffle to work to test his brewery's product and to get even more drunk. Somewhere around 1:00 Stanley could be found sharing his good fortune with a mistress or two. At 3:00 he arrived home to a knock-down-drag-out fight with Midge that included the foulest of language and the throwing of fists and frightfully expensive knickknacks. By 3:30 they would be in the master bedroom making love so passionately that they could crack the china in the next apartment. Precisely at 6:00 Kinsey would serve them a sumptuous meal with a heaping portion of guilt lecture. By 7:30 they were out painting the town till all hours.

"Kinsey had her own routine. She would go to bed early so she could be up by 7:00 to run the vacuum cleaner and loudly wash the evening dishes, just to drive the Meyers crazy. She had no other duties till the evening meal as neither Midge nor Stanley were up to eat breakfast or in to eat lunch.

"It was a relationship where the Meyers were destined to kill each other either with love or to merely kill one or the other outright. Midge loved Stanley. He was funny and had lots of well-healed friends. He was the most passionate and skilled lover in Manhattan. Stanley was also filthy rich, so Midge, having grown up with no boundaries and no money, was like a kid in a candy store with a thousand bucks to burn every day, which she did. Midge bought dresses and lingerie, jewels and fancy hats. She bought dynasty vases and expensive crystal to throw at Stanley when he came home.

"The one thing Midge could not buy was respect, and that was my salvation. Midge had the dough to walk into any salon, but not one society wonk would have a thing to do with 'that whore and her whoremonger.' The only people in her life were Stanley, Kinsey, the sales clerks, and the men who whistled at her on the street. She wanted the unconditional love and respect of her own child. As a result of an unmentionable illness from his past, Stanley could not give her a child of their own. Despite his open philandering she was faithful to her vows and never gave a thought to another man after she was married.

"It was Thanksgiving 1914. Kinsey made a special feast and shared it with Midge and Stanley on this annual day of truce. Father Collier joined them as he had the last two Thanksgivings. 'Feasting with the sinners,' he called it. He hated the wretched lives they lived but Father Collier loved the Meyers' honesty. He could let down his collar, so to speak and enjoy the day. Stanley was a lost cause but he liked the guy. Besides, how could he say he believed in miracles if he didn't keep praying for Stanley's salvation? Kinsey was a regular churchgoer, but it was her date pudding that made her a saint. Midge was the most sinful woman he had ever known, but there was a goodness in her soul that he readily saw and loved. To Father Collier, Midge was that lost kid that you always pull for.

"In the middle of the meal Midge blurted out, 'Father did you ever have kids?' Father Collier nearly choked on his cranberries.

"'Well, to be honest Midge there have been times when I wished I had a son or a daughter. I always get over it though when some brat makes a ruckus in the middle of one of my best homilies.'

"Midge and Stanley laughed: Kinsey did not. Father Collier knew exactly what Midge was trying to say. 'You should have a child, Midge.'

"Stanley blurted out, 'Oh, no Father we can't have kids on accounta I had the …'

"'Stanley!'

"'Oh yeah, sorry.'

"Then Stanley went back to eating his turkey. 'One turkey to another,' Kinsey thought.

"'No I'm not kidding Midge, you'd make a great mother.' Kinsey thought that Father had gone mad and began to pray for any poor child that would have the plague of this house.

"'The sisters run a fine orphanage, but I'd like you to consider the one downtown. It's a real hellhole and those kids need a break. How about it Midge? Come to the rectory Monday morning and I'll go with you.'

"Stanley didn't take it seriously, thinking Midge didn't have a snowball's chance of being allowed to adopt a kid. He made it clear that he had to go to work on Monday.

"When Monday morning came Midge drove Stanley crazy. She was up at 7 a.m. with Kinsey looking for clothes that made her look respectable, and not the look she normally took to the public.

"By 8:30 Midge was pounding on the door of the rectory, but she was told that Father Collier was conducting the 8:00 mass. Going to the church she got in line for the sacrament and asked the lady in front of her to hurry it up. When she got to Father she asked him to cut to the benediction. He didn't of course. If Midge were to have a child the first thing she would have to learn was patience. Father wondered if God was laughing as hard as he was trying not to.

"Immediately after Father Collier shook the last parishioner's hand, she grabbed him and dragged him to the street where she hailed a cab by waving her arm and pulling up her skirt. It had always worked before and this time was no exception. The cabbie was afraid to ask where they were going and was relieved to hear it wasn't a hotel.

"When they reached the orphanage, Father Collier asked for the director. To his utmost sarcastic pleasure, it was a person he knew quite well -- a real dangling ash of society.

"'Maggie O'Brien,' he said, with threatening satisfaction, 'I haven't seen you in church since you were nineteen.'

"Maggie defended herself. 'Well Father, I've been awfully busy with my ministry here.'

Mother Midge

"Looking at the glum faces of the children he replied, 'And I've come to rescue one of these children from this miserable ministry. Mrs. Meyer is here to adopt a child.'

"'You just can't do that Father there are rules!'

"'Well Miss Maggie, let me tell you MY rules. First of all, get back to church or you're going to hell. Second, if I were to call the child labor people you'd be going to jail, and third, this woman has a pile of money and wants a child TODAY!'

"Director O'Brien sputtered and fumed but Father Collier had her over a barrel. She reluctantly led them through the wards.

"'Boy or girl,' she said hatefully.

"'A girl, I think -- yes a girl,' Midge replied.

"'We ain't got no babies, but we're expecting a shipment soon.'

"'Oh, I think an older child would be better.' Midge looked at Father and he nodded his agreement.

"The director took them to the ten and up ward, where just outside the room I was scrubbing the hall floor. When I saw the three sets of adult feet, I apologized for being in the way. Being in the way of an adult was a good reason for a beating and no supper. I must have had fear in my eyes when I looked up at the pretty woman's face.

"The director glared at me and said, 'Come on, the floor's not wet over here.'

"The beautiful woman stood there and stared at me, and for some reason I said, 'Mother.'

"The papers were signed in half an hour, and the bribe was paid. On the way out the door Father Collier looked at Maggie O'Brien and said firmly, 'Confession, Thursday, four o'clock, BE THERE!'

"Midge, Father Collier, and I went back to the rectory, and as we climbed out of the cab Midge flat planted a big smooch on his lips and hugged him like he was her man. 'No man has ever made me this happy,' she roared as we stood there on the street where every passerby could plainly hear.

"Mrs. Hawley was on her way to the Women's Society and walked by just in time to hear it all. Sister Mary Francis was standing in the door of the rectory with a most unusual look on her face. Father Collier just casually smiled from ear to ear and gave Sister a pat on the shoulder as he sauntered past her on the path to the sanctuary.

"We still had just enough time to shop for a change of clothes for me and to meet Kinsey. Midge was thrilled to have the people in the store look at her like she was a proper mother.

"It didn't take long to figure out Kinsey. She told me I was the prettiest girl she had ever seen, gave me a sandwich, and scolded Midge not to 'screw this one up.'

"Stanley came home at his usual 3:00 to find out that things had changed. Kinsey had already warned me about the storm that was about to brew. Stanley blew his top when he found out what Midge had done, and he threatened to throw her out. He cussed Midge out something fierce, and she cussed him equally back and warned him not to use language like that around her daughter. Then he shouted, 'This is stupid' and tried to get Midge upstairs for their usual fling. Midge made it plain that Stanley wasn't going to get any more of that from her until he sobered up, gave up his other women, and started going to church regularly.

"Stanley came completely unglued. 'CHURCH -- are you out of your mind! Don't you tell me how to live!'

"'I'm your wife. Don't you treat me like one of your whores!'

"'Well that's all you were when I picked you up, and that's all you'll ever be! Now get out of my house and take that brat kid with you!'

"Now it was Kinsey's moment to open up on Stanley. She burst through the door with a rolling pin and chased Stanley from the house. He stood in the street and shouted to all of the neighbors that he was going to 'come back tomorrow and throw you whores out of my house.'

"The next day a server came to the house with an eviction notice. She read the judge's name and shoved the paper back into the server's hand with instructions to 'tell Your Honor that if he goes through with this, I'll be glad to improve his sex life by calling his wife to let her know how he likes it.' With that Midge went down to the courthouse and shared the same offer with every judge that she had ever jaded from her jaded past.

"Stanley was stuck. There was no throwing Midge out of the house, but because they weren't legally separated or divorced there was no law either that said he had to give her any money. It was only a matter of time until he starved them out, and Midge knew it. She pawned what she could in a short time and moved out. Before she did, she put one of Kinsey's good roasts in the upstairs bedroom and propped open the back door. When Stanley went back into the house, every dog in the neighborhood was chewing it to pieces.

"Stanley went on a total binge without Midge. He ruined his company, lost his wealth, and ate up his liver. He died in a flophouse before the war was over.

"Midge, Kinsey, and I went to the church to ask for help. Father Collier arranged to hire Kinsey to cook for the rectory. The general thought among the other priests and brothers was, 'Thank God -- Sister Mary Francis was about to kill us with her cooking.' Midge and I were allowed to stay until we could make other arrangements.

"I had a hard time knowing at first what to call Midge. My natural mother was the one I thought of as 'Mother,' and I felt odd calling her 'Midge.' I asked her about it and she suggested I call her 'Mother Midge.' That fit just right for me, and it made her feel good as well."

It was getting late and we needed to get up early the next morning. We were running low on paint and would have to get to Mr. Yoder's hardware before he closed at noon Saturday.

I hugged Great Aunt Alice goodnight and told her softly, "I will saw the wings off your Jenny if you ever do that to me again."

"I love you too, Great Nephew. Goodnight."

Chapter 16
Fighting Back

We were up at the crack of dawn to make the trip to Bauerhoff. We bought six more gallons of farmhouse white. Mr. Yoder had only two colors in stock -- farmhouse white and barn red. A slick salesman had once talked him into purchasing one can of yellow, but it sat there for two years before he managed to sell it to some depraved Methodist in the county, who in turn used it on the inside of his house so he could hide his fetish.

The trip was a quick one as there were no trains at Yoder's crossing. We were back in plenty of time to finish the east side of the house. The next step was to move the scaffolding to the west side. By then it was too late to start on that project, so Great Aunt Alice fixed a late lunch and we sat on the porch swing to go on with her story.

"By the second week of Father Collier's hospitality Mother Midge was worried that we had no viable plan, and that she was proving to be a poor mother. Nothing could be farther from the truth, but I did agree that we needed to do something to get on with our lives.

"We decided to start by taking inventory of what we had. Mother Midge had four good dresses, two of which were questionable for church property. She had one suitcase, one extra pair of shoes, and $500 in cash. I added to the treasury the two dresses that Mother Midge had purchased on our way home from the orphanage, one pair of shoes, and one satchel that had been released to me from the orphanage storage room -- but only after a divine threat from Father Collier.

"I hadn't opened the satchel in two years, so we made a great show of it as though we were uncovering a pirate's treasure.

"There was my father's shirt. I held it to my chest as if he were still in it. Mother Midge asked me about the shirt, and when I told her she took on the look of a lost child. She said sadly, 'I never had a father,' so I hugged her with the shirt between us. It felt good to hug a mother and father again. Mother Midge had the same fetching features of my mother, but she was shorter than Mother and not as thin as my mother had become. She felt more like the mother of my early childhood, and it took me back to a pleasant time.

"Having enjoyed the moment, we pressed on with our inventory. There was one change of clothes and two sets of underwear that I could no longer wear. I decided to throw them out, but Mother Midge wanted to have them for her first keepsake, as she had none of my baby clothes. The next item was my mother's dress. Mother Midge held it up for a few moments, and then she said, 'Thank You, thank you so much,' as if my mother were standing in that dress to hear those words.

"The next items were my father's razor and comb, three toothbrushes and tooth power, a bar of soap, and a soap dish from Titanic, which would be worth a fortune now. There was also my hairbrush, my mother's hairbrush, some makeup, and the locket with the dirt from her Grandfather's grave in Ireland.

"Then I shouted, 'Look my mother's journal!' Between the pages was the letter my grandfather had written about my mother's birth, the one Cousin Robert had given us in Ireland.

"Finally I pulled out my father's journal. Besides his writings, there were several of his sketches, some papers that proved he had founded the company, a warning about Mr. Self, a deed, paid in full, to our home on Jane Street, and a last will and testament giving me full ownership of his factory, his assets, and our home. 'I own a home! Mother Midge, we own a home!'

"The next morning we were on our way to Saugerties. We took the train out of Grand Central Station and followed the river. The farther the city fell behind us, the more at home I felt. Mother Midge was just the opposite. She had spent her whole life in New York City. She had never seen fields or hills or so many trees. 'Ohmygosh, ohmygosh! What is that thing?'

"'It's a cow.'

"'Are they dangerous?'

"'No, they eat grass.'

"'What do they do?'

"'We get milk from them.'

"Just about that time old Bossie raised her tail and gave Mother Midge the wrong impression of how we get milk. With a worried look she said 'So how do they make it white?'

"When I saw the station sign for Saugerties, my heart jumped. I took my satchel and ran ahead of Mother Midge. As soon as I reached the platform I knelt down and kissed those blessed boards. Then I ran into the station, where I saw Mr. Vought, the stationmaster. I jumped into his arms and gave him a passionate hug. He was taken aback at first as I had changed a bit, as girls do between eleven and fourteen. Then he recognized me.

"'Alice Howard?' I didn't think we would ever see you again. Where are your parents?'

"When I told him the story, he was shocked.

"'We didn't know, hon. Old man Self said your dad wired him that he was sick of small towns and wanted to chuck it all for better parts. He showed us the telegram. Your dad said he was giving up the factory and everything'

"I asked about the house on Jane Street, and Mr. Vought told me that it had been boarded up, and that Mr. Self had filed suit for some breach of contract, and he tried to get all of your dad's bank money and the house to settle. It all looked legal, but the judge didn't buy it so he locked down all of your dad's bank money and the house for seven years to give him a chance to come back and fight. Last week old man Self asked the town council to tear down your house because it hasn't been lived in for three years and he said it was an eyesore.

"I showed my father's journal to Mr. Vought to prove that Mr. Self was lying.

"I asked if we could get into the house, and Mr. Vought said that we would have to ask the judge first. With a worried look I asked Mr. Vought where we might stay until the mess was settled. 'You'll be staying with me.' It was the booming voice of Big Carl Johnson. I was so glad to see my father's best friend. Big Carl had been in the next room and had overheard me telling the story.

"Big Carl sat down on one of the passenger benches with his head in his hands, full of remorse. He told me that it was his urging that had encouraged my father to take the trip. He begged my forgiveness. I told him there was nothing to forgive. We had enjoyed a wonderful time in France and Ireland. Besides my mother would have died that winter if she had stayed in Saugerties, and my father would have been lost without her.

"When the emotions died down, I realized that I had failed to introduce Mother Midge. She had been standing just inside the doorway, uncharacteristically silent the whole time. I introduced her to Mr. Vought and Big Carl. Mr. Vought greeted her with a broad smile. Big Carl stood his full height and stared at Mother Midge like she was a vision. He was a good foot taller and perhaps fifteen years her senior, but Midge had a look and a smile that could light up a dead man. Carl was a handsome man for his age. He had a slender waist and broad shoulders. His graying blond hair only served to accentuate his penetrating blue eyes. I was enjoying the spectacle, when Mr. Vought broke the spell.

"'We've got a hot one here, Carl. We'd better get a jump on this before old man Self finds out that Alice is back in town. We've got all the proof we need. I'll call Donlon and have him get the Judge down here right now.'

"I've mentioned Mr. Donlon before, but I didn't tell you much about him. Mr. Donlon was the school principal, the constable, and the fire chief. He was one of those fellows who seemed even-keeled, and able to organize anything. Mr. Vought told him a little of the story and swore him to secrecy, which wasn't needed as Mr. Donlon was a square shooter. Judge Harper trusted Mr. Donlon implicitly and knew if he said it was an urgent matter, it was.

"Two hours later they walked into the station. Mr. Donlon looked at me squarely and said, 'Well, I see you don't slouch anymore.' I gave him a big hug and he smiled and hugged me back. I didn't hug the Judge because I didn't think one could legally do that.

"Judge Harper had thick coal black hair, bushy black eyebrows, and a cookie duster mustache. He was a good judge and as fair a man as I ever met. He knew the law. I was glad he didn't know Mother Midge.

"Judge Harper decided that the occasion called for a full legal investigation on the spot. We pulled the passenger benches together and he swore us all in 'So help us God.' Then he asked me to tell the whole story. He asked Midge a few questions and he asked Carl several questions as he had been in the middle of things at the factory and could testify to some private conversations he might have had with my father.

"After reviewing the written evidence that my father had left in his journal, Judge Harper seemed personally convinced that Mr. Self had committed a crime and that everything belonged to me, as I had testified. Still there was the matter of the telegram that my father had supposedly sent to Mr. Self giving up his factory. This would have to be investigated further before Judge Harper could make a final decision.

"Then, too, there was the matter of my father's death. No one in Saugerties knew that he had died except the people in our small group. There was no death certificate, no body, nothing except my story. We needed a record or an impartial witness or something. Self could still say that my father had sent me to Saugerties with my story while he was running a scam from France.

Fighting Back

"Mother Midge reached into my satchel and pulled out the soap dish and the bar of soap that was inscribed *'Titanic.'* 'There aren't too many of these floating around,' she said. It was convincing proof that I had been on Titanic. Judge Harper took my hand and said, 'I'm so sorry, Alice. It must have been terrible. Still we need ironclad proof. We need a report or a witness who may have seen your father on the ship after the lifeboats were away.'

"I thought about it for a minute, and then I thought of Mr. Bride, the wireless operator who had told me of my father's last moments. As his overturned lifeboat was the last hope, he could testify that my father was not onboard that raft and certainly lost.

"Mr. Vought went to the telegraph and wired his friend in New York, who was also a ship-to-shore wireless operator. He in turn sent the message to Halifax for better transmission coverage. The man in Halifax reached Mr. Cottam in Scotland, who in turn got ahold of Mr. Bride. Mr. Bride replied with the testimony that he had seen my father with a small boy heading for the stern when the ship foundered, and he was sure my father did not survive. Mr. Cottam also sent an independent message verifying that in Carpathia's wireless shack he had heard Mr. Bride tell me that my father was heading for the stern with a child when he last saw my father. Mr. Vought's friend sent back a message from the White Star Line confirming that my father was officially listed as missing and presumed dead.

"All of that took place over the space of four days. While we anxiously awaited the response, Mother Midge and I stayed with Big Carl. He seemed to enjoy the novelty of having women in his humble quarters, especially when Midge flirted with him. I quickly surmised that it was more from self interest instead of gratitude. She actually kissed Carl goodnight on the lips and gave him a womanly hug each evening. When Carl looked over her shoulder and saw I was smirking, he gave me the evil eye as if to say, 'Go away, kid.'

"Carl slept in the living room all draped over the end of the couch. Mother Midge and I slept in Carl's big bed. She would always remind me to brush my teeth and wash behind my ears, because she thought that was what mothers were supposed to do. I would remind her to say her prayers. Mother Midge had never really said bedtime or any other kind of prayers before. They went something like this, 'Hey, God, please bless Alice, and Kinsey, and Father Collier, and that nun.' Then it would fall apart with, 'and that dreamboat in the other room -- isn't he a dish?' I supposed that God would just have to be happy with what he could get. As we fell asleep I curled up behind her and held her like I would my own child.

"Carl and Mr. Vought had kept us under wraps, which is hard to do in a small town. Mr. Vought took the messages to Judge Harper, and the judge found the evidence strong enough to release the house, bank assets, and the factory to me. He also found cause to arrest Mr. Self for fraud. He called in Mr. Donlon to make the arrest and allowed him to take a posse. The posse consisted of all of us who had been at the train station for the initial hearing, minus the judge himself.

"We walked into the factory with Big Carl in the lead. The receptionist (Father never needed a receptionist) tried to stop us, so Mr. Donlon arrested her on the spot for interfering in a police action. This was to keep her from calling up a warning to Mr. Self.

"When some of the workers saw Big Carl and me, they started to cheer. Carl made a quick sign to be quiet, and we stormed the stairway to the offices. Big Carl strode up to the door of the main office and kicked it open, splintering parts of the frame. Mr. Self, who was meeting with his five board members, exploded at Carl. 'What is the meaning of this? Get out of my office! I'm calling the constable!'

"Big Carl just smiled and stepped aside to reveal a fourteen-year-old girl who said sternly, 'YOU, sir, get out of MY office!' Mr. Self fell back in my chair in disbelief. Mr. Donlon walked into the room and asked, 'You wanted to see a constable?' His posse laughed. 'Roland Self, you are under arrest for fraud, and you, gentlemen of the board are also under arrest for being accessories to the crime of fraud.'

Fighting Back

"Mr. Donlon had only one pair of handcuffs, which he wrenched tightly onto Mr. Self's wrists. The others and the receptionist were ordered to put their hands on their heads as they were marched out of the office.

"Mr. Vought ran to the rail of the balcony that overlooked the shop floor and hollered, 'Boys, you can shout all you want now!' The shop floor roared as Big Carl escorted Mr. Self down the stairs. Self was blood red and screaming that they were all fired. Big Carl had him by the collar and his feet were barely touching the floor. The other hoodlums followed Carl, with Mr. Donlon ready to give a club to the kidneys to anyone who drug their feet.

"Finally I appeared at the rail and held up my hands for quiet. 'I'm afraid Mr. Self is right, boys. You won't be working for his factory anymore.' They grew quiet, thinking they really had lost their jobs. 'Because starting right now you are working for Frank Howard's girl! And we're going back to a five-day work week. And as soon as I get old fat hat's scheme figured out, you're all going to get a raise!' Again they cheered till the skylights clattered. I finished by calling out, 'Carl Johnson! I'm going to need your help Monday. These boys need a good general manager.' The shop boys cheered their approval, and Big Carl shot both arms over his head with Roland Self still attached. He nearly killed the man. Midge had to fan herself at that show of strength.

"Judge Harper ordered the office closed for a criminal audit. This caused a problem in that much of the work of the factory would have to halt until the audit was complete. Midge had the solution. She knew the Secretary of State and could get his office to send an army of auditors to clean up the mess in a few days. Judge Harper asked her, 'So how do you know the Secretary of State?' I cringed as I waited for her response, and began to inch toward the door. 'A few years ago we had a real tight business connection. He was very satisfied with my work and said he owed me a favor. May I use your phone?'

"The judge let Midge use his office to make the call, and the next day there were six state auditors poring over the factory's books. By the following Wednesday the audit was complete. They found enough evidence to put Mr. Self and three of his board members, and two more associates in New York City, away for many decades. The auditors also found enough in slush accounts to allow us to raise the worker's pay to two dollars a day.

"At the trial it was learned that a crony of Mr. Self had spotted us on Titanic and wired him. The rat went down with the ship, but Mr. Self had a man on the docks in New York City to make sure my father didn't get off Carpathia. When Mr. Self was sure my father was dead, he had a friend in France send the telegram that was supposedly from my father. When Mr. Self received the call from Miss Quinn, the deal was sealed by setting me up for a long haul at the orphanage, which would give him time to legally steal all of my father's assets. With this in place, he sprang the news on the town and took over the business. The only sad end was that Bill Maryanski was forced to move on and was unaware that his firing had been avenged.

"Mr. Self was found guilty in twelve minutes. He was sentenced to thirty years. Three of the board members received twenty years each, and the other two members' ruined reputations kept them from getting any further work in New York State.

"The receptionist couldn't get work anywhere in town. I offered to let her do maintenance work in the factory. She did for a while, but the boys would have nothing to do with her. She was cute as a button, but the boys didn't even look when she climbed the ladder to change the lights. Eventually she gave up and said she was moving to New Jersey, but nobody cared."

Great Aunt Alice said that was enough and we should stop for the day. "Tomorrow is church day. Let's go to the early service so we can beat the Amish to Yoder's cafeteria."

"Afterwards, if the weather is good, we can take the Jenny up for a Sunday flight."

The preacher did a convincing sermon on miracles that day. It was July. I prayed for a blizzard.

Chapter 17
Bringing up Mother

Great Aunt Alice and I worked all day moving and setting up the scaffolding on the west side, so it was Tuesday before we did any more painting. When we did, we only worked until the mood left us. We stopped for an early lunch and spent the rest of the day in the lawn chairs beneath the oak tree while Great Aunt Alice went on with her story.

"The best part was going home to Jane Street. Big Carl pried the boards off the doors and windows. It was the first time in over two years that the rooms inside had seen the light of day. There was a lot of cleaning to do, but the house was sound and free from any major damage. Carl made sure the plumbing, furnace, and power were all working before he left. I had to teach Mother Midge the wonders of coal heat, but she was glad that my father had installed electricity and that the bathroom was indoors.

"We had covered the furniture, so the dusting chore was reduced quite a bit. Anything not covered had a thick layer of dust. The stairs were a chore. The carpeted floors had to be swept twice to get out all of the dirt. The kitchen counters took some work, but the floor mopped easily.

"One of the last things I did before we left for France was to mop that kitchen floor. It brought back memories. I would see memories everywhere -- my mother's needlepoint, the vision of her brushing her hair in the bathroom mirror, the hook where my father always tossed his hat -- they all played like a movie in my mind. I couldn't look at the front door without seeing my father burst through to exclaim the great news of our trip to France, or the chair that reminded me of my surprised mother being steadied by my father and the President on his whirlwind visit.

"When things got settled I wrote to Ethel Roosevelt. She hadn't heard from me for two years, and I knew she would be frantic. She sent me a return right away, relieved to know I was alive and back on top, and that she was so sorry for my ordeal. She had heard from one of her friends that we had been on Titanic and was sure we all were lost when she hadn't heard from me. Ethel was now living her dream of becoming a nurse. I never let a month go by after that without writing her.

"It wasn't long before my friends began to show up. I was shocked at how much Alice had matured. Eileen was the same good-natured soul and a little thinner. Molly had pretty eyes and had filled out well. George was gone; his family moved away when Mr. Self fired his father for being too loyal to my father. Tommy wasn't nearly as handsome as I had remembered, but Bud was becoming quite a looker.

"Since I had lost so much schooling during my time in the orphanage, Mr. Donlon held me back a year. My friends were all high school freshmen, and here I was an eighth grader, but I'll bet I was the only eighth grader in the country with my own factory.

"I was at home again among lifelong friends. On the other hand Mother Midge was a stranger in a foreign land. Time would tell if she and I would make new memories together and turn this house into our home. We each now had our separate bedrooms, but there were times when I would slip in and curl up with her to make sure she knew that I really loved and needed her.

"Introducing Mother Midge to Saugerties and vice versa was an interesting proposition. First there was the matter of church. She was convinced that a good mother always takes her daughter to church. I didn't have any problem with that, as I had been reared in the church and enjoyed the fellowship. On the other hand Mother Midge had but a vague idea of what one did in one of those places and only a morsel of experience to back it up. She was nervous as a cat the first time we went.

"'What if I don't know what to do?'

'Just look up at the stained glass and weep.'

"I had to teach her that Methodists don't genuflect and that 'Amen' was a better way to say, 'Yeah, buster, you got that right!' Looking back on the situation, I'm glad she didn't know the modern phrase 'Been there, done that.'

"Then there was the problem of the day-to-day routine. I would go by the factory early and check on things with Carl, go to school, and then again stop by the factory before going home to a kitchen full of smoke. On the other hand Mother Midge had nothing to do while I was in school. She had no friends to speak of. It wasn't that people didn't like her. Every man in town would tip his hat, even if he wasn't wearing one. The women in Saugerties are a genial lot and had no intention of excluding Midge. The problem was that there just wasn't that common ground one needs for a friendship.

"The only highlight for Midge was the evening visit from Big Carl. The three of us would sit in the parlor and talk over the business of the day. I noticed that she dressed in a most appealing fashion for Big Carl. I also noticed that my general manager had a hard time keeping his mind on business when she was in the room.

"As a side note, everyone in town knew that Big Carl was going to marry Midge except Carl, who didn't have a clue as to how to get the ball rolling. I would have to work on that one.

"The thing that most drew my attention was that Midge had a good head for business and was a big help with the bookkeeping. That gave me an idea. I knew she wouldn't work out at the factory. She could handle the work just fine, but she'd shut down production every time she went to the water fountain. I had a feeling that the fashion business was a good fit. She knew more about fashion than any woman in Saugerties, and she had shown that she understood the workings of business. So on the way home from school one day I stopped by Mrs. Branch's women's store.

"It was the only dress shop in town, and Mrs. Branch was getting quite old. As I looked through the underwear section, I asked her how long she had been in business. 'My land, child, my husband and I opened this store in the centennial year 1876. That's been a long time. Before that, I had worked ten years in the store in Albany. I was about your age then.' I asked her if she had ever thought of retiring. She said, 'Very much so -- it does tire me these days, and I would like to move to Arizona to live out my days with my son.' Such ideas were exotic for those times, and I wondered if I would ever see Arizona.

"I asked Mrs. Branch what she thought of selling the store and gave her my reasons. She seemed pleased that the store could outlive her, and she agreed it would be good for Midge and the ladies of the town. She gave me an estimate of the cost of her inventory and the expectation of income. I promised to make an offer as soon as I could. After checking with Big Carl and Mr. Polo at the bank, I decided that I could afford the outlay and made my offer the next day. It was almost three times what Mrs. Branch had expected, and it would keep her in good stead for the rest of her life. Midge was a little unsure of her abilities and also very touched by my faith in her.

"Two weeks later Mrs. Branch was on her way to Arizona and Midge Meyer was the proprietor of the Centennial Dress Shop. Things worked exactly as I had planned. Midge was soon making friends with the women of Saugerties. They in turn loved her spunk and flattering salesmanship, which gave the women in town a new sense of appeal. In time Midge added a 'special line,' which could only be viewed by private appointment, and only by married women. She kept it so discreet that I don't think any woman in town thought that any other woman knew about it. At any rate they didn't dare talk about it. I did notice that the women who took advantage of the 'special line' tended to have their husbands sitting closer to them in church.

"Every month or so Mother Midge and I went to New York City to buy clothes for the store. On these trips we would stop by the rectory and visit with Father Collier and Kinsey. Father Collier was always glad to see us and was especially pleased with the improvement in Midge. Kinsey seemed a little on edge. I think it was hard on her to be nice for such long stretches. She had secretly been teaching Sister Mary Francis to cook just so Father wouldn't condemn her to hell if she made a break for it.

"On one of these trips Mother Midge and I decided to right a few wrongs. Before we left we wrote to Mayor John Mitchel about the appalling conditions at the orphanage and how we might together work to correct them. I suggested a surprise inspection. I knew my way around and the most incriminating time for the raid. Along with our proposal, I sent letters from Judge Harper and some of the other Saugerties folks who were able to back up my story. Midge wrote a postscript at the bottom of my letter and sealed it before I could see what she wrote.

"When we arrived at the Mayor's office at the appointed time, Miss Quinn was in the outer office. She thought that she had been summoned to receive recognition for her devoted service. If she recognized me, she didn't show it. Imagine her surprise when the three of us were called in together. Inside the office I refreshed her memory and unloaded on her for the misery she had caused. I made sure she understood that she had called me a liar based on the story of a now convicted felon and showed her the proof of his crime. Miss Quinn reached for my cheek and started to say, 'Oh you poor . . . .' I cut her off with a violent look and a word I will not repeat. Mother Midge later corrected me on the use of the word and suggested a worse one that she would have used in my place. I've never felt so satisfied in my life.

"The four of us, along with a police officer and one of the Mayor's deputies, descended on the orphanage just as the boys would be returning from work. Father Collier met us out front and we marched in like we owned the place -- which at that moment we did. Maggie O'Brien dropped the cigarette from the corner of her mouth and turned farmhouse white at the sight of the Mayor marching past her office. Father Collier paused just long enough to reminder her that she had yet to come to confession and then hastened his step to catch up with the imminent explosion.

"I led them to the boys' dorm, where the girls were attending to the cuts and burns of the day. One boy had a broken arm, and another had a wound that was so infected that I would be surprised if he was able to keep his limb.

"Miss Quinn started to say, 'Oh you poor . . .' This time we said in chorus, 'SHUT UP!' The police officer declared the whole orphanage a crime scene and ordered all of the staff to the dining hall. Then he used the orphanage phone to call for a medical team and some detectives from one of the precincts. The Mayor's deputy called City Hall for a team of auditors to seal and investigate the books. Father Collier suggested that the children be moved to the Catholic orphanage as soon as the city could, and the Mayor offered to help pay for the added burden.

"Finally there was the matter of Miss Quinn and Maggie O'Brien. We adjourned to the director's, office where the Mayor fired Miss Quinn outright. The publicity that followed ruined her reputation, and she had to leave New York City to find a job.

"When the Mayor made it clear that Maggie would be arrested for her part 'in this crime,' Father Collier took him aside for a conference. As Father Collier whispered in Mayor Mitchel's ear I could see him shaking his head in agreement. The Mayor turned again to the director and said curtly, 'Confession, Thursday 4:00, BE THERE!'

"Her penance (along with some strong advice from the prosecutor's office) led her to become the most reluctant nun in the Roman church, where Maggie was assigned to work in the poorest slums in the city. A few years later, she contracted typhoid from a rat bite and died, cursing Father Collier with her last breath.

"Just before Thanksgiving we invited Father Collier and Kinsey to Saugerties for the holiday. Father declined, as he was on duty while the other priests were home for the holidays. Kinsey took the train home with us for a few days.

"At the station I introduced her to Mr. Vought, who called Big Carl to pick us up. Carl took us past the factory and showed us the sights of Saugerties, which didn't take long. He dropped us off at the dress shop and took our bags to the house.

"Kinsey seemed impressed with the work Midge had done with the shop and even more by the reaction of the people on the street who met us on the short walk home. Midge had finally earned the respect she could never have bought. Kinsey was proud and happy for Midge and told her so. However, she didn't want to get sick on it so she gruffly said, 'I'm fixing Thanksgiving dinner.' Midge retorted that Kinsey was her guest and it was her obligation. 'Not on your life, sister. I'm not going to put my fate in those sissy hands (Mother Midge did have beautiful delicate hands). We're going to that kitchen of yours to take inventory and then I'm sending little sis to get what I need. You do have a kitchen, don't you?'

"Thanksgiving was the best meal I had had in a year. We shared it with Carl, Mr. Vought, and of course the three of us. The conversation was a little stilted at first, with a lot of small talk about how the house looked and the delicious meal.

"Kinsey broke the ice with a sledgehammer. 'So, Carl, when are you gonna marry this dame?' Midge kicked her under the table.

"'What are you kicking me for? I've been around you long enough to know when you're head over heels, and this guy is obviously nuts about you. So how about it?'

"Carl only managed to say 'Well' and Kinsey cut loose again with, 'Well at least this year we only have one turkey.'

"Carl asked, 'What do you mean?'

"'Stanley.'

"'Who's Stanley?'

"'Midge's husband.'

"'Her what!'

"Carl was confused. I was trying to figure out where Kinsey was going with this. Midge was to the point of tears. Mr. Vought didn't know what to think, so he just continued to eat.

"'Stanley is her husband.'

"Carl was looking hurt and shocked. Now Midge was crying and imploring Carl not to hate her.

"Mr. Vought asked if there were any more dinner rolls.

"'Mr. Johnson, I want you to listen and listen well. Stanley is a drunk who cheated on Midge twice a day for the last six years. All that time she never looked at another man. She's separated from him because he tried to starve us out of the house. She gave up a fortune to be thrown into the streets, and do you know why? She did it to be a good mother to that little girl. She would have died for that sweet child, and if it didn't pain me so, I'd tell you that woman is a saint. She deserves to know that the man she loves is going to love her back and stand by her for the rest of his life, and here she sits broken hearted because you've never even asked her out for a cup of coffee.'

"Mr. Vought said that he would take more coffee.

"I decided to lie low for I was the one who had spilled the beans of their relationship to Kinsey.

"Carl pried the words out of his mouth, 'But . . . she's married.'

"'Midge, Stanley's dying. He's lost it all, and he's drinking himself to death. Father Collier goes to see him in the flophouses every week or so, and he still refuses the sacraments. It won't be long, Midge.'

"Midge took on a sad face. 'Poor Stanley.'

"'You see that, Carl? After all that bum did to her, she still feels sorry for him. You won't find a woman like that anywhere. So what do you say?'

"Mr. Vought said, 'Please pass the dressing.'

"Carl got down on his knees and took Midge by the hand. 'I don't care how long I have to wait, Midge. Please don't marry anyone else. I want to be your husband.'

"Midge jumped on Carl and knocked him flat on his back. She straddled him in a most unlady-like fashion and kissed him over and over, saying, 'YES!' between each kiss.

"Mr. Vought said, 'Great meal, Mrs. Kinsey. Did I hear someone say date pudding?'

Chapter 18

The Great Roscoe

Wednesday morning we resumed work on the west side of the house. Not only had Great Aunt Alice put up the sheets to make me feel less squeamish, but she also put one of those dog collars around my neck -- the ones dogs wear to the vet to keep from noticing other dogs. I would have been mortified if anyone had seen me, but I had to admit it kept me from looking down.

Great Aunt Alice again started at the peak of the roof, but it was a perfect blue sky and she was soon too distracted to work. "I'm going flying. Do you want to join me?" I pointed out that the west side gets the bad weather in Indiana and that I needed to stay and do more scraping.

This time she flew her primary plane, the one she called "Ethel" after her best friend Ethel Roosevelt. It was a one-of-a-kind plane, for which she had developed the design features and specifications. She had it built in the 1930's by the Spartan company. It was a sleek and brightly colored favorite at any fly-in, and no tower man could ever mistake the pilot. If any doubt remained, one could tell by the slow roll and the velvet touch landing that was Great Aunt Alice's aviation signature.

The original engines had been replaced, but the frame and body was the same, and it was maintained as new as the day she first flew.

The Great Roscoe

Great Aunt Alice had flown her Ethel to every continent and around the world. At Lindberg's suggestion, she had used his Great Circle route to cross the Pacific. She had often soulfully contemplated the mistake her friend Amelia Earhart had made by not using the same route to cross the Pacific. Great Aunt Alice had flown with Amelia in those early aviatrix days and described her as "only a fair pilot but an eagle of a friend." Great Aunt Alice could never speak of Amelia without shedding a tear, and lamenting "She was so young."

After a few hours of aerobatics, and chasing Mr. Yoder's cows, she put Ethel down like a feather, parked her in the barn, and sauntered to the house. It had been a good day for Great Aunt Alice.

As she walked past the scaffold, she told me to find a stopping point. She said, "I'll fix us some lunch, and then we'll talk about Roscoe."

After a sumptuous meal of egg salad sandwiches and cantaloupe (musk melon is the more Hoosier word), we sat in the glider under the sycamore and she continued her story.

"Almost two years passed before Stanley's miserable life ended. Midge saw to it that he had a decent burial, and she thanked Father Collier for his faithfulness to the old reprobate. Carl and Midge married the next spring, and Carl moved into our house to stay. I became the only kid in the world who owned both her own factory AND her parents' house.

"Kinsey also moved in to stay, to keep us from starving to death. She would never admit it, but it was fun to watch 'her' Midge blossom into the happiest woman in New York State. Kinsey was still a crusty old broad, and we loved her too. She spent her spare time keeping company with Mr. Vought, and making sure he was well fed. He in turn taught her Morse code and let her send a few messages while he sorted the mail.

"Midge still had her shop and was a popular part of Saugerties. The factory was prospering under Carl's steady hand, to the point where most of the workers were pulling in the enormous sum of three dollars a day. They in turn splashed that money across the town and made Saugerties a great place to live.

"I was doing well enough in school that Mr. Donlon let me move up to my normal grade so that I could graduate with my friends that May. I hadn't the slightest idea what I would do upon graduation. I had all of the money I needed. I had no special need or desire to go to college. I was almost eighteen and older than my mother when she married, but I had no real love interest.

"After graduation Molly went off to take nurses training. Eileen married some fellow who had been courting her all the way from Poughkeepsie. Bud joined the Army, but the war was over before he had to go overseas. Tommy took a larger role in his father's store. Alice had another year before she would graduate, but she already had her heart set on teaching.

"It seemed like I was the only one who didn't have a goal. Then a year later, in August of 1919, I met Roscoe.

"One day I went to the drugstore for Midge, and as I passed Mr. Grover's newsstand I saw a flyer for 'The Great Roscoe's Flying Circus!' These were the early days of the barnstormers, the most exciting entertainment of its time. I begged my parents to let me go. Can you imagine an eighteen year old today begging their parents for any kind of permission?

"Mother Midge said, 'Of course' and told me that she would like to go as well. Carl said that God would have given us wings if he had meant us to fly, and Kinsey just shook her head and frowned.

"The flying circus was to do its show on Saturday at the Heffernan farm. The circus consisted of two surplus Curtis Jennys and four flying Veterans from the war. Harley Keller and Roscoe Burke were the two main pilots, with Slim Walker and Felix Herman specializing in the stunts. Among them they had shot down more than twenty enemy airplanes and seven balloons during the war. Felix had dueled with the famous Red Baron, or so he said.

"The boys came into town in grand fashion on Friday afternoon. To publicize the show, they did a dogfight over the

The Great Roscoe

Hudson and came in low over Main St. Everybody who could rushed outside, and some of us drove to the Heffernan farm to greet them. Kinsey went along with us 'to have something to do.' When she saw the 'skinny boys' she told them they were going to eat with us that night.

"Felix was the talker of the group and seemed to have more adrenalin than blood. Harley was the fancy dresser and seemed to be a little on the wild side. Slim was a little heavier by comparison and ate plenty of Kinsey's good cooking.

"Roscoe was a dreamboat. He was a slender six feet even with coal black hair and brown eyes. He had a ramrod-straight slim build that made him look even taller. He was more graceful in his movements than any man I had ever seen. He was quiet, and when he spoke at all he was very polite.

"Mother Midge caught me looking at Roscoe and realized that she might have to work a little magic to keep Carl distracted. As I grew closer to the edge of the nest, Carl was becoming more of a father and after the barnstormers left he made a big show of it. He didn't like those boys at all, 'No sir! Flyboys, drifters, and fellows who would woo a girl and leave her ruined in some God-forsaken pasture -- that's what those fellows are.' Fortunately for me, mother Midge was a good magician.

"Other townsfolk had invited them to sleep in their homes, but the boys wanted to stay close to, and work on, their planes that night. Roscoe, Slim, and Harley slept in Mr. Heffernan's barn. Felix slept outside under his plane.

"On Saturday people came from as far away as Albany, paying twenty-five cents each to see the show. They began with a wild 'dogfight' between Roscoe and Felix. After those two landed, Harley, the steadier pilot, took over Felix's JN-4 and Felix moved to the front seat.

"Back in the air, Harley's Jenny came from high out of the sky, heading straight toward the crowd at what seemed like a head-high pass. Several in the crowd dropped to the ground, and then the Jenny completely disappeared. Roscoe drew our attention back to the front with a roaring loop. After a few seconds the crowd was shocked into wild cheers as Harley's Jenny hopped the trees behind us and skimmed over our backs. A split second after that surprise, Roscoe roared across in front of us inches from the ground. Making a hard left he skimmed the crowd again and came around for a second pass. As he did, this time from the right, and inches from the ground, Harley came in from the left sure to hit him. At the last second Harley pulled up and skimmed the top of Roscoe's plane. The crowd was flush with applause and cheering.

"As Harley passed over the field, the engine sputtered, and Felix climbed up from his cockpit as though he were trying to jump out of the doomed plane. The crowd gasped at the impending crash. Instead Harley smoothed out the engine, and Felix climbed onto the top of the wing. Harley slowly climbed into a wide circle and Felix stood there with his arms outstretched. Then Felix went into a hand stand, finally standing on one arm on top of the Jenny. It was beyond comprehension.

"Roscoe made his final pass, with Slim hanging by his legs on the axle between the landing gear. Roscoe came within inches of crushing Slim's head on the landing field. Then he climbed on a fast spiral to the heavens. One could see Slim being pried from the machine by centrifugal force and the duration of his dangling. High in the air, Slim could hold on no more and came hurtling to the ground as the crowd shuddered and prayed. His arms and legs flailed helplessly. Some turned away, some fainted, and the rest of us stayed glued to his fate. At the last possible moment, Slim pulled a parachute and ended with a swift, solid, and safe landing.

"Slim gathered himself and ran to the megaphone to announce, 'Ladies and Gentlemen! R o s c o e ' s F l y i n g C i r c u s!' As he made the announcement, Harley and Roscoe brought the two planes down in perfect tandem. Roscoe, Felix, and Harley walked toward the cheering crowd with their arms locked and raised to the sky. Harley took the megaphone and stirred up the crowd again with a, 'Salute to the Flying Eagle S l i m Walker!'

"For the rest of the afternoon, Harley and Felix worked the crowd while Roscoe and Slim took all takers up to see the Hudson

The Great Roscoe

River and all of Saugerties 'for one thin dollar.' Several people paid the dear price for this once-in-a-lifetime chance to see where they lived from the air. Some people left, and others watched the planes and their friends while their families picnicked on the grounds.

"Mother Midge went up for her first flight and loved it. Carl and Kinsey wouldn't do it for love or money. Mr. Vought had been eating some of Kinsey's fried chicken and took a piece up to enjoy, as he saw from the air his train station and its far stretches of steel and ties. I've often wondered if that chicken wing was the first in-flight meal.

"I of course paid my fare and made sure it was with Roscoe. He asked if I had ever been up before and I related the story of the Wilbur Wright flight when I was ten. He was impressed and gave me a little schooling on the controls before we took off. Once in the air he let me fly the plane for a few minutes on his instructions. It was fun to be in the air again, especially with Roscoe.

"As the crowd dwindled I asked to go up once more, but this time I wanted to parachute to the ground. Roscoe agreed to take me up. I was to unfasten my safety belt at his signal and not before. Then I was to stand in the forward seat, with my arms folded across my chest, and make sure my feet were not hooked to any part of the cockpit or seat. Then he would flip the Jenny over so I would have a clear exit from the plane. I was to count to five and pull the ripcord. If it failed, I was to immediately release the main chute and pull the ripcord of the reserve chute.

"I was ready. My heart jumped to my throat as I stood on the Jenny's seat. Then Roscoe flipped the plane and I was free. I was a bird, and so caught up in the experience that I missed my five seconds. I continued to 'fly' until Roscoe roared past me. Coming to my senses I pulled the cord and was on the ground with a thud that knocked the wind out of me.

"The boys all came running and shouting. I tried to shout for joy, but I couldn't get the air in or out. Roscoe landed as close as he could and joined the boys surrounding me. 'Did you see that?'

Slim shouted. They all agreed, 'That was something!' When I was able to breathe again, I asked Roscoe what they meant. 'We've never seen a woman free fall that far before opening the chute. Very few men will do what you did.' Roscoe looked straight into my eyes (I nearly emptied my bladder) and asked me, 'Do you want to learn to fly?' I said, 'I do.'

"Roscoe and his circus moved on, as such enterprises must, but Roscoe himself flew into Saugerties every few months to see me and to give me flying lessons. Mr. Heffernan was nice enough to let us use his pasture anytime we needed an airstrip.

"By my fourth lesson Roscoe declared me ready enough to solo, so much so that he trusted me do it in his own JN-4. I rose like a butterfly, soared like an eagle, and landed with a bounce, a hop, and a perfect ground loop. Roscoe walked slowly to the plane with his usual undecipherable expression. When he told me to get out, I thought I was in deep dutch for the bad landing. With his calm demeanor he asked one question, 'Are you still walking?'

"I said, 'Looks like it.'

"Then he said, 'Good landing, pilot' and pinned his Air Corps wings on my chest.

"'I'm a pilot?'

"'Yes.'

"I jumped in his arms, kissed him full on the lips and promised that I'd keep his wings in the family."

Great Aunt Alice reached in her pocket and pulled out the wings that Roscoe had pinned on her that day and showed them to me. We looked them over for a while and she returned to her story.

"Roscoe smiled and I noticed that he didn't fully let go of me right off. We walked hand in hand all the way back to Jane Street and supper. As we walked he made it plain that now that I was a pilot, it was time to teach me to fly. I wasn't sure where he was going with that one, but I didn't want to talk just then. All I wanted was to lean upon his shoulder and walk beside this graceful quiet man.

"In the weeks to follow, Roscoe taught me the simple Chandelle. He taught me the Immelmann and the Split S, which he said would be useful in air combat. I hoped he wasn't serious, but it was always hard to tell with Roscoe. From there we mastered the Flat Spin, the Snap Roll, the Inside loop, the Outside loop, and something called the English bunt.

"The graduate studies focused on wing walking and the aerobatics that made Roscoe's circus rule the sky. When I had mastered these, it was time to master his love.

"Roscoe was a man who had to have precise control. I don't mean to imply that he was domineering, for he was anything but. Precision and control were the oxygen and blood of his life. Half an inch the wrong way on the stick, an untaught wing wire, or a single misfire at the wrong time could mean death for himself, but more importantly for someone else. He had seen enough death in his short life. He had avoided his own not only by his moves in the air, but also by making sure every wire, nut, and bolt of his plane were in top order. I have no doubt that he was as wildly and passionately in love with me as I was with him, but 'wild and passion' could get a man killed -- or worse kill the one he cared for most.

"My task was to prove to him without doubt that I could not only live his vagabond life but thrive on it as well. He had to know that he could rely on my every move and motivation for my own survival. Mostly he had to know that I could outlast the shock of his possible sudden death. While most women had to lure their men with romance and temptation, I had to win Roscoe with logic and reactions.

"Winning the approval of my parents was also vital to Roscoe. Indeed he was on trial observation by Carl and Midge all during our courtship. To my surprise, it was Carl who was most on my side. Roscoe was like no man that Midge had ever known. Her arsenal of skills would have never worked on him, and she didn't understand his reactions. Roscoe had a mind that only an introspective man like Carl could understand. Roscoe was a curiosity to Carl, but the things Roscoe did and the few things he said made perfect sense to Carl. This time it would be Carl who would work his magic on Midge, and believe me there were times when Carl could leave Midge speechless.

"The final test was to prove to Roscoe that I could survive without him. This would be the only time I had to lie to him. I accomplished this in a language he would understand. We took the plane up for practice one day and I deliberately made a rookie error on a routine that I had more than mastered. When I put it down I didn't give him time to lecture me. I taxied to a stop, turned to him, and shouted in his face 'GET OUT!'

"Now flying solo, I took to the air and performed to perfection every maneuver Roscoe had ever taught me. I finished with one of my own. I cut the grass inverted, no more than a yard from the ground, climbed to elevation, did a perfect slow roll, and put it down like a feather. Then I taxied to the barn and chocked the wheels.

"Roscoe strode up behind me and grabbed my arm. On the march from Heffernan's farm to Jane Street, I don't think my feet hit the ground twice. The only problem was that Roscoe hadn't thought of a word to say, and he couldn't compose a single phrase. We burst through the door, much as my father had for our trip to France, and stood straight and speechless before Carl's chair. Carl looked at us then he looked at Roscoe, who was just standing there holding my hand so tight that it was turning blue. Without a word from Roscoe, Carl stood to his full height, shook Roscoe's hand, and said, 'Of course, son, we'd be proud.'"

Great Aunt Alice said, "I will never understand the way men talk without talking." I said nothing.

"Midge came into the room with a look of 'What's going on?' I gave her THE look, she squealed, returned THE look, and grabbed me, adding an appropriate kiss on the cheek."

I thought about what Great Aunt Alice had just said about men talking without talking and decided it would be wiser to withhold my comments and let her go on.

"Midge kissed poor Roscoe as he had never wanted to be kissed before. Kinsey passed through the room as if on cue, shook her head, and muttered, 'It's about time.'

The Great Roscoe

"As a little girl I had imagined a large church wedding, the kind that men hate. The forces that had shaped my life and especially the last year had caused me to consider a better course. It was Monday. The boys had a show in Columbus, Ohio and would have to be there for their publicity flyover and ground check on Friday afternoon.

"We chose Wednesday at 1:35 in the afternoon, which would represent the upturn of the hour and our lives together. We would hold it at the Methodist church, and by word of mouth we invited all who would be able to attend and wished to share their friendship, 'but no gifts please.'

"Roscoe flew back to the boys who were camped out at Corbin's field, a small airfield in Pennsylvania, used by mail pilots and barnstormers needing a base while drifting between air shows. They arrived on Tuesday evening and Mr. Richardson was nice enough to open his men's store so that Midge could marshal them into the 'Sunday best' that they had never owned.

"Roscoe's brother Charles, your grandfather, lived on this farm back then with his folks and didn't have time to make the trip, but he sent us a nice letter and enclosed twenty dollars, which was a huge sum in those days.

"Ethel Roosevelt arrived Wednesday morning to be my matron of honor. I was so excited to see her, and I had never met her husband, Dr. Richard Derby, whom she had assisted on the battlefields of the war. The most telling thing I could say about him was that he 'fit her well,' and I was pleased with her happiness. They brought with them their two oldest children, Richard Jr. and Edith, who reminded me a little of myself at that age.

"Sadly Richard Jr. died that very year of septicemia. I was devastated for her when I heard the news. Roscoe flew me to Oyster Bay to visit for a few days and console my friend, but of course one can really do nothing but show love and support at such times. Roscoe had arranged for Frenchy Miller to loan us his JN-4 for our travel, so the boys could put on a command three-man performance for the good folks in Duncan, Oklahoma. The extra time gave Ethel a chance to know Roscoe better, and for us both to get to know Richard better. My time with Richard only confirmed my first assessment of him.

"Dr. Derby and Roscoe had a special bond from the war. Roscoe had looked into the faces of boys being killed and wounded. Richard had looked into the faces of the wounded and dying boys. During one of their 'man conversations' Roscoe suggested that Richard and he take a 'walk.' A 'walk' to Roscoe meant flying.

"He took Richard over his home and the town. He flew gracefully over the water and land that blessed Oyster Bay. He flew Richard over the grave of his son. The mound was still fresh and visible from the air. For the next several minutes he just flew, saying nothing, as Dr. Derby poured out the emotions that a man is not allowed to have. When Roscoe was satisfied that Richard was composed enough, he landed softly on the Derby lawn. That night Richard spoke only, with a melancholy smile, of the boys pointing and running after the plane, and he finished the account with, 'Ethel, we should have a man inspect our roof. I believe I saw some tiles that may have been damaged in that last storm.'

"Well, I suppose I've drifted a bit from the subject at hand. Most of my school friends were there for the wedding. Eileen and her husband Mike came up from Poughkeepsie. Carl closed the factory for the afternoon so the men and their wives could attend. Miss Wilson and Mr. Donlon were there. Judge Harper and his wife attended. Mrs. Branch sent a telegram from Arizona, which Mr. Vought brought to me. He sat with Kinsey during the service.

"Carl gave me away and sat next to Midge. They allowed two open places against the aisle to represent my mother and father. I was deeply grateful for their gesture. Ethel was her radiant self as she stood next to me. The boys stood shotgun with Roscoe, who was nervous about standing in front of the well dressed crowd and of having to say more than two words in the same hour. Thanks mostly to Midge's work, he was so handsome and I was so in love.

"There was one more witness I had insisted upon. I never explained the reason. It was the parson's cat."

Chapter 19

Newlyweds

It took us several days just to scrape the west side of the house as that was the most weathered side. We stayed with the painting for the rest of the week, as the almanac had predicted a wetter forecast for the last half of the month. We managed to get the west side finished before the rains came. We didn't have time to take the scaffold down but we would not need it for the north and south sides, as the roof lines were closer to the ground and Great Aunt Alice could reach them easily from the ladder.

When the rains began we had several days to share the story of Great Aunt Alice's new life:

"I spent my honeymoon night in a barn at Heffernan's farm. The boys slept under the planes that night to give us some privacy, but they needn't have. I could tell that Roscoe was unsure of how to handle our situation. I was reasonably sure he knew the basics, but his life revolved around delivering marvelous results without harming anyone. He wanted to plan it out. He wanted to make it special for me, and he was too tied up in the details. Besides, the last several hours had been 'a whirlwind of the most magnificent sort' and we were both tired.

"Roscoe fumbled nervously with my clothes. I turned to my husband and whispered to him 'Relax, take a few days. Get used to the feel of me. For now you must concentrate on your performance in Columbus. We will be married many years, my love. When the time is right you will know, and I will be ready.'

"I could feel his body relax and his face swell with a smile as I lay curled in his arms. For years I had wanted a man to touch me where his hands were at that moment. I was so glad that I had waited for those hands, and that man.

"There was so much to do on Thursday. I played it up for the boys with a look as if Roscoe had absolutely ravaged me. My hair was tousled, I had a silly smile, and I walked a little bowlegged. I walked straight to the coffee pot, stretched my arms wide with as much 'up' work as my chest could muster, and giving a big yawn, I said 'I hope at least you fellows got some sleep. It's a long flight to Columbus.' Then I shot down a cup of hot coffee to keep from laughing, and burned myself good with my own joke. I wanted my husband to look good in front of his friends. Item one on my checklist was complete.

"We went home for one of Kinsey's great breakfasts and visited with my family and Ethel's, as they had stayed with my folks. By 9:00 it was time to fly out of Heffernan's farm for Zimmerman's field, which was a vagabond airstrip in range of Columbus. I kissed everybody several times over and cried almost as much as Mother Midge. The boys each kissed Kinsey right on the smacker. When it was Harley's turn, he dipped her.

"Just before 10:00 we were in the air. We made three passes over Saugerties as I waved to my dear friends and family below. Of course, I cried like a fool.

"As we passed over the spot on the Hudson where I nearly died as a child, I could swear I saw Flood looking straight up at me through a space in the trees.

"I would have to earn my keep on this venture. Before there were four pilots and four seats -- now I had to sit on someone's lap. Roscoe enjoyed the time with his bride, but there were times when he just wanted to fly. Felix and I were the smallest of the crew, so we fit well together. Slim was just a little too big for comfort, so we didn't try that combination much. Harley was more than happy to accommodate me, but he had a bad habit of placing his hand on my leg.

"Slim had ingeniously designed and built eight storage cases, each the size and shape of a bomb. We used these for the few items we would need and could afford to carry. We attached these to the bomb racks making them functional and impressive to the crowds below as we entered towns.

"Needless to say, of all the boys I liked Roscoe best. Slim was a good ole boy from Texas who loved the cowboy life. He was hard working and simple in his needs. One could really depend on Slim. Harley was a lot of fun and a steady pilot, but he could sure get us in dutch with some of the local fathers. I dearly loved Felix -- he was so enthusiastic, he was a great listener, and he was always a gentleman to me.

"Felix, as I would learn, had a dark side as well. Felix was the top ace of the group, and the war memories would sometimes change him into a solitary figure. He always slept in the open under the planes, or in a part of the hangar or barn by himself. The boys had long ago learned to respect Felix's moods and let him be.

"All of the boys had their nightmares. We didn't talk about them. I had read enough about these things in my letters from Ethel, like the sad nightmares Jean Louis would always have about shooting Günter. I could hear the boys cry out in the barns at night and would make sure they were not in a position to hurt themselves, but I knew not to touch them or try to wake them up. When Roscoe had his dreams I would slip away and nestle back next to him before he woke up so he would not know.

"The one thing I insisted on was that we would go to church as often as we could. For one thing it was the right thing to do, but it was also good for business. A good image was good publicity, as the letters from one town would ignite interest in relatives and friends in the towns ahead.

"Roscoe got along fine with God, and the church was a good place for the quiet reflection that restored his complex mind. If the preacher was a little dry that day Roscoe would think about a new maneuver or do a mental check of the planes or the schedule.

"Most of us had figured that being on God's good side was pretty important in our line of work. Being a passionate man, Felix was also a very devout man. Hailing from Texas, Slim was a natural born Baptist.

"Harley was the exception. If anyone asked, we would say that we needed someone to guard the planes lest some mischievous child get it in his head that he could fly, which could result in a terrible tragedy. Fortunately there were enough mischievous children in these towns to make our lie plausible. More likely Harley would be 'guarding' some poor town girl who might be wishing a few months later that she had gone to church that day

"Our weekly routine went like this. We flew into town on Friday afternoon to stir up interest. Saturday we would do the show in the morning and give rides for 'one thin dollar' in the afternoon. That 'one thin dollar' was a little thick for most folks, but it was plausible for a once-in-a-lifetime deal. Sunday morning we would go to church, and if the parson approved we would sell rides in the afternoon. Sometimes we would take the parson up for free to help him decide, and on other occasions we would give ten cents from each dollar to the local churches to improve the town's goodwill.

"Mondays we would rest in the mornings and stay in the local field, if we didn't have to move on to a vagabond field, or if Harley didn't do something to inspire a hasty retreat. Monday evening we would share any troubles the pilots had had during the show, and service the planes. Tuesdays we would practice the show and talk over any new maneuvers to add. Wednesday would be a free day if there was no additional practice needed, or if we didn't need an extra travel day to our next show. Thursday was a travel day for sure, and Friday we would fly into the next town.

"The Columbus show was a great success. We made enough in that show to give us a cushion for the few that barely broke even. The week after the Columbus air show also went exceptionally well. The planes needed very little service, Tuesday's practice was right on the money, and we didn't have to move on until Thursday afternoon.

"Tuesday night Roscoe was relaxed and happy. He took me for a walk to watch the sun set over the Ohio plains. As night fell, we kissed and he softly led me to the far end of the field. Without a word he was letting me know it was 'time.' Midge had shared with me that woman-to-woman talk and had given me advice on how to satisfy Roscoe. In an act that is rare to this day, but never for Midge, she had pulled Roscoe aside and had given him advice on what I would need.

"We ended our walk at the end of the field where Roscoe turned and kissed me. I took one step back, dropped my dress in a free spirit manner, and kicked it aside. There I stood in total surrender. I told him that everything I had was his to take, then I pulled him near and undressed him with my kisses. Roscoe was so gentle and I was completely receptive.

"That was the way it was throughout our married life. We never worried about what we took for ourselves. His goal was my satisfaction and mine was his. As a result we both received more than we gave."

I have to admit that I was a little embarrassed to hear Great Aunt Alice reveal such intimate details. After all she was my Great Aunt.

On the other hand it was a low time in my life. The press of dwindling time and the things that I had never touched outside of the pages of my books were really beginning to matter. Listening to her stories stirred desires in my heart that I had always been afraid to pursue.

I wondered if I would ever be a "Roscoe" to any woman. I slept a little lonely that night.

Chapter 20

Vagabond Days

Great Aunt Alice woke me up early the next day. It was still raining and we could have slept in, but she wanted to give me a taste of what it was like to be a barnstorming vagabond.

Before we could do this without interruption, we needed to drive to Yoder's in Bauerhoff for groceries. We did this in Great Aunt Alice's '33 Flatbed Ford. It had come with the farm and had been in the barn for years. With only a little bit of restoration, Great Aunt Alice had it rebuilt and kept it in showroom condition. It was a real eye catcher, but with a standard stick transmission, standard brakes, and standard steering it took a real man to drive it. That's why Great Aunt Alice did all of the driving.

In Bauerhoff we made the usual rounds. We picked up a few things we needed at Yoder's Hardware, and then we made a stop at Yoder's Sew shop, where one could get everything for making clothes except zippers.

I figured we would drive home after buying the groceries at Yoder's, but Great Aunt Alice decided to treat me to lunch at Yoder's Amish Kettle Restaurant. We both ordered the breaded pork tenderloin sandwich, which was a sight to behold. The buns were larger than the average sandwich bun and baked fresh every day. The tenderloin itself was as large as a dinner plate. The milkshakes were smooth and almost straight from the cows at Yoder's Dairy.

Arriving back at the farm, we put the supplies away and began our "vagabond" days.

It was Monday, and the vagabond schedule called for us to work on the planes. Great Aunt Alice showed me the intimate details of her sky blue JN-4, and the things that Roscoe would have inspected, tightened, patched, and lubricated. Before I came to the farm I knew very little about her Jenny. In time I would be promoted to Great Aunt Alice's crew chief.

Over the next few days we would live the life of her vagabond days, doing the things that they would have done. That evening we cooked a kettle of beans over an open fire behind the barn. We added a little dried pork for added flavor and that, with a pot of coffee, was our supper. We slept in the barn that night, and in the morning she told me more of her story:

"I've already told you the general schedule. That was tough enough, but it was the details that made our life so austere. First there was the food. We could usually count on a few eggs from the farmers who would let us use their pastures. At the vagabond airfields food supplies were even scarcer. Any meat we had was dried, and we couldn't carry much at a time. Any vegetables could be found in season, but on a day-to-day basis only. I made sure the boys ate them too, usually to a chorus of, 'Ah Ma.' Apples were plentiful in the fall, and when I could and I would fix the boys a sort of fried apple dumpling. Nothing could be baked. Everything had to be cooked over an open campfire. We could usually count on a good home-cooked meal once or twice during the weekends we were in a town, and more likely to be invited by some local host. Campfire kettle beans could be eaten three meals a day, and coffee was the universal elixir.

"Our wardrobe consisted of the outfit you were wearing and the one you were washing or mending. We couldn't afford to carry any more weight. I was pleased that the boys choose to do most of their washing, mending, and dishes. They never treated me as their 'woman servant,' but always as 'one of the boys' -- an equal in the venture.

"The 'ladies room' consisted of an outhouse, when I was lucky, and if not a slit trench -- even on cold and rainy days. The boys were always gentlemen. Roscoe, Slim, and Felix kept an eye on Harley to make sure of that.

"During the summer we would work the shows in the North, Midwest, and East. By late fall we worked the South and Southwest. The schedule was hectic, but we preferred it to the few weeks that had no show. Those weeks threw off our timing, and left us eating more beans.

"We could have lived better, as I still had plenty of income from the factory. I chose instead to give Roscoe the dignity of supporting our marriage from his role as a provider, and budgeting within his means. He was not a vain man, nor a cave man, but he had his pride, and a husband who has his dignity is a loving husband. Carl arranged for my share of the factory's profits to be deposited into an account that Mr. Polo managed very well for our 'retirement.' We lived that wonderful vagabond life for the first two years of our marriage.

"Within six weeks of our wedding, I became more involved with the show. In practice, I showed the boys that this girl could do any maneuver in the show as well as a picture-perfect inverted grass cutter. I was billed as the 'Angel of the Air,' and I was worked into the act between the dogfight and the spectacular main event. It turned out to be a big draw, and we were being booked for bigger and better shows.

"1925 was a banner year for us. We were wealthy by barnstormer standards. Finances were so good that the boys pitched in and bought me my own JN-4. At last we could travel in comfort and carry more supplies. She had a sky blue paint job with a set of angel wings painted on each side. She was christened the 'Blue Angel.'

"We also added a new wing walker act that featured Slim in a modified tuxedo and me in a very short and tight 'wedding dress.' Harley piloted Slim while Roscoe was my pilot. Felix would narrate from the ground as we danced in the sky in a sort of courtship. We would then fly side by side in a wedding ceremony. After that we went into a terrible fight with wild gyrating gestures. The climax was when we 'divorced' and walked away from each other, and right off the wings of our respective planes. As we free-fell, we would reach for each other in remorse. On landing we ran to each other's arms in reconciliation. Slim liked that part and sometimes really played it up, especially in practice. To tell you the truth he was a great kisser. As part of our practice Slim and I would stand on the wings while the planes were on the ground and work out our choreography. The boys really liked my short 'wedding dress,' and they would often stand beneath the wing to make sure I was doing it right. They never seemed to care how Slim was doing.

"At the shows my short dress would cause a stir among the wives. Felix would cover us by turning toward some woman in the crowd who had an indignant look on her face and would 'spontaneously' and loudly lament that it was so sad that I had to wear that blushing creation, then add that it was aerodynamically necessary to maintain my balance and keep from being swept from the wing and to certain tragedy. 'I know it is terribly embarrassing for the poor girl, but she would endure anything to cheer the crowd and to promote that a woman can do anything these days.' Felix could tear your heart out when he spoke in that tone. This brave sentiment would repeat through the crowd giving each man below the green light to stare all he wanted. I often wondered how much the population of these towns increased nine months after one of these performances.

"Slim and I won the hearts of the crowds, but Felix owned their nerves. He became more daring with each season, and I will always consider him the greatest wing walker of all time.

"In February we did the Dallas show and were showered with praise from the press and public. Harley loved Dallas. Actually he loved Dallas too much, but that part was not covered by the press. Felix was a little uneasy with the big city, and the public attention, and he was feeling closed in. Slim was in Texas and that was enough for him.

"We made good money and publicity from the big shows, but it was the small towns that we enjoyed most. The small townsfolk seemed to appreciate us more, and their roots were so much closer to our own humble beginnings.

"The biggest problem we ever had in a small town was our own fault. We were ready to leave Goldthwaite, Texas where the people had treated us so nicely. That morning we attended a first-rate service at the Baptist Church and a pitch-in dinner afterward by the church folk.

By 2:00 the rest of us were packed to go and waiting on Harley, when he came galloping full out on a 'borrowed' horse. He gave the frantic hand signal to 'wind 'em up', and we took the warning to heart. As the three engines roared to life we saw a rancher bearing down on us in his pick-up truck. We hit the air as one unit and heard the 'BLAM BLAM' of his shotgun. No one was hurt, but Harley spent the evening patching the holes in Roscoe's plane. That night as we all bedded down and things got quiet, Harley asked in a frustrated tone, 'Well don't you want to know?' We all replied in unison, 'NO!'

"I finally got to see Arizona when we did a show in Phoenix. We did a full show in Duncan, Oklahoma to make up for the three-man show that Slim, Felix, and Harley had performed there when Roscoe and I went to see Richard and Ethel. From Duncan we did shows in a wide variety of towns -- Albuquerque, Stillwater, Abilene, Robinson, Keithsburg, Dayton, Anderson, Detroit, Kenosha, Chicago -- all leading to the 'big one' that July in St. Louis.

"St. Louis promised to be the show of shows, with barnstormers from across the world competing for the top prize of $5,000 and the Eubank cup.

"On Friday we crossed the Mississippi and circled some kind of courthouse that still stands near where the Arch is located today. There were scores of barnstormers in the skies over St. Louis. We gathered at Lambert Field for the show the next day and found our assigned field space. During the afternoon we mingled with the other crews and admired each other's planes.

They were all shined to glory, and the spirit of the place was higher than a cloud.

"There were barnstormers from 37 states, Poland, Italy, Germany, France, Canada, England, and Mexico. We were fed like kings, and each team was photographed. That evening we drew for show position and were given some safety rules. The committee wished us luck and we shook hands all around.

"Felix had left the briefing early, as he couldn't stand the crowds. He seemed especially uneasy around the German team. It might have been that he was stirred by looking at the very type of planes that he had dueled in the war. I also noticed him looking at one German pilot in particular. The German clearly noticed Felix but would not look him in the eye. As usual Felix slept by himself, but not very much, as he was very fitful that night. For that matter, nobody really slept that night. The competition was too worrisome for sleep.

"The morning was even more worrisome, as Harley was running a fever and was sick at his stomach. We decided to substitute Felix for Harley and let Harley do the ground commentary. We cut the dogfight, as we figured several of the other vagabonds would do something similar. We went with my Angel of the Air, the Amazing Felix, with Roscoe as his pilot, and The Wedding, with Felix as Slim's pilot, and Roscoe as mine.

"The Germans had flown two teams ahead of us and were clearly leading the competition in their bright red powerful Focker Triplanes. The call was made for 'Roscoe's Flying Circus!' and all eyes drew to my 'Blue Angel' and its cutie-pie pilot. I headed down the strip and shot into the air. I pulled G-forces that would have blacked out some of those pilots still on the ground. My loops and spins were pin-point precise. I topped the sky with a 'Roscoe Roll' and finished with a final ground sweeping inverted pass. Roscoe said I was only eighteen inches from the ground and my tail was little more than six. The roar of the crowd followed me like a tidal wave.

"As I taxied to our staging space I watched Roscoe roar into the air with Felix already standing in the cockpit. Felix was like a man possessed. He did stunts that would kill any other man, and Roscoe had his hands full trying to compensate for Felix's fragile balance, while keeping the flying precise and clean. They too landed with the crowd in their hands and the competition squarely in our court.

"We had won the admiration of our worldwide peers. Now it was time to take their hearts and their laughter. The crowd was mostly composed of men, and when I walked to my plane the guys began to whistle. I gave them a little Midge move that really sent their blood pressure sky high. They were already cheering, and all I had done so far was to walk to the plane.

"We rose in tandem, gently and in style. On the way up Roscoe told me about my grass cutter, and I was a little shaken to think I had been that close to the ground. Then he told me how near Felix had come at one point to falling off the wing.

"When we gained altitude Slim and I took our positions on the top wings for the first pass. It was the flirty-look pass. This was to be followed by another head-on pass, where we blew kisses to each other.

"Suddenly something was very wrong. Felix came around this time in an Immelmann, a combat move, and too high. Slim was now down on the wing and hanging on for dear life. I could see him looking back at Felix, and I could see the wild look in Felix's eyes as he dove sharply at Roscoe's plane. I dropped to the wing and felt the whoosh of his landing gear inches from my ear, and I heard Slim screaming Felix's name. We all knew what was happening now. Felix was having a war flashback and was out to kill us all.

"When Felix looped high above us for another pass, Slim fell off at the top of the loop and deployed his chute immediately -- not taking any chance that he might black out.

"Roscoe shouted, 'ALICE! . . . GO LEFT! . . . LONG COUNT!' And then he shouted his last words to me, 'ALICE, I LOVE YOU!' With that he dipped his wing left and gave me a bump to shove me farther from Felix, who grazed the belly of Roscoe's plane and stripped his landing gear.

"As Felix came around again he found the drifting Slim in his sights and clipped his legs off with the top of his wing. A cloud of blood exploded into the sky, and a trail of blood followed Slim to the ground. If he was still alive when he hit the ground, it would be the most painful landing of all time.

"Roscoe had only two options -- fly his plane into Felix's JN-4 to kill Felix and himself, or run him out of gas, where they might both have a chance to crash land and survive. In either case it had to be as far from the crowd as possible. Roscoe maneuvered to pull Felix to the north of the field and away from the crowd. He did all he could to minimize the situation, but there was one option that he could not fully control. That remaining option was that Felix, the slightly better pilot, would ram and kill Roscoe first.

"I held the count as long as I dared and pulled the cord. I landed with a hard thud, and Harley came running over to me. He jumped across my face to shelter me from the sight of the sound I would hear a second later as Felix hit Roscoe and they both exploded in midair.

"Slim bled to death, either in the air or shortly after landing.

"A moment before, Roscoe's Flying Circus ruled the skies, as the roar of the crowd lifted us ever higher. Now the boys were gone. Slim was dead, poor tormented Felix was dead, my husband was dead. I had no body to kiss one last time. I had no body to bury. He was just gone.

"Before the sound of the sickening crash and the gasp of the crowd, I was the 'Angel of the Air.' Now, in morbid silence, I was a twenty-four-year-old widow."

Great Aunt Alice walked away from our campsite and into the farmhouse. I put out the campfire. Our vagabond days were over.

Chapter 21
Widow

Great Aunt Alice remained in her room for two days. When I knocked, she refused to answer. When I went in, she was sitting in her wicker rocker, facing the window and hugging her bed pillow. When I asked if she was all right, she said nothing. I took her a little food, but she ate very little of it. Every now and then she would go to the bathroom, and then return to her chair, holding her pillow, staring out the window.

I fought with myself and racked my doctorial brain for the words that would bring her back to the living. She had dredged up for me the most painful memory of her life. Unlike the Titanic episode, which she had cautiously eased into, she had not mentally prepared herself to retell this tragedy. It was as much a mental shock to her now as it had been then.

For all of my life I had failed as a man. I was no good at sports or fixing things. I never had a real date in high school. I had never been loved by any woman or respected by any man. I was a geek and a freak -- just a laid-off professor of pre-Georgian literature. Great Aunt Alice needed a man. She needed Roscoe.

Completely out of my nature, I pulled her to the bed. I placed her on her side. I curled up behind her. I held her like I thought a man should hold a woman.

"Was that the first time he said 'I love you?'"

"It was one of the few times he said it with words."

"He was saying goodbye -- you didn't get the chance to tell him goodbye."

I had finally found the opening. She exploded with emotion.

"I didn't get to say goodbye! There was nothing! He was gone! There wasn't a bit of bone or flesh -- NOTHING! When your man dies of cancer you can fall on his chest and wail your heart out. Even Slim . . . oh dear God . . . the fear in his eyes . . . his body was as white as my dress."

"What did you do?"

Great Aunt Alice went on with the story with halting pace -- as if it were someone else's nightmare.

"Frenchy Miller was there. He found me some clothes and helped me change. He held me a lot. Frenchy telegraphed Midge and Carl. Mother Midge took the next train to St. Louis to bring me home.

"Harley flew the 'Blue Angel' to Saugerties and with his permission parked it in Mr. Heffernan's barn. Then he took the train back to his home in Detroit. He didn't wait for my return. I never saw him again.

"I stayed in total seclusion in my home on Jane Street for a month or more. Carl, Midge, and Kinsey placed a complete hedge around me. I couldn't handle flowers, or cards, or sympathetic voices -- no matter that I appreciated the caring they represented. The fellows at the factory were lost. Ordinarily there would be a collection for flowers or they would attend the funeral, but it did not apply in this situation.

"The people of Saugerties did not feel bad that I had seemingly rejected their good will. They understood. There was only one thing they could do. They prayed. The people in my church prayed for me. The men at the factory led their families in prayer for me. The shopkeepers prayed for me. Mr. Vought prayed for me. Judge Harper prayed for me. The children in the school prayed for me. Barnstormers all over the country prayed for me. The people we had befriended in the small towns all across America prayed for me. Father Collier prayed for me. Mr. Bride and Mr. Cottam prayed for me. As the word spread of my need, people everywhere prayed for me. I could feel their hands. I could feel a million hugs. I could feel Flood's hand on my back. I could feel my mother's arms around me. I could feel my father's hand on my heart.

"I don't know how it works, but I knew, I knew.

"After a while Mother Midge thought it best to take me to Oyster Bay. Ethel would sit next to me on the balcony facing the sea. She would talk some, but mostly she would just listen. I said very little; she listened even more.

"Richard would come home at night and give me the biggest hugs and kisses. He would show great affection around Ethel, for he knew that I would see this in others in the world and must accept that love continues whether we have it in our lives or not. I was glad to see him do this. I needed to feel a man's hug. I needed to see that all love in the world did not die with Roscoe. The children were so sweet. They would bring me tea and flowers and little paper hearts. Ethel's five-year-old would walk up to me and put her head on my tummy and hug my leg.

"When I returned to Saugerties, I began to get out of the house. The townsfolk knew not to press me. Instead I would feel an occasional light hand on my shoulder or my arm. Alice sat next to me in church and held my hand. She said not a word except to pray the Lord's Prayer or sing as the worship called for such. Alice had a beautiful voice.

"All of these acts of kindness were so good for me, but something was still missing. For months to come, the world lived on, but I only existed from moment to moment.

"Finally one day I heard an airplane engine. An hour or so later there came a knock at our door. It was Orville Wright. I had renewed my friendship with him after one of our Dayton shows. He had seen me fly and wanted to meet this 'Angel of the Air.' He was of course surprised to find out that I was 'Frank Howard's little girl, all grown up.' I found out then that Mr. Wilbur had died of typhoid just forty-five days after my father. He was just at the cusp of the first practical designs, and Mr. Orville would live to see two world wars with their powerful machines, and to see Chuck Yeager break the sound barrier.

"Mr. Orville never really stated his business. We just talked, and as we did so I put my head on his shoulder and he put his arm around mine. We talked of things that only fliers could understand. It was like the boys and their nightmares. I could only understand so much. It was their world, from which I would always be excluded no matter how much I sympathized."

Great Aunt Alice rolled on her back and snuggled up to me. Her mood was still melancholy, but her tears had stopped, and as she told this part I could feel the tension lessen in her body.

"Mr. Orville spent the afternoon and was invited to stay. He accepted and thanked us for our hospitality. He slept in my room and I in the room off the kitchen. About 6:00 I woke to the strong fragrance of aviator's coffee. I can't tell you how it is different, but the smell of a vagabond's coffee pot is unique. Perhaps it was the fact that the smell of this pot was coming from the backyard.

"I looked out the window to see Mr. Orville sitting on a log at the edge of the fire pit with both hands around the warm cup. I put on my jacket and walked out in my nightgown and slippers. I poured a cup, as barnstormers do without comment, and sat across from him with the fire between. I looked at him and he at me with a loving, understanding smile in our eyes, but no expression on our lips. We said nothing. We drank our coffee. We set our cups down. Then Mr. Orville said just two words, 'Get dressed.'

"As I walked into the house to do as he had requested, he put out the fire with the aviator's coffee, as it would be no good for normal folks' consumption. I came out in my flying suit. As we walked, the town was coming to life. The factory boys were walking to work. The shopkeepers were opening their shops. The children were forming their play adventures. Mr. Orville was well known at that time and the word began to spread that 'Orville Wright was in town, and that he was walking with Miss Alice, and that she was in her flying suit.'

"Children began to follow, shopkeepers closed their shops, factory men stopped walking to the factory, women in aprons left their homes, the pastor stopped his morning vespers, and we became a magnet drawing the whole town from a respectful distance.

"We walked straight to Heffernan's farm, where I saw my 'Blue Angel' standing before the barn like a faithful pup. She was freshly wiped down, her oil changed, and her tank full. I started to run to her like a mother who had found her missing child, and then I stopped.

"I hadn't seen her since the day I lost my Roscoe. Mr. Orville stood a few steps behind, with the crowd reverently back and silent. I took one slow step and then another. I quickened my pace, but not to a run. When I reached her side I climbed into the cockpit and kissed her controls.

"CONTACT!"

"Mr. Orville pulled the propeller, and she roared to life. I taxied to the pasture, where I took her to the sky. I flew as high as I could, right into the arms of my Roscoe. As if making aerial love to my husband's spirit, I came down into every maneuver Roscoe had taught me. Then I finished with my inverted grass cutter, pulled her up, and circled for a feather soft landing.

"When I taxied to the barn there was no applause, for this was God's performance for me. I jumped out of the plane, threw my goggles down, and ran to Mr. Orville. We both fell to our knees, and I buried my head in his chest and cried, and cried, and cried. My Saugerties friends gathered around us silently in a circle. They dropped to their knees and held their hands out to me in prayer and love."

I kissed Great Aunt Alice, left her in the bed, and went out to paint the north side. A few minutes later she joined me, and we painted in silence the rest of the day.

Chapter 22
The Great In Between

We were closing in on the end of our painting project. There was only one more side to paint and we would be finished with the house. The barn was too large to finish painting in the time we had remaining before the bad weather set in, so it was useless to start.

I knew that soon I would become a liability to Great Aunt Alice. If a college were going to pick me up for the fall start, they would have contacted me by now. I was starting to feel pretty blue. Great Aunt Alice asked me about my mood, and she told me of her "in between" days.

"Mr. Orville was my savior. While the others kept me going with their love and prayers, there remained this hump that only a pilot could understand, and Mr. Orville knew how to lift me over the barrier.

"I was back. It was my time to grow strong again and lend my prayer and support to others in need, but I didn't know where to start. I had plenty of income from the factory, but that was Carl's job to manage -- I was just the owner. Midge had her dress shop. Kinsey had our family to feed and harass -- and Mr. Vought to keep in line. I just didn't know where to steer my new life.

"There was always barnstorming. Frenchy Miller had heard of my 'conversion' and, 'would be happy to add me to his boys.' I was tempted, but my barnstorming heart had left me at St. Louis. I've often wondered if I made the right decision by refusing Frenchy's offer, but I think I did.

"Aviation was changing. The days of the barnstormers were on their way out. The vagabond boys were beginning to get respectable jobs flying the mail. More and more women were learning to fly, with their minds on cross country races and records. I wanted none of that, but I would hang out at the fields and made lots of dear friends among the women pilots, and I was glad to see their progress.

"I asked Frenchy about Harley, and he said Harley had gone back to Detroit and was working in the factory. He wasn't very happy, but he didn't want to be happy. He held himself to blame for St. Louis. He figured that if he had been in that plane instead of Felix, we would have won, we would have been happy, and we would be alive. I wrote several times to Harley and told him it wasn't his fault, but he never returned my letters.

"I decided I would fly to Cook Field to apply for the mail service, but the postmaster there was an absolute pig who flat out said that women weren't qualified to handle such a dangerous job. I flew off in a huff. Boy, was I mad! I came back around and buzzed his post office tent flat around him. I waited until he crawled out, and then I chased him down the field till he fell flat on his kisser. I finished with a third run right through his open hanger, and then I landed on his field.

"I jumped out of Angel and strode right for him like I was going to kill him, and he did the same towards me. When we got close enough I yelled, 'YOU OWE ME AN APOLOGY, BUSTER!'

"'ME? LISTEN, GIRLIE, GO BACK TO YOUR DOLLIES BEFORE I . . .' He raised his hand like he was going to spank me, so I grabbed him by the tie and punched him in the gut. He folded like a house of cards. I turned and with a brush of my hands I said in my sweetest girlie voice, 'But that will do as well.'

"About that time one of the mail pilots who had watched it all sauntered past the scene with his mail bag and the postmaster gasped, 'Call the police!'

"'Oh, did the little girl beat you up?'

"'You're fired!'

"'OK.'

"The pilot tossed me his bag and said, 'Here you go, Angel, Gresley field.'

"'Thanks, Ralph.'

"It was Ralph Kern, whom I had known for years. Ralph flew a Spad in the war and was a lean, tall, blue-eyed, heart-breaking son of a gun. Everybody loved Ralph. He could step into any plane for the first time and fly it like he was just putting his pants on.

"As I revved Angel's engine and took off down the field, the postmaster staggered to his feet and waved his right arm while he held his stomach with his left. He was shouting, 'Stop (huff puff) that girl (huff puff) she's stealing (huff puff) the mail.' I couldn't hear a thing he was saying so I turned around to hear him better. I didn't want to be rude. The trouble was that it takes longer to get in the air with the wind at your back. I clipped him pretty close to get the Angel up. This time he fell flat on his rear. I've never seen a man with such a poor sense of balance. He clearly didn't have what it took to be a mail pilot.

"I flew over to Gresley field and pulled up to the pilot's shack, where I found Gusty Hollimon. I asked Gusty where to put the mail bag. Gusty gave me this long smile so I scolded, 'Now, Gusty.' He chuckled and pointed to the postmaster's tent.

"When I walked in, the tent was empty. I stepped outside and looked around as I heard the door snap on the Ops shack. This fellow was coming out of the shack laughing so hard he could barely walk. He pointed at me standing there with the mailbag and laughed, 'You're the girl. . . Ralph just called . . .' The poor man was laughing so hard he could barely get it out. He pointed to the pilot's shack and said, 'Come on. We gotta tell the guys.'

"'Aren't you going to arrest me?'

"'Are you kidding? I wanna kiss you. Everybody hates that . . .' I won't tell you what he called him.

"At the pilot's shack we saw Gusty and Norm Tiefel and told them the whole story, which they just loved. Norm had been a part of Frenchy's boys for a while in '22. He could do an inside loop and hang at the top for what seemed like an hour. Gusty was a good ole boy from Arkansas. He was very tall and thin as a toothpick. He had the most beautiful singing voice I had ever heard and had written several catchy hymns. Gusty's mama taught him well, and every night at 7:00 on the dot he would sing a hymn and read out loud from the Bible, whether the boys liked it or not. For the most part, they didn't mind as there wasn't anything else to do, and any job too dangerous for a girl to do called for a good relationship with the Lord.

"I added that last part myself.

"Gusty was a slow talker and a slow walker who impressed a person as one of those country boys who could always make a fool out of a city slicker with a Ph.D."

"Sorry, Great Nephew."

"No offense taken, Great Aunt."

"The boys laughed and laughed as I told the deadly details. There was a knock and the sheriff walked in ready to arrest me for stealing the mail. He had received a call from the sheriff on the Cook end. The postmaster here told him that I had delivered the mail as expected and there was nothing wrong as far as he could see. He tried to introduce me, but he didn't know my name. I interjected 'Mrs. Burke' and the sheriff tipped his hat. 'Pleased to meet you, ma'am.'

"Then the Gresley postmaster asked the sheriff if the Cook postmaster had said anything about an angel and indicated that the Cook postmaster might be having one of 'his episodes.' The sheriff said he didn't know and asked to use our phone to call the Cook sheriff. He asked about the 'angel' reference, and the Cook sheriff confirmed that he had said something about an angel. The Gresley postmaster told our sheriff that it sounded like an 'episode' for sure, and that he might want to have the Cook postmaster taken in for the night to make sure he wouldn't hurt himself or some other poor fellow. Our sheriff passed along the message and bade us goodnight.

"A few minutes later we got a call from Ralph, and from our postmaster's reaction we could figure out where the Cook postmaster was going to be spending the night. When the post office found out that one of their postmasters had been arrested for mental problems, they let him go.

"When things settled down, Norm took the mail on to Worchester, and Gusty and I had a good visit.

"Gusty told me about a group of business fellows in New York City who needed an on-call fellow to fly them various places, and that Frenchy could fix it for me if I were interested. I told him thanks, and we put it aside for talk of the 'old days.' We reminisced of his near miss in Greenup and our second air show in Duncan.

"When 7:00 rolled around, Gusty began to sing, 'I've heard an old, old story 'bout a savior came from glory.' I joined him in a swell duet, and we finished with a reading from Ephesians and a prayer for my safety. Gusty let me sleep in Norm's bed that night, and I flew home in the morning.

"I hadn't settled a thing in my life, but I had enjoyed my time with some of the boys who knew me by my vagabond name, Angel. It felt good to get a little air under my wings again."

Chapter 23
The Business Pilot

It was a lazy day. We ate a light breakfast, let the dishes go, and said to heck with the painting. I relaxed with a good book while Great Aunt Alice took Ethel up for a "walk." She told me that the cornfields were starting to turn and in a few weeks they would look like one of those brown woven doormats that you see here and there.

School hadn't started yet, so there were lots of kids playing. She buzzed the little league diamond in Orland, which always delighted the boys and drove the coaches crazy. She did a loop over Yoder's pond for the Yoder boys, who were fishing. There wasn't a fish within forty miles of Yoder's pond, but boys (and, most of the time, men) generally fish for the fishing, not for the fish. She took one more pass at Yoder's cows and brought it "down on the house" to let me know she was home.

"I'm hungry for ice cream, Great Nephew. Let's go to Yoder's Drive-in." It's hard to describe an Amish "drive-in" except to say that every parking spot has a hitching post and you have to watch your step if you get out of the truck. I would try to describe the Amish buggy hops, but you wouldn't believe me if I did.

On the way into Bauerhoff I asked Great Aunt Alice if she had ever found her niche in life.

"Not right off. I subbed for some of the airmail boys when they couldn't work, and I bummed around the airfields with the new gals. I helped Carl when he needed me, and I was involved in the Methodist Women's Society activities.

"I caught up with Frenchy Miller at River Bend and the subject of that private pilot's job came up, the one Gusty had told me about at Gresley Field. Frenchy told me that it had been filled, but the pilot had recently married and the haphazard schedule was digging into their wedded bliss, so he was looking for a nine to five. He said it was a good time to get in, as they were trading in their Fairchild 71 for a brand new Bellanca CH-200.

'These guys must be loaded.'

"'They are, and they won't be looking for any old barnstormer. They need someone who can navigate them from town to town in a straight, quick line. How are your navigation skills Angel?'

"I had to admit that I mostly followed the railroads to get around, so I asked Frenchy if he knew any pilot who could give me some advice. He started to tell me about a mail pilot they called Slim, who worked out of Lambert in St. Louis. Then he realized that was the field where Roscoe died and he paused awkwardly as if he had really goofed. I told him it was OK and that a good pilot can't be a mental prisoner all their life because of a bad landing.

"'I think about him everyday Frenchy. I'll never forget the look in Felix's eyes, or Slim's pale white body. I have those dreams all the time now, like you fellows have. It broke my heart, Frenchy, But I can't let it destroy my mind. Besides, I've have all of you guys loving on me.' Frenchy and I fell into a mutual hug and he said, 'You got that right, Angel. We love you a lot.'

"'So how about this other 'Slim' fellow? That's a pretty common nickname in our business.' Frenchy couldn't think of his last name, but he said I would know him. 'He used to fly with Klink.'

"'Leon? How's he doing?'

"'Leon hurt his back. He can't pull the G's anymore.'

"And then it hit me, 'Daredevil Lindbergh? How do you figure him?'

"'Yeah, that's the one. He's making a try for the Orteig Prize, and he's been working on what to do when he runs out of railroad tracks to follow.'

"I thanked Frenchy for the friendship and the lead and decided to fly to Lambert the next day. As I flew over the river and spotted the courthouse, I could see in my mind all of those barnstormers filling the skies that day we entered the city. Looking back on it, we would have had a field day with that arch they have now. As I came over Lambert Field, I saw the spot that still held the ashes of Roscoe and Felix and their locked planes. I blew them a kiss and landed.

"At the Ops shack I asked Lou about Lindbergh. Lou was an interesting character. He was one of those fellows everybody knew, but nobody knew anything about him, not even his last name. He always seemed to be in the Ops shack, and he had the answer to any question one could throw at him.

"In response to my question, Lou said that Slim was on his way back from Chicago, but that Tom Nelson and Bud Gurney were in the pilot's shack. The other pilot, Phil Love, was in St. Louis for the night.

"I didn't know Tom, but I knew of Bud Gurney, and Phil was a good friend. I asked if I could walk out 'there.' Lou knew what I meant and said, 'Sure, do you want me to . . . you know.'

"I said, 'Thanks, Lou. I want to do this one alone.'

"'Sure, Angel, anything you want.'

"I walked first to the spot where I had landed. I lay down on the grass and looked up this time to an unobstructed sky. There was no smoke, there was no blood, there were no angry engines or gasping crowd. In the peace of that moment I prayed. I prayed for Harley, and Felix, and Slim. I prayed for all of the pilots I knew who died before and who had died since. I prayed for all of the little kids in the crowd who saw what Harley had covered from my eyes. I prayed that I could one more time feel my Roscoe pressing upon me.

"From there I walked to the spot where I saw Slim's body. Where I had once seen a gruesome display of death, there now was a small patch of Texas Bluebonnets about the size of a human body. Bluebonnets are not native to Missouri.

"It was about a mile to the place where my Roscoe and Felix impacted the ground. I kept my eyes down, hoping to find part of Roscoe or his plane. The crater was well along with the process of healing. The boys had placed a marker for Roscoe, which I appreciated immensely. There was none for Felix. as he was looked on as some sort of Judas. Two years later I came back with a marker for Felix.

"Bits and pieces of the two planes could be found half buried in the soil and the weeds, but no human remains as far as I could tell. Then I found a fragment of the top wing of Roscoe's plane. I knew it was his -- I recognized a part of the red mark I used to judge my position when wing walking. Harley's plane had a blue mark.

"Something possessed me to stand on that mark, close my eyes, and spread my arms. When I opened my eyes again, I was in the air. Harley and Slim were passing our plane in the part where we blew each other kisses. We did the whole routine and I ran to jump off the wing.

"As I was 'falling' to the ground I saw something gleam. What I found was a gold band, badly mangled from the impact and the fire. Inside there were enough letters to determine it was bought at Halpert's, the jewelry store in Saugerties. It was Roscoe's ring! I fell to the ground on that spot and went to sleep with my head on Roscoe's chest.

"A few hours later I heard the mail plane. It was Lindbergh returning from Chicago. I went to the pilots shack to meet him and to give him a general idea of why I was there. He remembered me and shook my hand. I felt funny calling him Slim or Daredevil, and I knew he didn't like Charlie, so I'd always referred to him as Charles.

"I asked Charles if I could meet with him in the morning after he had some sleep. He thanked me for my courtesy and said that he was very tired and would be glad to talk with me over breakfast around 6:00.

"Lou let me sleep in the Ops shack that night. I stayed up and talked to the boys for a while and thanked them and the others responsible for the marker. I showed them the precious ring and they were glad for me. Lou came up with the leather string I still use to carry it around my neck."

Great Aunt Alice pulled the ring out and showed it to me. It had a special beauty in its malformation. I can't describe it, but it was truly special.

"I met with Charles the next morning over a plate of heavy cholesterol and high-octane coffee. When I explained the job I was after and the need to navigate without the ground landmarks, he understood.

"'You aren't going to use this against me for a Paris run of your own, are you?' I assured him that I never wanted to see the Atlantic again as it had taken my father on Titanic. He showed no remorse for making the statement, as he had no time for sentiment or apology. I'd always respected that in Charles. You always knew where you stood with him.

"Charles bluntly told me that he was 'following the rails till they ran out.' Then he would use shipping lane charts, a watch, and a compass from there. He had already surveyed the landmarks or had gathered information from other pilots or wireless men on this side of the ocean. The conversation triggered an idea. I asked him if it would be possible to create a chart of our major cities showing the latitude and longitude of each. Then I could use compass and watch, as well as known landmarks, to chart a more direct route overland. He didn't see why I couldn't do that. I thanked him and wished him well on his plans, and bade him a flirty, 'See ya, Daredevil.'

"Charles shot back with 'Bye, Angel' and he gave me a wink. He did have a carefully guarded sense of humor. It was a sign that you were on his trusted friend list.

"With this new information in hand, I had Phil Love drive me to the St. Louis Library, where I worked for nine days looking up the precise longitude and latitude settings for each major and mid-sized city in the country and making a set of charts.

"During that time I also wired Orville Wright for information on who might be able to give me the air speed of the Bellanca CH-200 Pacemaker. To my surprise, he put me in touch with Mr. Bellanca himself, who answered all of my questions on the aircraft.

"The remaining unknown would be the winds aloft. I could determine the wind speed at the point of departure and calculate some possible wind drift, but the upper winds might be very different. Knowing this, I went back into the library for another twenty-seven days and calculated cities or landmarks every ten miles along the major routes and every twenty-five miles along the minor routes.

"Armed with my charts and the special mathematics tutoring my father had given me in France, I calculated a course, using the Jenny's air speed, from St. Louis to Memphis, to Nashville, to Indianapolis, to Chicago, to Cleveland, to Buffalo, and finally back to Heffernan's farm in Saugerties. I predicted a date and time when I would touch down in each town and finally Saugerties. When I had landed at Heffernan's farm, I was off by only seven minutes and had drifted off course a total of less than two miles.

"I was ecstatic and wired Lindbergh of my success. Charles asked me to calculate a course from Roosevelt Field to Halifax for comparison to his figures. I did so, and he responded that mine matched his to the mark. He said he would think of me during that section of his attempt, and thereafter kept me in the loop when he had discovered anything new in navigation, which later included his Great Circle Route to Japan.

"The last piece of the puzzle was to learn how to fly a Bellanca. Mr. Bellanca was very nice in that he invited me to Dayton to see and learn to fly his marvelous design. I accepted at once and learned much from the experience. It was faster and larger than any plane I had flown, with room for six passengers. I wished Mr. Wilbur Wright had lived to see this advancement on his achievement.

"It wasn't hard to fly, but it was different in its feel, and I needed a few hours to master the plane. Mr. Bellanca was nice enough to give me six days of intense training, and he actually asked me to test its abilities with some of my barnstorming maneuvers. In a sense it was an even swap, where I was the test pilot for Mr. Bellanca and he was my flight instructor. When I left Dayton I could fly the Bellanca like a professional, which had been my goal.

"I also wired Frenchy, told him of my newfound prowess, and asked him if the Bellanca job was open. Frenchy told me that someone else had the job, but he too was having trouble with the on call hours and was looking for another job.

"A few weeks later I got the wire from Frenchy to make my move. He sent a telegram to each of the gentlemen telling them that a top-notch pilot by the name of Burke had some interest in the Bellanca job. He just kept it at 'Burke' so the men would not know that 'Burke' was a woman and therefore prejudice their thinking.

"After an exchange of contact information, I found it almost impossible to arrange a common interview meeting with these busy men. I proposed instead that I should take each gentleman on one free trip to the place of their choosing. This way they could evaluate me in the actual job without any loss of time or investment. My only stipulation was that I should know the destination in time to plot a course. They seemed pleased at my innovative thinking and conspired among themselves for a test.

"The Bellanca was jointly owned by Dr. Horace Jones; Monty Tabor of Tabor, Steepe, and Long; and Rowe Montillo of Goode Productions.

"Mr. Montillo was first. He asked me to meet him the next morning at Roosevelt Field for a flight to Claremore, Oklahoma where he was to meet with Will Rogers. We would be in Claremore for at least three days, and I should pack accordingly. I was pleased. This would be a milk run, I loved Oklahoma, and I might get to see one of my personal heroes.

"When I met Mr. Montillo the next day, he was surprised on two accounts. The first of course was that this 'Burke' of the telegrams was Mrs. Burke, and not a bad looking female at that.

Then I finished the coup by saying, 'Pleased to meet you, Mr. Montillo. We will arrive in Claremore at 4:58.' No other pilots had ever made such a precise prediction of the arrival time, or had predicted that they would arrive so quickly.

"Mr. Montillo had happy eyes and a calm good sense of humor. His company was pleasant and conducive to easy friendship. I could also see in him a man with a take-charge ability and a command presence if he had to use it. Mr. Montillo told me that his friends called him Rowe, and he asked me to do the same. I responded that my name was Alice but that my flying friends called me Angel and he could call me either. He seemed to prefer Angel, which put me further at ease.

"Rowe asked me how I knew Frenchy, and I told him of my barnstormer days. When I mentioned Roscoe's Flying Circus, he lit up.

"'Did you fly a light-blue Jenny?'

"'I still do.'

"'Oh, my gosh! That was you! I was in St. Louis. I saw that inverted grass cutter -- unbelievable! That was the most amazing move I've ever seen. Who was that girl in the wedding dress?'

"'That was me.'

"'Nice legs, kid. Gee, that had to be awful. So you and Roscoe were married?'

"I pulled the ring from my bosom. 'I still am.'

"We talked about what I had been through since the crash, and he was fascinated about the visit of Orville Wright. Rowe said he was sorry, but he wanted first dibs on the movie rights if I ever decided to write about it. Rowe said he had served in the infantry during the war and had caught the bug of aviation watching the pilots duke it out overhead.

"He asked if I knew any other famous pilots, and I mentioned Charles Lindbergh. Rowe was very excited and asked if I could wrangle a meeting for him. I told him that Charles would never consent and I wasn't about to violate his trust.

"Rowe kept an eye on his watch, and as we spotted the airstrip at Claremore he announced that I was way off on my projection. 'It's only 4:57.' I told him that we hadn't landed yet and made a big circle over Claremore. Then I cut the engine, which really shook him up, and explained that a good pilot needed to execute a dead stick landing without a moment's notice. Much to his dismay, I had used the term 'dead stick.' Much to his relief, we landed like a feather and coasted to the Ops shack. With a broad smile on his face, Rowe shook my hand and said I had his vote.

"I parked the plane and walked back to the Ops with my bag and Rowe's. He apologized that in the excitement he had forgotten to get it out of the plane. I told him that was part of the job, which impressed him all the more.

"Rowe sent a telegram to the other two to tell them of our early arrival and his approval. Then he called the Rogers home, but Will was not in -- he was expecting us later. The Ops man was Ward Stilson, who knew me from our shows in Claremore. Ward told me that Shady Bright (barnstormers have weird nicknames) was around somewhere and that he would find him to take us to the Rogers home.

"Rowe was impressed with my connections -- and even more so when Mrs. Rogers saw me and said, 'Hi there, Angel. How have you been?' She gave me a big hug. We had met after one of our shows in Claremore, where Will and Slim had hit it off to the point where we were invited for supper and to stay the night.

"Will walked in a few minutes later and kissed Betty. She said, 'Look who came to visit.' Will walked straight to me and completely ignored Rowe. 'Angel, darlin,' it's good to see ya.' We gave each other a big hug. I kissed Will on the cheek and buried my head in his chest. I said, 'I hope you don't mind, Betty.' She said, 'Na, gal, I've been tryin' to get some woman to take him off my hands for years.'

"We all laughed, and then my laughter turned into uncontrollable tears and I shook in Will's arms. I was having one of those 'Roscoe' moments, along with being back with two people whom I dearly loved, and who had been so kind to us in our lean years. Betty came over and the three of us hugged like ma and pa and daughter.

"As I came to my senses, I realized that my potential boss was being left out and probably thought I was pretty unstable. I introduced him as Mr. Montillo. Will hadn't quite figured out the connection and asked if we two were hitched. Rowe turned quite red and launched into a sheepish smile. I quickly corrected the situation and told Will that I was trying out for the part of pilot and Mr. Montillo was the fellow who was here to work Will into one of his shows. Will told Rowe straight out, 'Well, sir, if you hire that gal I'll sign anything you want. If you don't you can fly your own plane back and she'll stay with us.' Rowe tried to explain that there were two other partners who would have to agree first, and Will made it clear that he had better be on 'good speakin' terms with the other two boys.'

"Will had no more said this than the phone rang. It was Dr. Jones. He needed to be in Haiti the next day. I had not figured my charts for anything outside of the forty-eight states, so I asked Betty if they still had that globe I had seen the last time I was there. They did, and it had enough information to get me the extra distance from Miami. I plotted my course, with Rowe and Will looking on with great interest. I apologized to Betty for having to leave so soon. She threw together two sandwiches and a thermos of coffee and I was out the door.

"Back at the field I'm ashamed to say I poured out Betty's good civilian coffee and replaced it with Shady's aviator's brew. Then I filled the Bellanca's tanks and asked Ward for a funnel, a length of hose, and a good-sized bottle. He asked me what it was for, but I told him it was none of his business."

"It's none of your business either, Great Nephew."

"Trust me, Great Aunt Alice. I really don't want to know."

"There is no way I could have flown to Roosevelt Field on time without flying all night, and there is no way I could have flown at night at all without my navigation scheme.

"I arrived at Roosevelt with an hour to spare. I topped off the tanks and did a complete inspection of the aircraft and went inside to freshen up. I filled the thermos with Roosevelt Field coffee, which is the strongest coffee in the world. Back at the plane I lay down between the seats and fell asleep for the first time in twenty-one hours.

"I woke to the air from the open door and a rap on the frame. It was Dr. Jones. He asked if I was able to fly. I said that I would in a moment. I opened the thermos and quickly drank down a cup of the evil stuff. Five minutes later we were in the air and I was wide awake.

"Dr. Jones was more business-like than Rowe. He favored a young version of President Wilson in appearance, but he was in no way a dour man. At the tender age of thirty-three, he seemed more mature than a man should be at that age. His conversations were cordial but brief. Dr. Jones was more than a doctor -- he was a healer. Here he was leaving the comfort of New York for what is still one of the most backward countries on the planet, and all for an unknown waif who needed relief from a malformation that would be commonly cured here. He would receive no compensation, not even public adulation, for this heroic deed.

"We were loaded to the gills. We had the medical supplies that he would need, as well as some extras for the local clinic's inventory. We had a shortwave wireless that would transmit at least as far as Miami. We had food and general supplies for the local villagers -- things they could not otherwise readily obtain.

"Our conversations came in short bursts as we flew south. He asked my name and I told him as I had offered to Rowe. He chose to call me Alice. In turn he never offered to let me call him anything but Dr. Jones, so I continued to call him by his proper title. He told me that Mr. Montillo spoke well of me. I told Dr. Jones that I was pleased with Mr. Montillo's company and that I hoped that he too would also see me as a favorable pilot. Dr. Jones didn't respond. 'You're not following the coastline like the other pilots.'

"'This is a more direct route.'

"'How did you fly at night?'

"I explained my method of plotting and staying on a direct course.

"'Interesting. It's a long flight. If you need to use your bottle I won't mind.' I tried to play dumb.

"'What bottle?'

"'The one under your seat. Good thinking on your part.'

"'How did you know?'

"'When I boarded the plane I observed yellow ice on the strut. No need to worry -- I am a doctor and quite familiar with the female anatomy. I shall be a gentleman.' I didn't want Dr. Jones to think I was faint of heart, so a few minutes later I did precisely as he had suggested.

"When we stopped in Miami to refuel the plane, I was slightly behind my estimated arrival time. I attributed this to the extra weight of the cargo and added that to my calculations for the leg to Haiti.

"We also stretched our legs and had a bite to eat. Dr. Jones prayed before his meal, and I thanked him. I have always admired that in a man. I pointed out to Dr. Jones that we had another four hours to Haiti, which would force us to land at a strange field in the dark. I suggested that we wait until dawn to continue the flight. Dr. Jones agreed it was the safer course of action and would still fit his schedule.

"The next morning we arrived in Port-Au-Prince where we registered our presence in the country. From there we flew to the remote village where the operation was to take place.

"The Haiti I saw was a kaleidoscope of hope and fear. There were places that were as safe as Saugerties and places of dread. There was the enormous wealth of magnificent villas, and mud hut poverty. There were places of distance between Christianity and Voodoo, and other places where the two were one. In general, there was peace in the country, but armed bandits ruled some of its remote parts. The overwhelming descriptor was 'STARK,' -- stark beauty in the land, stark love among the families, stark poverty lacking the very least of what we call essential, and the stark beauty of the children we saw.

"Dr. Jones would be performing his miracles for the next two weeks through operations, examinations, and treatments. I needed to get back to Claremore in two days to pick up Rowe. I had figured on a good rest in the Haitian sun before my return to Oklahoma, but that went to pieces with a shortwave call relayed from Mr. Tabor who had to be in Toledo the next afternoon.

"Three hours after I first landed in Haiti I was back in the air headed for New York. I lifted off the short village airstrip that shot a narrow beam between two sharp mountain peaks.

"Reaching Miami about 5:00 p.m., I topped off the fuel tanks and filled my thermos with the evil brew. I landed at Roosevelt Field with just enough time to top off the tanks and for an hour's nap. At 5:30 I hit the restroom and headed for the Ops shack to pick up Mr. Tabor.

"Mr. Tabor was all business and a bit cynical. He had seen the dark side of man and was jaded by it all. He didn't have the need to 'like' anyone and for the most part kept his own company. He was a good attorney who won his cases. That was all that was required, and he expected to be paid for his results. He called everyone by their last names, so to Rowe I was Angel, to Dr. Jones I was Alice, and to Mr. Tabor I was just plain Burke.

"Mr. Tabor said nothing the whole flight, short of our initial curt introductions. He read and took notes the entire time, except for the hour he slept. That was torture for me. I had traveled over 6,000 miles in the last four days. More than anything, I wanted to take a just a short nap.

"On landing at the Toledo airfield, Mr. Tabor stepped out of the plane and said, 'Be here in two days, same time.' He walked away without the slightest comment on my flying or even a simple goodbye.

"The only compensation was that I was closer to Claremore, where I was scheduled to pick up Rowe. After topping the tanks I wired the Rogers that I would arrive at 6:30. I had one fuel stop in St. Louis, where Lou fixed me a quick sandwich and Phil Love gave the latest news on Lindbergh's efforts while I fueled the plane.

"When I arrived at Claremore, I asked Rowe if he wanted me to fly him back to New York that night. To my relief he said we could fly out the next morning. This had been some test. I had flown all of those almost continuous hours without a dime of pay or knowledge of my status. I would not know that until I had returned all three gentlemen to Roosevelt Field and they had a chance to discuss and vote on my fate. Little did I know that the easy part was behind me.

"I hadn't been on the ground thirty minutes when Ward Stilson came running out to where I was refueling the plane. He had a phone message for Rowe that Dr. Jones was in trouble. The word was out that a large gang of bandits had heard of Dr. Jones' mission work and was headed for the village to kidnap and kill him. That's precisely how they operated. The bandits would kidnap a foreigner and hold him for ransom. Regardless if the ransom was paid or not, the bandits would then kill their victim. Rowe and Will arrived about the same time as the message.

"Without comment Will used Ward's phone to call his friend J.M. Davis, who opened his museum and rushed over with a B.A.R. and six boxes of ammunition. I called for Ward to get me a box and a cargo net to secure the weapon and the ammunition, as I didn't want them to be bouncing around in case I hit an air pocket. I ran to the pilot's shack to fill my thermos and to quickly calculate my course.

"Rowe jumped into the plane without his briefcase or suitcase, which Will promised to ship home. I quickly hugged him and told him to share it with Betty, and we were off.

"As we raced through the night to Miami, Rowe told me that he and Will had managed to get on each other's good side right off and had signed a set of deals that worked out for their mutual benefit. The other days were spent enjoying life with the Rogers. Rowe thanked me for opening the door for him with the Rogers, but I minimized my part of the deal. I may have opened it a crack, but Rowe was the kind of guy that everyone just naturally wanted to have as a friend.

"There was one detail I had left out in my plans. I told Rowe to turn his head.

"He asked 'Why?'

"'TURN YOUR HEAD!'

"When he heard the sound he muttered, 'I don't believe this.'

"When I said he could turn back, I thought of taking a swig to shake him up, but I didn't. I had definitely been in the plane too long.

"After a refueling stop in Atlanta, we reached Miami around 9:00 in the morning. I did a quick refuel to make sure I had enough for some extra flying. In Miami we received the message that the bandits had camped that night within ten miles of the village and would be on them by midday.

"We raced as fast the bird would fly. I skipped the formalities at Port-Au-Prince and flew straight to the village. If I was going to register my presence in the country it would be in a less bureaucratic way.

"We arrived over the village around 3:30 p.m. with the bandits on the village airstrip and Dr. Jones in their possession. We couldn't very well shoot our way in. I had to separate the good doctor from his captors. In an act of delicate aviation brain surgery, I decided to put the Bellanca on the deck in hopes that they would release their grip on Dr. Jones long enough for me to play a little pilot sheepdog.

"Dr. Jones diagnosed my actions and stood as tall as he could as I came in at what I hoped was seven feet off the airstrip. Dr. Jones turned toward my pass so his captors would have to face me as well. If I flinched, or if he flinched, the trick would not work. If the bad guys didn't flinch, it wouldn't work. I was taut as a strut wire as I made my pass, waiting for the dreaded bump on the fuselage. It didn't come, but Dr. Jones later said I missed his head by a foot or less.

"The important thing was that it worked. Even the bravest of the bandits let go, and Dr. Jones ran for the brush, where many of the villagers were hiding for a chance to surprise the bandits and save Dr. Jones. Three of the bandits got up and chased after him. As one of them lifted his weapon to shoot the fleeing Dr. Jones, the villagers rose up to pummel him and the other pursuing bandits to the ground with rocks. Once the bandits were down, the villagers mobbed and killed them with their bare hands and took their weapons.

"We now had a seam to work with, and I put it down even lower as Rowe cut loose with the B.A.R. By now we had cut the force down by almost a third and had taken some gunfire damage ourselves. We had to stop these guys now or they would be back to destroy the village.

"Having taken courage at the shots they had put in us, the bandits regrouped at the end of the runway. I knew better than to face their massed firepower, so I flew away behind a mountain. Thinking that I had cowered or was low on fuel, they marched on the village unafraid. That's when I swooped in from behind as we had done in the air shows.

"Rowe finished off all but five of the bandits, but one of them got me where it really hurt. He shot up Betty's thermos, which was still half full of my life's-blood coffee. I was half mad full of adrenaline and the other half just mad. I told Rowe in no uncertain terms to stow the weapon, put on his seat belt, and hang on. I rolled the plane over for the most aggressive inverted grass cutter of my life. The remaining bandits were so confused that they ran right into the angry villagers, who finished them off.

"The landing strip was too littered to land, so Dr. Jones and the villagers pulled the bodies to the side as I circled. When the strip was clear, I put her down as though nothing had happened. When we stopped, Rowe's eyes were as big as saucers. There was silence for a moment and then he let out with a war whoop, followed by one of my own. We hugged each other like we had just won the big game, and in the midst of it I began to cry and wail, as our mad celebration turned to relief and then just plain delayed reaction fear.

"Over the next few days, Dr. Jones finished his work while we stripped the bandits of their weapons and buried their bodies. Rowe taught the villagers how to use the weapons and plan for any future invasion, although they had already performed superbly in their defense of Dr. Jones. They had fought armed bandits with little more than raw courage. These simple villagers were the bravest of heroes in my book.

"On our return to Miami, Dr. Jones and Rowe put the three of us up in a seaside hotel for a week for my 'combat' pay. They also gave me money for a few changes of clothes and a swimsuit that both men seemed to appreciate. Relaxed and relieved to be alive, we were sitting on the beach one day when I shot up and shouted, 'Mr. Tabor!' I had left him in Toledo far beyond my expected return.

"He was furious when we met for my confirmation meeting. Tabor berated me up one side and down the other for my neglect. The other two defended me with the facts, but he would have none of it. I had let HIM down and I was OUT! That's not the way the other two saw it, and Tabor was told to find another pilot and plane. He told Rowe and Dr. Jones that they couldn't do that, and Tabor filed a lawsuit.

"Fortunately, Midge knew the judge. Furthermore, at the trial, when the judge heard of the Haiti rescue he was furious at Tabor's pettiness. He threw the case out and levied the highest court costs on Tabor that the law allowed.

"In addition, there was plenty of bad press for Tabor, and the law firm was so embarrassed that Steepe and Long voted him out of the partnership. Tabor was so publicly disgraced that he could no longer get a good client in Manhattan. In fact, he never again won a case in New York City."

"Well, Great Nephew, that was a lot of flying. Let's call it a night and work on the south side in the morning."

"But did you get the job?"

"Oh, yes, I did, and I almost got the man."

She winked and smiled, and left me hanging.

Chapter 24
We Did a Lot of Praying

By now I didn't mind the painting. I had learned how to paint without it running to my elbow. Great Aunt Alice had found that old hat in the barn, and that kept the farmhouse white off my hair and glasses. I had learned how to clean the brush so it wouldn't be stiff as a rock the next day. It was the scraping I didn't like. It was monotonous as, well, watching paint dry. I was getting better at scraping and could now take off the old paint with hardly any wood.

All of this work had improved my manhood as well. Now when I flexed my arm you could almost feel a muscle, and I could stand way up on the first rung of the ladder without feeling faint. I had even considered standing on the second rung, but I decided it best not to take unnecessary chances.

It was a blistering hot August day, so we gave up at noon. After a light lunch and the cleanup, Great Aunt Alice went on with her story:

"1929 proved to be quite an adventure. In my travels with Dr. Jones I would meet the rich and famous, who clamored for his expertise, and the poorest of the poor, who could pay him little but needed Dr. Jones the most. He had patients over a wide range of this hemisphere, but his main practice was still in Manhattan, so my schedule for him was, for the most part, on-call.

"Dr. Jones did insist that I know enough about medicine in the event I was needed to assist him on one of our travels, so I spent most of one month following him on his rounds so I could learn his habits. His head nurse, Virginia Loftus, grilled me in the basics of first aid and general nursing. Nurse Loftus was as tough as Roscoe. She had high standards and insisted on perfection, which made her mentoring highly valuable.

"While I learned a great deal from Dr. Jones and Nurse Loftus, I was able to give back as well. There was a man pretty high up in the banking business and a long-time patient of Dr. Jones whose daughter was badly burned in a kitchen fire in their remote cabin on Lake Champlain. We flew there as fast as we could to prepare her to move to the burn unit at St. Vincent's hospital in New York City.

"On the way up I told Dr. Jones of a treatment we had used on the burns suffered by the orphanage boys. We called it Ludwig's solution. It consisted of a mixture of vinegar and glycerin. When we used it on even third-degree burns, it allowed the skin to heal without the normal scars of burns. Dr. Jones had never heard of the treatment, but it sounded as though it had merit, and he trusted my first-hand witness accounts of the actual cases. He also knew that existing processes had not fared as well, so judging that it would do no harm he decided to give it a trial. We stopped in Albany to purchase sufficient quantities of glycerin and vinegar, and I instructed Dr. Jones as he mixed the solution in flight.

"When we reached the cabin, the poor girl was in misery. She had third-degree burns to her face and the upper front part of her torso. The slightest touch sent her into screams of pain, as her poor parents could do little but watch. Dr. Jones saturated the inner bandages with the solution and wrapped her wounds as gently as any human could and applied a finish wrap to keep the solution in.

"Thankfully she passed out as we tried to move her, and we were able to load her onto the plane with less awareness of her pain. Her parents prayed the rosary, and Dr. Jones did what little he could for the suffering child. It was imperative that we transport the girl to the hospital as soon as we could, and that was my job.

"Roosevelt Field was a long drive from the hospital. It would be a Godsend if we could find a way to land closer and get her into treatment sooner. There was a thoroughfare in front of the hospital broad enough for a landing. I had previously studied the possibility of landing there in an emergency situation. I knew of a gap where I could come in low enough to clear the remaining power lines, but the street would have to be completely cleared, in and beyond the landing zone.

"I told Dr. Jones of my plans. He agreed it would be a great help to the child, and expressed his faith in me, but he left it to the parents. They indicated that they would sooner die with their child if we crashed than live without her if we delayed her hospitalization.

"Fortunately Dr. Jones had insisted that we add one of those new aviation radios to the Bellanca, which I was able to use to contact the office and Nurse Loftus. I gave her the specific instructions of what I would need, and she contacted the hospital and the police to clear the street. After Nurse Loftus worked her magic, there wasn't so much as a scrap of paper in the street from curb to curb.

"We secured the girl as best we could, and I warned everyone that I would have to do a steep descent to come in under the wires. I made a pass to check out the landing area and to again judge the wires. I raised a quick silent prayer and in we came, sharp to clear the wires and a yard over the street to a long soft landing nearly in front of the entrance.

"We were immediately met by a medical crew with a gurney which the mother ran beside, unable to hold her little girl's hand. I handed the Ludwig's mixture to the father and told him it was her life's blood, as he ran to catch up with his daughter.

"Then I turned to the plane and thought, 'Now what?' I guess that's when I noticed the crowds cheering behind the police barricades and the reporters rushing to surround me and the Bellanca. The reporters asked my name, how I felt, if I thought we might die, if I had ever flown before, and even if I was married. I gave one response. I pointed to the hospital and said, 'Pray for that girl.' That became the headline in the next day's paper. The part of my statement that they didn't report was 'and anyone else who gets in the way of my propeller.' Immediately after saying that part, I climbed in, fired up the Bellanca, and did a ground loop that sent the reporters scurrying.

"The police came to my rescue, and I shut off the engine. It would have been a needless risk to try to fly out, so I worked with city officials to figure out how to get the plane back in the air. After some discussion it was decided that we would truck the Bellanca on a flatbed to a nearby pier. The pier, which was about the size of a World War II aircraft carrier deck, was cleared. I revved the engine to full power and held the brakes. I said a prayer and let her go. We went the entire length of the pier and dipped almost to the water before she began to rise. I said 'we' because that day the Bellanca and I were a team. We did a victory lap and an inside loop over the city before I put her down for a well deserved rest at Roosevelt Field.

"In the weeks to follow, the girl would have to be painfully undressed and redressed many times, but the end results were good. She had a few minor scars, but nothing that some light makeup couldn't conceal. The Ludwig's solution had worked, and I could finally see some good from my miserable days at that orphanage.

"Through my work with Rowe, I managed to travel to California on several occasions. This is where the future of entertainment was beginning to center. He still had his links to vaudeville and the Broadway stages, but we were seeing more of the Golden State and the majesty of our country as we traveled between the coasts. Thanks to Rowe, I could get seats to any show in town, and he introduced me to a host of stars from those days.

"On Broadway I met Fred and Adele Astaire, who were just as charming in person as Fred would appear in his movies. However there was nothing 'charming' about their work ethic. They drove each other to exhaustion to make their dance routine look effortless. There was not a cross word between them, just a lot of sweat and hard breathing as they practiced single steps over and over. Ray Bolger was a delightful man, who seemed to have fun just living. He wasn't concerned about perfection in his dancing -- he just wanted to enjoy his work, and his audiences were the beneficiaries. I also met a very young Buddy Ebsen and his sister Vilma as they danced a simple routine to the delight of the patrons. Entertainment back then was designed to make one enjoy life, not to drive some political agenda or to plunge one into fear and gloom.

"In Hollywood Rowe introduced me to Katharine Hepburn, who asked if she could take a flight with us. She was fascinated that Rowe had chosen a woman pilot.

"We went out over the ocean, and I let her take the controls for a short distance, showing her what to do at each step. When she found out that I was a barnstormer, I asked her if she wanted to walk the wing. Rowe was afraid that she would do it and relieved that she declined, but she wanted me to do 'some of those fancy flip flops.' I told her to buckle up and hold on as we did some basic loops, flew upside down for a while, and finished with the 'Roscoe roll' that Roscoe had invented for the flying circus.

"As we pulled straight and level Katharine and Rowe were whooping it up, but I became very silent. Katharine, being a woman, asked me what was wrong. I told her the story of Roscoe, and she stroked a tear from my cheek and told me I was a lucky woman and wished that someday she would find a man who would stir her soul as Roscoe had mine. From that point on, we were Angel and Kate to each other, and Kate would do anything she could for Rowe.

"Rowe also introduced me to Clara Bow, Mary Pickford, Vilma Banky, Charlie Chaplin, Louise Brooks, and Greta Garbo. Some of them were plain as toast, while others had a mystery about them that they didn't give up even in casual conversation.

"The most dramatic role was the one Rowe and I played as we flew back to New York after one of these Hollywood trips.

"I had always been a little leery of the Rocky Mountains. If I had to land in a hurry where would I go? Also, if I had to land in the mountains how would we survive for the several days it might take to find rescue? For this reason I carefully studied the terrain as we flew across in the summer months, for landmarks that I might have to use. I also checked the plane over with extra care and made sure we had survival provisions.

"Our luck ran out on an early spring day as we were flying over, of all places, Mt. Alice in Utah. An ice storm rolled in and showered the Bellanca. I couldn't go around it or over the storm, and I sure wasn't going to drop down with all of those mountain peaks. I was losing control with the ice build-up on the wing. I needed to find a landing spot and fast. I found a break in the clouds that allowed me a quick look at a plateau that might work, near what I later found out was the intersection of current day Utah 10 and what is now Interstate 70. I quickly spotted a small town and part of a road to the north and brought her down as close as I could. There was deep snow on the ground that brought us to a rapid stop. The plane rolled over on its nose and almost crossed the tip point before settling back on its tail wheel with a shock. We were lucky for the moment.

"After checking to be sure we were both all right, I went out to check the plane. Everything looked airworthy except for the ice on the wing. I fired up the engine and it roared to life. As far as I could tell, we could get her in the air if we could get enough of a strip cleared for takeoff. That was the problem. There was nothing but deep snow and large rocks between us and the air.

"The radio worked, but we were blocked by the mountains and I wasn't sure we were getting out. I knew we weren't receiving a signal so I had my doubts, and I decided to hold off on using it lest we run the battery down.

"I looked over my charts and decided that we were within five miles in a straight line of Emery, Utah. I could see smoke in that direction. Rowe suggested we make our own smoke to let people know we were here. Rowe somehow pulled together enough firewood to make a pretty good signal fire. That night we used it to cook one can of hash between us. We both agreed to make our five days of rations stretch to ten for now.

"That first evening we decided that there were two options. We could drag the radio to the top of the nearest mountain and hope to get a message out, or we could try to hike to Emery. The most certain of the two seemed to be the walk to Emery. Although the distance was relatively short, the conditions suggested it might take several days to accomplish.

"That night as we huddled together under the blankets, Rowe could very easily have taken advantage of the situation and I wouldn't have fought very hard. He was a good man and we had become quite fond of one another. He chose instead to remain a gentleman and kept his mind on sheltering me and saving us. I will always be grateful for that good strong man and our friendship.

"The morning was clear and slightly above freezing. I suggested that we try to extricate the plane and see how far we could taxi. To my surprise, we were able to roll about fifty yards before we got stuck again. With the snow now packed down, we pulled it free and tried it again back along the path we had created, this time rolling several feet beyond our original landing spot. We had the beginnings of a runway, but something told me to investigate further. When I did I found that there were boulders just under the snow on both ends of our trench and that we would not have enough room to launch the plane. We had wasted a whole day that we could have used to walk to Emery. I was pretty low that night, but Rowe insisted that he too thought it had been worth the try.

"The next morning we headed out in the direction of the smoke. At Rowe's suggestion, we stoked our own fire with scrub brush that would make a lot of smoke that we could use for a bearing in the event of needing to turn back. We also took enough provisions to camp along the way, as it might take several days to reach Emery. By noon it appeared that we had made almost no progress at all in the deep snow and the rough terain. By 3:00 it was time to make camp. Together we made a half-faced camp with the wind to the back and built a fire to the open side. We were cold, but it was not unbearable.

"The fourth day was windy and cold. Visibility was too poor to see the Emery smoke, but I had my compass to guide us with the fix I had taken the day before. We spent the night in the cleft of a boulder with ancient Indian pictures carved into the rock.

"It was the fifth day and we were through half of our rations. It was getting harder to walk. By midday we were close enough to see the road I had spotted from the air before our landing. It was a good sign, and we tried to reach it before giving up for the day. We set another fire that night, but there was very little shelter. During the night it began to sleet.

"As the dim first light of the sixth day began to touch the sky, I was finished. We had to be within two miles of Emery, but my mind could not comprehend taking another step. We were exhausted by hunger and exposure. The only thing we had going for us was the temperature. It remained near the freezing mark, but we had not experienced the deep bitter cold that this part of the country could issue. I told Rowe that he should go without me. He said that he couldn't. He was counting on me carrying him. I returned a feeble laugh and told him I wanted to kiss him, but in the cold I might stick to his cheek.

"'I can think of worse, Angel.'

"Then we heard an animal. We could barely see it in the dark and thought it might be a wolf or a coyote. Had we come all of this way to be eaten alive? As it drew near I realized it was a golden retriever, and behind it was an old man with a lantern. His first words to us were, 'Well, I'll be. The missus was right. The other day we heard what we thought was an airyplane engine up on the mountain, and over the next few days we could see your campfire smoke. She told me I should go looking for you, and she was right. We live less than a mile from here. Well, I'll be. Do you think you can walk?'

"At that point I was ready to run. We left anything we didn't need and followed the old man back to his warm cabin where 'the missus.' fixed us a hot bowl of oatmeal and the best coffee I had ever tasted.

"Harry and Leatha Ford were a hardscrabble pioneer couple who had lived in Emery about as long as Emery had existed. They were nice enough to let us stay for the two months needed to melt the snow and for the ground to harden sufficiently to fly out. For their trouble we helped with the chores and later resupplied them for what we had used.

"A few days after our rescue, Harry lent us two horses to go back to the plane. We wanted to recover what supplies we could, and we needed to get a message to the outside world that we were both safe and would be delayed in our return. There were no phone or telegraph lines in the area, so we had to use the radio. It would take some work, but Rowe found a peak that allowed us to transmit. It took about two hours to move the radio by horseback and on foot to a position where Rowe worked the generator, while I tried to find a frequency that would connect. We finally made contact with a man in Salt Lake City who promised to relay our message.

"When the weather cleared, two young fellows from Emery helped us move enough stones and boulders to fashion a suitable runway. In return we offered to take them and Harry and Leatha up for their first plane ride. Leatha was rather matter of fact about the experience, but Harry was like a kid at Christmas. I think they got a kick out of seeing their house from the air and watching their old dog, Red, carry on as we flew over. We landed in a pasture near the edge of town, where Red ran to greet us.

"We thanked our hosts and promised to stop by on our next trip, which we did with a load of supplies to replace double what we had used. I bought a red hat from Midge's store for Leatha. It looked good on her, and she beamed from ear to ear when she saw herself in the mirror.

"Before the incident in Utah, Rowe was somewhat a driven man. He lived and died by his schedules. That all changed when he was faced with our death, and I don't use the word 'our' lightly. I sensed that he would have been fine with his own death, but if he had to live with the thought of causing my death it would have been too much for him. In that sense he was very much like Roscoe.

We Did a Lot of Praying

"Instead of losing business due to our absence from 'the world,' he gained new clients. His established clients were just glad that he was alive. It's funny how we humans take our friendships so casually until faced with the ultimate separation. Rowe was also more relaxed in general, allowing that natural comfortable style of his to blossom. His clients enjoyed doing business with Rowe more than ever, and they looked forward to his visits.

"1929, like 1912, began as a year of limitless joy and possibilities, and like 1912 it came to a devastating crash. We did a lot of praying that year."

"I'm getting tired, Great Nephew."

Great Aunt Alice kissed me goodnight and went to bed. I was restless and felt like sitting in the dark for a while. I was feeling pretty blue. In taking inventory of my life, all I could come up with was that I had obtained a Ph.D. in a field that nobody else cared a whit about. I was almost finished painting a farm house, but I was really more of a burden than a help.

Recording Great Aunt Alice's life was the most important thing I had accomplished in my life, but when I compared my story to hers I was nothing. I was lonely. I was insignificant. My heart ached so badly I wanted to die, but I needed to finish the south side of the house.

I fell asleep in the chair.

Chapter 25
The Great Depression

In the morning I was still in a sad mood, and I had a crick in my neck as well from sleeping in the chair. It was raining, a miserable gray all-day rain. Great Aunt Alice sat in the chair next to me and pretended not to notice my mood as she read her daily devotional. She knew more than I did that I was just like my grandfather. Great Aunt Alice put down her book and stared out the window, as I was doing. Then without any obvious prompt she started talking about Grandpa Charles.

"I haven't said much about your grandfather. It was just as hard on Charles to lose his brother as it was for me to lose my husband. While Roscoe was the daring ace, Charles was the awkward farm boy who could never quite seem to find his place. His parents were hard-working Christian farm folk, but they were quiet and slow to praise. Roscoe was Charles' big brother, his hero, and his escape from the dull life of the farm.

"The truth was that Charles was the more accomplished man. He became a farmer and fed thousands of people in his life. You don't get any trophies or applause for that, but can you think of anything nobler? Many years passed before Charles found the woman of his dreams.

"Your grandmother was a saint. She bore two boys and your mother, all in her later bearing years. She watched both boys die

The Great Depression

in the same farm accident, one trying to save the other. After that she woke up every day only by sheer will power. She cared for her brokenhearted husband and your mother, and did so with love and a smile, while wanting nothing more than to die. Your grandmother was my hero, and in his way your grandfather was a very successful man.

"After Charles and Katherine died, your mother inherited the farm -- but she had no use for it. She was no farmer, and there were so many bad memories of her lost brothers and the sadness in the family. On the other hand, this was the only home that Roscoe had known. Both he and Charles were born in what is now my bedroom. Your mother sold the place to me. It helped her financially, and it keeps me close to Roscoe and with a good place to store my planes."

I didn't acknowledge anything Great Aunt Alice had said. She wouldn't have wanted me to do so. Instead I indicated to her that I was putting my funk aside by asking her to continue with her story.

"You said that 1929 ended badly -- what happened?"

"History tells us that the stock market crashed in October and caused the Great Depression, but that's not entirely true. It was the beginning of a series of events that sank our country deeper and deeper with each passing month.

"It didn't affect Rowe or Dr. Jones as much as other people. Their incomes were of necessity decreased, but they still maintained a higher standard of living compared to the rest of the nation.

"There would always be a need for medical help, regardless of one's ability to pay for it. By this time Dr. Jones had made his fortune and could afford to accept more charity cases, which he did. He never worked for free, as he believed it was imperative to a patient's pride to 'pay' for services rendered. Sometimes his pay would be a pie, or repairs to his car, or some much needed mending. For his poorer cases he would often wear a shirt missing a button or a suit jacket with a small hole in the elbow to give the patient the option of suggesting the barter of a repair for the medicine.

"On the other hand, Rowe continued to do about as well as he had been. The movies went on as before, except they were now in the business of mending the souls of the nation. It was the optimism and hope expressed in the movies of those days that gave cheer to the overburdened minds of the American people. Inside the theater the good guys always won, while outside that was a less sure outcome.

"We didn't fly as much, so I lost some income there, but that was the least of my worries. The real trouble was in Saugerties. The factory orders dropped almost overnight. At first we had to cut the workers' salaries in half and our own by two thirds to keep the factory afloat. By 1933 we were able to work the men only three days a week. The town businesses, of course, suffered as well. Midge cut back her hours, and finally was open only one day a week.

"There was a run on the bank, but Mr. Polo locked his doors until cooler heads prevailed and the government was able to put safeguards in place. Mr. Polo had invested my money well and in return this money was enough to help see me through a good portion of the crisis. He had invested about half in good long-term stocks and the other in bank loans. In general I took quite a beating, but in the long term most of these companies had the ability to survive, if only barely. The investments rebounded during the war, and by the end of the second war I had regained it all and about half again as much. I can't say that I actually went hungry during Depression times, but there were lean times for everyone, and I did what I could to help others.

"That was the secret of the Great Depression. It was not the government that saved us but the people who worked together to help each other through. The day after the run on Mr. Polo's bank, the town's civic, business, and spiritual leaders called a town meeting to talk over what we could do to stem the crisis. Just about everyone came. We opened our books and laid it out for everyone to see. This was how bad it was and how bad we thought it would be. Then we took inventory of what everyone in town could do and set up a barter system.

"A fund was collected from everyone in town according to their abilities. I started it with half of my fortune and Carl put up half of his. The people followed. Even children gave their pennies.

"This fund would be used to purchase any raw materials that we couldn't produce with our own hands. The merchants used some of this money to haggle for good prices on bulk items that were shared equally with the townsfolk. Carl figured out how much coal we could give up from our factory reserves to share with the homeowners. We fired up the old saw mill to produce lumber for repairs to each other's homes. We also built a generator that could work off the old millwheel to supply a limited source of electricity. Those with extra ground to till organized large gardens. The children tended the weeds, and the folks who knew how to can and preserve did so for the food pantry.

"Local farmers pooled their livestock operations, and men who knew how to butcher did so for the pantry. Material for clothes was purchased in bulk, and those who knew how to sew would set up shop in the local churches. They would make what was needed from a list provided by the Community Chest, as the project became known. Those who produced more than their 'assessment' were allowed to keep the excess, thus encouraging production.

"Still there was precious little extra, and the work of the Community Chest was never ending. While most folks adhered to our agreements, we still had the demon of human nature to deal with, and it took a lot of sacrifice and discipline to keep things going.

"1933 was a hump year for Saugerties. We had a drought that severely cut back our produce. Hoof-and-mouth nearly destroyed our milk and meat supply, and too much hunting had pushed away our wild game supply. Most of the building repairs had been made and we had all of the furniture we needed, so some folks looked upon the men who had performed those functions as freeloaders when they took what was rightfully theirs from the food pantry. Those of us who could at all put a little more money into the Community Chest, and we barely survived.

"1934 was slightly better on a national and local level, but with almost imperceptible improvement.

"1935 was downright stagnant, no better no worse, except that America lost its best friend. In August, Will Rogers and Wiley Post, a brilliant aviation pioneer and personal barnstorming friend, were killed in a plane crash in Alaska. Afterwards I spent a month with Betty consoling each other, one aviation widow to another.

"Hope was so fragile in those times. It shattered for me personally in 1936. That was the year that broke the factory and our family. Carl did everything humanly possible to keep the factory open, but he could not. Again we opened the books to all of the fellows who worked there and none of them could argue with our fate -- we were beat and we had to close.

"Carl solemnly shook hands with each of the remaining workers, and I exchanged hugs with several of the men. We thanked them for their hard work and dedication, and they thanked us for trying so hard to keep the place open and for giving up most of our own money to keep them working. After the boys left, Carl left – his head down and a thoroughly defeated man.

"I stood alone on the balcony and cried my heart out. I thought of all of the activity I had witnessed from that balcony. I saw my father working with the men. I saw Big Carl managing the floor and lifting great loads. I saw the boys in triumph as we ran Mr. Self out of the factory in handcuffs. I told my father I was sorry that I had let his dream slip away, and then I cried some more. During the second war the factory was donated for scrap, and the land was eventually reclaimed for other projects. No sign of it exists today.

"Then things went from tragic to worse. On the path home I found Carl face down in the street. Dr. John told us it was probably a catastrophic stroke. Midge was devastated, as Carl was more than her man -- he had been her savior.

"For weeks after Carl's funeral Kinsey and I tried to console Midge without success. Not a day passed, rain or shine, that she did not go to mourn over his grave. Then one day she returned from the cemetery and said, 'I want to see Father Collier,' so we took her to New York City.

"Father Collier was now Bishop Collier and it was harder to get in to see him, but not for Midge. She told the secretary to tell Father Collier that 'his woman was here.'

"'It's Bishop Collier now and I will do no such thing.'

"'Well, listen here, buster.' It was good to hear some of the old Midge.

"'Madam I am a fully ordained priest and you will address me as Father.'

"'Well, listen here, Father Buster. I want to see Father Collier!'

"'It's Bishop, it's Bishop!'

"'Father Bishop?'

"The Father Secretary let out a scream like he was going through an exorcism, and the intercom on his desk lit up, 'Come on in Midge.' Midge gave the Father Secretary the raspberries, and Kinsey told her that she was going to hell for sticking her tongue out at a priest.

"When we entered, Bishop Collier stood up and walked toward us. He said, 'How are you, darlin' -- it's good to see you,' and he gave Midge a big hug. Kinsey knelt down to kiss his ring, and Bishop Collier pulled her up and hugged her as well. Kinsey had a funny look in her eyes as she had never hugged a Bishop before. I wasn't sure what a Methodist should do with a Catholic bishop, so I shook his hand and curtseyed. Bishop Collier gave me a kiss on the cheek and called me 'little Alice.' Kinsey didn't know if Bishop Collier could go to hell for kissing a young woman on the cheek in a greeting, so she kept it to herself.

"Bishop Collier asked us to sit down. Father Secretary called over the intercom to ask if we needed anything. I think he was checking to make sure Bishop Collier wasn't being brutally pummeled by Midge. 'So what can I do for you, Midge?'

"'Father Collier, I just had to talk to you.'

"Bishop Collier knew it was futile to try to correct her, so he just encouraged Midge to go on. Midge told him about Carl and how much she loved him, and how much she missed him, and how she was lost without him. It was Midge's habit to let out her soul in one long sentence connected with several 'ands'.

"Bishop Collier tried to point out how much Kinsey and I loved and needed her, but she would have none of it. I was now a grown woman and didn't need a full-time mother, and Kinsey had Mr. Vought to gripe at. We tried to tell her that Bishop Collier was on target with his words and that we needed her a great deal. Actually Kinsey's words were, 'I don't mind having you around, Midge.'

"'Father Collier, I think I ought to be a nun. What do you think?' We heard a click over the intercom followed by a thud in the other room, but nobody moved a muscle to check on the situation.

"'I think you'd be a fine nun, Midge.'

"Kinsey muttered something to the effect of 'God help us.'

"'There's just one thing that worries me, Father. I don't like rats, and I heard what you did to Maggie O'Brien. Would I have to be one of those rat nuns?'

"'Don't worry, Midge. I have a special assignment in mind for you.'

"I can only imagine how the sisters worked to transform the hard-loving girl born in a whorehouse into a sanctified nun, but there she was a few months later, dressed in her habit and ready to go.

"Their biggest problem was fitting her into a suitable name. The sisters tried to explain that when a woman enters the Community she takes a new name -- her 'religious name.' They explained to Midge that her baptismal name would be changed to symbolize that she was giving up the world and to show she was being born into a new life, the life to follow in the footsteps of God.

"That was a perfectly good description of the process and would have worked just swell with any other woman, but this was Midge, and her reasoning came from a different realm. She

The Great Depression

insisted that her name had always been Midge and she saw no reason to change it.

"They even brought out the big gun, Sister Sylvia, to convince Midge. Midge loved and respected Sister Sylvia more than any other Catholic, aside from Bishop Collier. Midge told me that Sister Sylvia was the kind of nun who 'really knew her stuff, and didn't make you feel stupid.' But not even Sister Sylvia could make Midge understand 'that name thing.'

"Bishop Collier had been asking about Midge's progress. The sisters finally got to the point where it wasn't going to get any better, so they brought Midge before the bishop as he had requested, and she blurted out, 'Hey, Father, how do you like the outfit?'

"Bishop Collier tried not to laugh. The sisters gasped and told Midge that it was 'Bishop' and that she was supposed to kiss his ring. Midge responded, 'Oh, that's okay girls. Father Bishop and me go back a long time.' She turned back to Bishop Collier and asked, 'So what do you want me to do?'

"'Midge, we have a need for someone to take over the reins of our orphanage, and I can't think of anyone who would be a better mother to those children.'

"'Are you kidding, Father? I'd love to do that. When do I start?'

"Bishop Collier told her that she could start when he knew how to introduce her. He asked her name. She gave a quizzical look and replied 'Midge,' as though she thought Bishop Collier had forgotten her name.

"'No, no, Midge, your religious name.'

"'Oh that stuff – well, these girls tried to stick me with every name under the sun. Can't it just be Midge?'

"'But, what do you want the children to call you?'

"'Mother Midge,' she said, as if it were the most obvious answer in the world.

"Bishop Collier laughed. 'Well, you know, Midge that doesn't sound half bad. Mother Midge it is. Sisters take Mother Midge to her charge.'

"Under her unorthodox care, the children thrived. Mother Midge made sure the children were well fed, educated, and sheltered. If they didn't behave she told them what would happen to them -- in terms not usually employed by a nun.

"She played with the children, cared for them when they were sick, and read stories to them at bedtime. I'm sure the love advice she gave the older girls was nothing any other nun would have told them.

"Kinsey moved to the orphanage with Midge to do the cooking and to gripe at the kids. Mr. Vought became very lonely, or at least very hungry, so he moved to the orphanage to be their caretaker. My school friend Tommy became the Saugerties stationmaster.

"When things settled down, I was alone in the old home. It was the first time since my orphanage days that the house had been so quiet. There were a lot of memories in that house, but memories no matter how sweet are of the past and it was time to move on with my life.

"1937 was a good year for Rowe. By then he was living in Hollywood most of the time and traveling only occasionally to New York. He had arranged to buy Dr. Jones' share of the Bellanca so that when I flew at all it was for Rowe and his needs. Rowe decided one day to trade in the old Bellanca. He called me and told me to have a plane built to my specifications, color and all. I was thrilled to take on the project.

"I started asking around and received many good responses, including one from Lindbergh. Charles was never one to socialize, but when I had an aviation question he was quick to respond with some well-thought-out suggestions. He told me about the Spartan Aircraft Company in Tulsa, which had a plane they called the Executive 7W. It held fewer passengers than the Bellanca, but, boy, could she fly. It had a Pratt & Whitney 9-cylinder air-cooled radial engine that could cruise at over 250 miles per hour. It had a range of 1,000 miles, 200 more than the Bellanca, and it could fly at 24,000 feet.

"All it needed was the red and yellow color scheme of Roscoe's plane and a few interior arrangements, and we were set. I had them add a cargo hatch for longer items and arrange for the seats to either fold flat or be removed for extra cargo.

"The cost was over $20,000 and I wasn't sure Rowe would want to go anywhere near that high. To my surprise, he didn't blink an eye. All he said to me was, 'Pick out a good one and load it up the way you would want it equipped and painted,' -- so I gave the Spartan folks the green light to build her.

"When it was finished I flew it to Hollywood to hand it over to Rowe. He was impressed. 'That's the most beautiful plane I have ever seen. Let's take her up.' Rowe was working with Clark Gable at the time and asked him to go up with us. Clark had seen a standard model 7W and was impressed with the modifications I had made for extra cargo. Rowe asked Clark if he would want me to fly him to some hunting trip sometime to take advantage of 'Angel's cargo arrangement.' Clark thanked us both and said he sure would.

"When I put the plane down, I handed the papers to Rowe. He in turn signed the back and said 'Here you go Angel. The plane is yours.' I couldn't believe it! I told him it was too generous, but he pointed out the millions I had sent his way with my charm and connections. Rowe reminded me that I had literally introduced him to Will Rogers, and how Kate Hepburn raved about me after that flight. 'People love you, Angel, and it has reflected back on me.' 'People love you too, Rowe.' I hoped he knew what I meant.

"Several months later I flew Clark and Carole Lombard to a Montana hunting trip just before they were married. She was a beautiful woman, but not a prima donna movie star. Carole was a lot of fun, and we got along great. While we did indeed have good times together, I also gave them their time alone. It was during those times that I became uncharacteristically jealous and moody. I hope I was able to hide my true emotions. Their love made me think of Roscoe, and only a few months before I had lost another man that I dearly cared for.

"Rowe was at a party at Cary Grant's house when he collapsed. He literally died in Cary Grant's and Irene Dunne's arms as they carried him to the sofa. Kate Hepburn called me, and I flew out as soon as I could. Rowe had no family, so his Hollywood friends looked to me to make the arrangements. We had a beautiful wake and funeral, with full military honors at the gravesite.

"I had Rowe buried in Forest Lawn, where his friends could visit his grave. For years later I would visit the grave at least once a year. I was always pleasantly surprised when I saw another decoration from one of his Hollywood friends. On one occasion I arrived at the same time as Gary Cooper. We hugged each other as we paid our respects to Rowe. It was good to see Coop, but he was looking mighty frail. A few months later he joined Rowe, while I was still banished to this life – far from my friends and loved ones.

"After Rowe's funeral, Kate asked me to stay with her for a while, so I did. We talked about love and cried. We talked about death and cried. Sometimes we just cried. Mostly I put my head in her lap, and she stroked me like she was my mother or I was her cat. For being such a tomboy, Kate had the gentlest hands. I will never speak ill of Kate Hepburn.

"A few weeks later I received a call from Rowe's attorney. Rowe left one third of his fortune to the Actor's home, one third to Dr. Jones for his charity work, and one third to 'His Angel, Alice Burke.'"

The mood was quiet after that. I pulled Great Aunt Alice's head to my lap and stroked her like a cat until she fell asleep. Then I covered her with a blanket and went to bed.

Chapter 26
World War Alice

We finished painting the house today with just enough paint to do one large doghouse. Great Aunt Alice had never had a doghouse so, she built one. She didn't have a dog either, but she reasoned that the big doghouse would scare off intruders.

For the life of me I didn't know where she got that idea. We were so far off the beaten path that no intruder could have found us. Plus we were surrounded by Amish, who despite their gentle reputation have "persuasive methods" of dealing with such matters.

She had a little barn red paint left over, so we poured in a half gallon of turpentine to get it loosened up to paint the imaginary dog's name above the door. It was decided that 'Brutus' would do the trick.

Then, from out of nowhere, she began to tell me another story.

"Did I ever tell you about my fighting days, Great Nephew? It was December of 1941. I was already ticked off about turning forty-one, and then those miserable Japs attacked our boys at Pearl Harbor.

"I later found out that my school friend George was in the Navy and was standing on the stern of the Battleship Tennessee when U.S.S. Arizona exploded. George was badly burned and died a month later of his wounds. He was one month shy of his Navy career retirement. That was so sad.

"Well, anyway when I heard the news of the attack I went from ticked to hopping mad. On Monday I took the train to Albany to enlist, along with Tommy's boy Tommy Jr., who looked so much like his dad at that age it was scary. His buddy Bud Fox (no relation to the Bud of my school days) joined us, along with Eileen's boy Bob. The boys tried to tell me that the military wouldn't take me, but I refused to listen.

"The Army recruiter must have thought he was having a nightmare when we showed up to enlist. For one thing, he was overwhelmed by the line of volunteers that stretched completely around the block, with one angry woman standing in the middle of it all.

"That day marked the start of a long war for Sgt. Stadler. Sgt. Stadler had been a buck sergeant since the last war. He was good at it, and that's all he ever wanted to be. His greatest fear had been that he was coming up on retirement and he would have to leave the only home he had known since leaving the farm. Then this Pearl Harbor thing came up, and his greatest fear became your Great Aunt Alice.

"Sgt. Stadler was too old to fight in this war, so he got stuck with recruiting duty. It had already been a long morning with a constant line of boys and men of every type -- all wanting to get out there and whip the Japs for what they had done to our guys. Sgt. Stadler was looking down at his desk when he said in a tom-a-ton voice, 'Next,' and then, 'Name.'

"He was shocked back into reality when a woman's voice said, 'Burke.' Here before him was a forty-year-old bird of a woman insisting that she can out-fly and out-fight any man in the Air Corps. Sgt. Stadler politely told me that he appreciated my patriotism but that there were no women in the Army.

"I flew off the handle and demanded they take me, and that I wouldn't be shoved aside just because I was a woman. I told him that I was the best pilot he would ever see and that I had real combat experience in Haiti. I listed my family's war history.

I told him that I knew Teddy Roosevelt. Sgt. Stadler finally had me forcibly evicted.

"He regained his composure and called for the next recruit in line, which was Tommy Jr. He asked, 'Have you been standing behind that crazy broad the whole time?'

"Tommy meekly replied, 'It's worse than that, sir. I've known her my whole life.'

"Sgt. Stadler reached across the table and shook Tommy's hand, 'No problem, pal, I can get you in.'

"Tommy went to the Army and survived the worst of the fighting in North Africa and Italy. He was wounded in the Normandy invasion but was back in action for the Battle of the Bulge. Bob was a waist gunner on a B-17 and was shot down over Germany. Bud joined the Marines.

"Alice Burke on the other hand was on Sgt. Stadler's doorstep every day for the next several months. I figured that persistence was the only way to get this old goat's goat and get into the action. I even wrote to Ethel to see if she could get some traction, and she in turn wrote to her cousin Eleanor to put a bug in the President's ear.

"Then one day I received a letter from Jackie Cochran inviting me to join something called the Army Air Force Women's Flying Training Detachment. We were to be the instructors for the new recruit hot dogs. First we had to go to Houston to be 'trained to fly the Army way.'

"My first flight instructor was a guy by the name of Lt. O'Dale. We called him 'Old and Dull.' He was the most patronizing man one could imagine. He hated the idea of women flying, and it showed in his instruction. We were trained in every aircraft under the sun, and believe it or not they put me in an ancient Jenny JN-4. On my first few training flights I was a good little girl, but when he tediously went over and over the steps for a chandelle, I almost puked. He finally let me take off and he asked me if I 'remembered step one.'

"'Gee, Lieutenant, I don't remember for sure. I think it was something like this.'

"I launched into every maneuver that old Jenny could do without tearing off the wings. Lt. O'Dale commanded me to 'land at once!' I cut the engine and let her dead stick to a feather landing on the airstrip.

"When we got out of the plane, Lt. O'Dale began to chew me out something fierce, but he had to stop in mid-sentence to puke his guts out.

"I also got a lecture from Jackie Cochran on how we were trying to impress the brass, not kill them, and that I needed to fly the 'Army way' if we were to make progress with the higher ups. I solemnly apologized for my behavior and she accepted. Then we both broke into a laughing jag, and Jackie said, 'Damn! I wish I had seen that!'

"Eventually things settled in and we became known as the Women Airforce Service Pilots -- or W.A.S.P.

"I did a stint for a while training new pilots. Some of the boys didn't like the idea of training under a woman, while some of those half-grown Casanovas wanted a woman to train under them. I had very effective teaching tools for either category.

"It wasn't long before the sentence 'That crazy old (woman) tried to kill me!' became widely used. My commanding officer, Col. Norris, backed me all the way. Whenever he overheard some cadet use that sentence he would say, 'If you're smart enough to listen to her, that crazy old (woman) is going to save your hide,' only he didn't say it quite that way.

"Some days I pulled the targets for gunnery practice. I had one group who routinely shot too close to the tow plane. On my suggestion Col. Norris ordered that one gunner would go up with me for each practice, until everyone had a chance to be the target. It's amazing how much better they became when faced with the muzzle end of those 50 calibers.

"When my top fighter pilots felt they were ready for the real thing, they had to go through me one-on-one for their graduation. I played the bad guy and didn't give them any quarter as we tried to out-dogfight each other. No pilot ever 'shot me down,' but the ones who came close enough became some of the best aces of the war. I eventually heard that my guys put a small angel on their flight suits to signify that they were one of Angel's boys. That made me proud. Of all 'my boys' only two were shot down, and one of those two survived to fight again.

"I was just as tough on my bomber pilots. I would play the opposing fighter pilot, and come at them from every direction in my Mustang. I would fly with the crews and cut their engines. It was my job to create as much chaos as possible. I would blindfold them and make them fly by the information fed to them by one of the gunners in the event that both pilots would be blinded by an explosion during a combat flight. They had to fly with 'wounded' legs or arms. They flew with missing hydraulics and any possible hindrance I could throw at them, and no one graduated my course without doing a dead stick landing, where I initiated the time and place.

"My navigators could plot a course to within a tenth of a mile to any spot on the planet under any conditions. My gunners could react to any situation. They used less ammunition and hit more 'bull's-eyes,' and my bombardiers were dead on target.

"The boys who came close but not close enough were disappointed but willing to go through the extra training to become one of 'Angel's boys.' I worked very closely with each one until they were up to my standards.

"The ones I hated to cut were the boys who had their hearts set on flying and who just didn't have what it took. I justified it in my mind by saying that I would sooner wash out a boy than bury him, but as someone who understood the love of flying, it was hard to disappoint them.

"After a while I was tired of training. The Army Air Corps had quite a supply of good pilots and no longer needed as much training, so I asked to transfer to the ferry service. I wanted to travel again and hone my navigation skills. Col. Norris was hesitant, but he was nice enough to let me go.

"My first assignment was to fly a B-24 bomber to England. It was a dark and stormy night when I landed in Thule, Greenland. For being the largest island in North America, it was still a pinpoint under those conditions. Greenland was cold. Greenland was deep in snow. Greenland was not green.

"Actually I had arrived in the better days of the Greenland war. They now had decent quarters and plows for the airstrip. I met a friendly young Army doctor by the name of Scea, who was from somewhere in the Dakotas. Dr. Scea told me that when he first arrived on base, the poor soldiers had to use shovels and brooms to keep that 'mile of salvation' open -- 'Isn't that right, Childers?' 'Yes, sir, and I have the blisters to show for it.' I asked Childers where he was from, and he said 'Florida' as though he was about to cry.

"I got a good night's sleep. In fact that was the only thing you could get in Greenland those days. The next day cleared enough to fly on to England. When I landed it wasn't snowing, but it was cold and wet. I remember saying to myself, 'Welcome to Florida.'

"After securing my delivery, I headed for the Ops to find out where I was to be assigned. The nice thing about a foreign air base is that even a forty-year-old girl can get a whistle if she had anything at all. Just for fun, as I passed a hangar where some fellow was painting nose art, I struck a pose to mimic his design and asked if he needed a model. The boys in the ground crew got a kick out of that one. I sauntered over to the shy dirty mechanic and gave him a kiss. My father always said that no man's hand is too dirty to shake, but he never said anything about kissing a dirty man's cheek.

"In the Ops I ran into a little trouble. It seems the sergeant didn't have any orders for 'no female pilots,' and he wasn't inclined to look for any. Furthermore, he didn't seem impressed by 'no female lieutenant.'

"I was about to show him my less feminine side when in walked an old friend, Jimmy Stewart. Rowe had introduced us at a party, and we had a good conversation on aviation. I was surprised that he remembered me.

"'Well hi, Angel. What are you doing here?'

"'I'm just looking for the war.' I turned toward the sergeant and added, 'AND A PLACE TO STAY.'

"'Well, you've come to the right place, Angel. I've seen plenty of the war and you can stay with my crew, if you don't mind roughing it.'

"'I'll have to tell you about my vagabond days. Back then a blanket, a barn, and a pile of hay was a luxury hotel.'

"'Well now, I'd like to hear about that. The boys are always up for some fresh conversation. Let me finish here and I'll take you over to our quarters. You can freshen up and join us for dinner.

"'SERGEANT! I believe you forgot to salute!"

"'Yes, Sir, Captain!'

"'Not me, you idiot, her!'

"I let his arm get very tired before I returned his reluctant salute with a glare and a SNAP of my own.

"I don't want you to think that Jimmy Stewart was one to throw his rank around. Jimmy was a good and tested pilot and a regular Joe to all of the fellows on the base.

"That evening we went to dinner and I got to know the boys. I knew better than to ask about the war, as they had had enough of that, so we talked about some of my adventures. I was surprised at how much Jimmy knew about me. We had only met on that one occasion. He told me that Rowe couldn't say enough about me, and that he had been 'on the verge,' but he didn't think I would want a guy his age. I was surprised to hear him say that. Rowe was only eight years older than me. He had so much going for him that he never really showed his age.

"Jimmy asked me if I still had the Spartan. I asked him how he knew about that. He said that Clark had told him about the time I took Carole and him to Montana, and how much he raved about my custom design improvements. I told Jimmy that I did and invited him to fly it anytime he wanted. In 1951 he and Gloria joined me for a vacation 'to see America.' We flew to the Grand Canyon and then up to take in the faces on Mt. Rushmore. Jimmy did most of the flying and paid for the car rentals, meals, and lodging. Gloria was a doll. I can understand why they never gave a thought to one of those Hollywood divorces. They were a great couple.

"I asked about Clark, and Jimmy told me that he was with a B-17 crew at a nearby base, and that he would hook us up if he could. Then I asked if I could go on a mission to see if those boys I had trained had learned anything. He told me 'absolutely not.' He was sorry but there was no way he could get a woman on a combat flight.

"Four weeks later I still had no orders and pretty much did what I pleased. Jimmy arranged for me to be temporarily assigned to his bomb group and gave me a duty that took an hour or two to perform each day. The rest of the day I did pretty much what I pleased. I took in London and saw a lot of the war damage. My hat's off to the English. They took a real beating and still held on.

"Eventually I caught up to Clark Gable. It was a bittersweet meeting. I told Clark that I had been so jealous of their love when we were on that Montana trip, and now Carole was gone just like my Roscoe. I asked Clark to forgive me, and he said that it was all right and that it was nice to talk to someone who understood the way he was now feeling.

"I had first seen Clark at the best time of his life, and now I saw him at the worst. He was a beaten man. He was no longer the heroic Rhett Butler, and I truly believed that he had entered the war to feel like a hero again, and maybe die like one to relieve the ache. I was no Carole Lombard, but I did what I could for Clark. I held him like a woman holds her man. He neither spoke nor sobbed, but I could feel the moistness of his tears forming on my neck. I honestly would have given him anything that he wanted at that point if it would have eased the pain. I knew it wouldn't and I've always wondered if he ever found any peace. I never saw Clark again.

"Two days later at 0500 a sergeant woke me up and told me to get into a flight suit that he left at the foot of my bed. I was then to go to a B-24 called 'Bums Away,' and I was to ask no questions or talk to anyone on the way. By 0700 we were in the air and headed for France.

"Some of the fellows acted a little funny about having a broad on board, but most of them loosened up after they got to know me. The co-pilot had actually seen one of Roscoe's shows when he was a kid and remembered my 'Angel of the Air' routine.

"To my surprise the ball turret gunner was Lester Holt, one of my students. He wanted to be a fighter pilot so badly, but he didn't have the stuff, so he was transferred to be a bomber gunner. Les was one of the worst gunners of all time, but by the time I was finished with him he was a crack shot. One of the waist gunners told me that Les had taken down four German fighters. Over the headset Les said, 'I owe it all to you. Miss Angel.'

"'You owe it to yourself, Les. You're the one who made the big turnaround.'

"It is impossible to describe the bomber group as it rises from all over the English countryside and begins to form into a drone of death. The logistics and execution of just forming the group is an astounding feat.

"Going into the target we were hit from all sides first by the fighters. Les got a piece of one, and the tail gunner took another down before one of the Me-109s hit our plane. It didn't do a lot of damage, but it knocked one of the waist gunners out. He was hurt enough that he was finished for the mission, but his injuries didn't seem life threatening.

"I jumped to his gun and clipped the tail of another 109. The nose gunner finished him off. I helped take out yet another German fighter. He was hit by the gunners from two or three planes, so it was a toss-up as to whose gun had actually taken him out of the air.

"The flak over the target was murder. The way it worked was that there were clusters of guns that consisted of four 88s pointing straight up. They would fire one, two, three, four, and reload in the same order, so that at least one of the four was firing all of the time. Multiply this by fifty to a hundred clusters and you can get a feel for what it was like over the target.

"The worst part was on the bomb run itself. We were locked into a period of a few minutes that seemed like hours, where we had to hold our line and could not take evasive action. I saw the tip of a wing shot off of one plane, and three planes disintegrated as one of them took a hit in the bomb bay before it had dropped its bombs.

"Almost simultaneously with our bomb drop we were hit with a massive jolt. Flak took off the front of Les' turret and blew a hole in the lower left of the plane and out through the roof. We were lucky the tail didn't split off right then and there. For the rest of the mission, the chances would remain pretty high of it breaking off before we could make the massive emergency field at Dover. Les was stunned and had several bits of metal in his body. But he was alive. No one else was hurt.

"By the time we had reacquired our fighter cover, it was agreed that since we were still in the air we would try for Dover.

"We might or might not make it back, but there was one certainty -- Les was doomed. With the hydraulics out and the ball jammed, we couldn't raise the ball turret or spin it around to let him out. The clearance on a B-24 is so low that if we landed without the turret raised Les would be crushed. The pilot would have to kill him to save the rest of his crew. Even if we bailed out, Les would be trapped in the spiraling plane.

"I looked the situation over and offered a suggestion. The hole in the plane was large enough that I could get my smaller body out with a parachute on. It was right above the hole in Les' turret. The hole in the face of the turret was too small for him to get out with a parachute on, and a parachute would have had to be lowered to him from the outside anyway. Many ball turret gunners left their parachutes in the plane, as there was so little room in the ball.

"The only solution was for us to cannibalize Les' parachute and to use those lines to lower me through the hole in the plane to the face of the turret. I could then tie on to Les and pull him through. Once I was secure to Les, we could cut the lines and we could ride down together on the same chute.

"Everybody argued against the idea, even Les, who knew his fate. They told me that even if it worked we would likely be captured, and being a woman, my treatment would be worse. I argued that I had gone through tougher stunts in my barnstorming days and that anything the Germans did to me was nothing compared to the mental anguish we would all feel for the rest of our lives when we felt the bump of Les being crushed on landing.

"There was a long silence, except from Les, who kept arguing that it was okay and that he wouldn't hold it against anyone, and that we had all signed up willingly for this gig.

"'No, Miss Angel, don't do it!'

"All the while he was protesting I was unpacking Les' chute and cutting off the amount of line I would need, plus a little. I decided to break his harness off and rig it so it could attach to mine. The flight engineer came back to help the radio operator, the unwounded waist gunner, and the tail gunner lower me through the hole, and to ease me into position. They also had to make sure the jagged metal from the hole in the fuselage wouldn't cut the line.

"The flight engineer paused before we began to say a short prayer for us and everyone said 'Amen.'

"Using the intercom I told everyone including Les precisely what needed to be done and the order of each step. The pilot slowed the plane down as much as he dared, and I was lowered through the jagged hole above the turret.

"It took me a pass or two to grab the opening in the turret. When I did, I handed the harness to Les and he put it on. Les moved to a sitting position on the edge of the opening with his feet dangling in the air. I clipped his harness to mine and told him to hold on to me. As we were dangling in the air, I secured him more firmly to me, making sure I could still work the ripcord.

"I had it in mind to fall as far as we could to avoid detection, but not as far as my barnstorming days, as I figured it might take more time to slow down and break the fall of what would be more than double my body weight. Being a ball turret gunner helped, as Les had to be small to fit into the turret.

"I repeated my plan to Les so he would know precisely what to expect. There was no room for anything but scientific execution. I thought of Roscoe, 'Wild and passion could get a man killed.'

"Les still protested, saying that I should just cut him loose and have the boys pull me back into the plane. The two of us linked could not fit back into the hole. I said, 'Are you kidding? Those boys would kill to be tied chest-to-chest to a hot dame like me.' He blushed and smiled and told me I was right.

"I gave the signal to be pulled up so they could cut the lines short to keep them from tangling in the parachute. I remember thinking, 'I hope we can really do this.' I felt them cutting on the lines, then snap, the roar of the plane faded quickly to the peace of a freefall.

"As we dropped I could feel Les' heart beat like a jackhammer, or maybe that was mine. I had never been responsible for another life in a freefall, and I wasn't sure it the chute would work for both of us. One of the P-38s on our wing dove toward the coast to draw German attention away from our chute. We must have been within ten miles or less of the coast, as I could see the English Channel.

"We landed in a pasture and quickly headed for the tree line, where we buried the chute. It was a hard landing, but neither of us was hurt.

"At the last second I had thought to put a compass in my pocket, so we had the necessary direction of travel. About a mile along we heard voices, so we dropped. This was before the Normandy invasion, so any voices we heard were likely to be ones we didn't want to hear. A German patrol wandered past us no more than fifty feet away. We were lucky that time. When the voices subsided we decided to travel farther, as it was still bright daylight and we could make better time. Thirty minutes later we heard more voices. These were French, but I had learned enough French from Madame Furnet to realize that they had seen the parachute and were looking to turn us in for the German bounty.

"We decided to lie low until dark before we traveled farther. I took a bearing on the compass and tried to make out as many landmarks as possible. We huddled together for warmth, and shared part of a D-bar that was in Les' pocket. We were close enough to a stream to get water, but we weren't sure it was safe to drink, so we held off on our thirst for now.

"While we waited for the cover of night, I put into play my nurses training from the Bellanca days and picked through Les' wounds. Les was a bloody mess from cuts all over his body from the flak. As far as I could tell I was able to pick all of the flak fragments out of his body, but I knew he would be sore for several days and I was worried that the cuts might become infected before we could get proper medical aid.

"Sometime after 2300 we started for the coast. Dr. Jones had taught me well in the art of observation. While we descended, I had noticed two villages and a rail yard leading to the channel, with a large city right on the coast. I had it figured that we could use these as landmarks but that we should stay as far away as possible to avoid populations and possible detection. If we stayed to the right of the towns and the rail yard and went to the left of the city, we might be able to commandeer a boat and row back to England. Les' biggest fear was that we might wander into a mine field near the coastal defenses.

"We made it past the first village without incident, and also the second village, as our hours of opportunity were expiring. We had it figured that the prime time to travel was between midnight and 0400, when most people would be asleep.

"Early dawn was fast approaching, and we needed to put more distance between us and that second village. The terrain was much too open to hide in, so we settled for a culvert under what had to be a main road toward the rail yard.

"During the day we heard a little German military traffic and some local civilians in horse carts. I was afraid that the Germans might make a routine inspection of the culvert, but Les pointed out that it was overgrown with weeds that should have been trampled if it had been the subject of routine inspections. We ourselves had 'fluffed' the weeds that we had disturbed to enter the culvert.

"As one German truck passed, we heard something fall off. We dared not check it by day. I hoped we could find it at night and that it would be food. The D-Bar was gone, and we had had no water for more than a day. Two Frenchmen passed near the culvert, and I heard one tell the other that there was one checkpoint about a kilometer north, but that the road was clear from there to the rail yard. It turned out to be a good day for intelligence gathering. We had direction, we had obstacles, and hopefully we had some useful supplies.

"By 2100 it was dark enough to explore for the fallen crate. It took us about thirty minutes to find it in the dark. Les found a hole in the road and figured the crate would likely be close. He was right, and we hit the jackpot. It was a case of canned tomatoes. Not only did we have food, but we also had plenty of juice to drink. We used our p-38s to open one of the large cans, and had our fill. We decided to take one other can with us, but they were too large to carry more than one. We made sure the can we had opened was well hidden, as we didn't want the Germans to find a can that had been opened by a GI can opener.

"That night we traveled about half a kilometer along the road and decided to leave the road until we were sure we were past the checkpoint. It was moonless, and I couldn't read my compass. We soon became disoriented. Discouraged with our aimless stumbling about, we decided it was best to lie low along a creek bed and wait for enough light to reconfigure our course.

"That was before we heard the roar of a flight of British Lancaster's, obviously headed for the rail yard. The searchlights and the German 88s lit up the sky and gave us a bearing on the rail yard. We knew that in the confusion we had a chance to pass by without detection. We were about a kilometer off course, and on the left side of the yard and not the preferred right side, but it was a bearing. We had to thread a line between the rail yard and the flak gun crews, which we did without detection. We were now north of the rail yard, and only a few kilometers from the coast, but very far from our landmark city. We were off our plan now and would have to do our best from there.

"As the daylight began to appear, we found ourselves in completely open territory. We were doomed if we couldn't find a place to hide. We found several large haystacks in a French pasture and decided to hide in one of them. As we settled in, I had the distinct feeling that we were not alone. A mouse crawled across my face, and all I could do was let it pass. Still there was something else, something larger. I had the dread fear that a snake was hot on the trail of the mouse. I looked at Les and I could see that he too had detected something. We could feel the warmth of a human sized body, and we could hear his shallow breathing. He was obviously trying to hide from us as well. I reasoned that a German wouldn't be trying to hide in a haystack, so I whispered 'Yank.'

"A few seconds later a hand stirred the hay and almost stopped my heart. I saw two eyes appear and heard, 'Blimey, a Yank, a bird Yank!' Keeping our conversations low, we determined that there were three other Brits in the haystack from a Lancaster that had been shot down the night before. We were all afraid that the Germans were on the prowl for them and agreed to remain quiet until dark, when we could move on.

"Somewhere around 2130, we heard a noise outside of the haystack. My first thought was that this was it, the Germans had found us. But then I heard a French voice call for us to come out. We hesitated and suddenly a stick appeared within an inch of my nose. Then we heard 'Résistance,' and we all climbed out.

"Waiting for us were three men and two women dressed for some military night action. I spoke with them in French, and I found out that there were many mine fields ahead and that they could get us through and to a boat that we could row to England. As it turned out, there were many such boats that were let loose near the coast by the Allies for such operations and to replenish the ones the Germans destroyed or evadees had used.

"The travel was treacherous. We threaded around some mine fields and through others to avoid detection. At times we were as close as twenty yards from German troops. We made not a sound and held on to the belt of the person in front of us. I swear that one of the Brits got in an extra squeeze on me in the dark. I guess you get what you can in war. I noticed that Les couldn't take his eyes off one of the French girls.

"As we ran out of darkness, we could smell the channel. The French directed us to an underground bunker, where we would have to spend one more day. They gave us a little food and some much needed water, and we gave them what we could spare from our weapons and supplies.

"The French girl treated Les' wounds with iodine and found two more bits of flak that had worked their way to the surface of his skin. Les gave his French girl the St. Christopher medal his mother had given him. She smiled and kissed him.

"It was determined we would head to the beach around 0200, as the guards we would have to pass would likely be asleep then. I guess that was not uncommon before our invasion, as the Germans who were stationed in that area had grown lax with the soft duty. At the agreed time we were met by another Frenchman with the boat. We exchanged goodbyes and climbed in. It was clear from the start that none of us were sailors but we managed to get far enough out to avoid being sighted by the German coastal gunners.

"We fought the dreary, choppy English Channel for more than two days. I had lost my compass somewhere along the line, and the sun and stars were mostly hidden by the clouds. For one of those days we couldn't see France or England, and weren't sure of whether we were drifting toward safety or peril. For all we knew, we were headed for the open Atlantic. With little food in our stomachs, we were all seasick at one time or another.

"While we were still barely in sight of France, we spotted a German patrol boat. I thought we had had it, but they seemed to not see our small craft in the rough water. Later that day a lone Stuka spotted us and did a strafing run. Bill Brown, one of the British airmen, was hit. His injuries were minor, but a small hole was punched in the boat at the water line. Every time we dipped it took on water, so we decided to stuff an undershirt into the hole to stop the leak. They all looked at me and I gave them a dirty look."

"I'd take it back if they would look at me that way today," Great Aunt Alice mused.

"I guess I should tell about who we had in the boat. I mentioned Bill Brown. Bill had been the top mid turret gunner on the Lancaster. He had been a printer before the war. I was surprised to hear this. I had figured Bill to be a business or political leader. He was definitely officer material and was clearly the 'leader' of his surviving crewmates.

"Ed Govan was the tail gunner. He had been a poor orphan most of his young life, and he had joined the corps for a chance at a better or at least a different life. I liked Ed. There was an abiding goodness in the man. He had a strong desire to do the 'right thing,' and he was trying to educate himself on just what the 'right thing' was. I thought of the great contrast between Midge's Stanley, who had started with everything and squandered it all, and this young man, who started with nothing and was fighting to improve every aspect of his life.

"I was shocked to find that the third airman was related to someone I knew well. His name was John Bride. The others called him 'Sparks.' John was the navigator and also worked the radio-related operations of the Lancaster. He had gone to the tail of the plane to check on an intercom problem when a German 88 hit the Lancaster just behind his navigation station. The nose broke off and all of the men forward were lost. The men in the back were in the section with the wing and in a sense were still flying. The engines ran for a short while, and their part of the plane turned and carried them almost five miles from the burning nose section. They managed to jump about a mile from the haystacks and had been in them an hour or two before we arrived.

"I asked John if he was related to Harold Bride of Titanic fame, and he told me that he was indeed Harold's son. I told John of my personal contact with his father and how I had seen him on the overturned lifeboat.

'Well, blimey sakes. Father had always told us that story and we thought he was pulling our leg. Do you mean to tell me that he really did spend the night on an overturned boat in the mid-Atlantic?'

"I assured him that I had seen the sight with my own eyes. 'Well, blimey sakes.' That seemed to be John's pet phrase. I asked about my friend and told John how his father had later helped me regain the factory. He told me that Harold was now a salesman living in Scotland, and that he was declining some in general but was still the agreeable friend of my past.

"After our rescue Les and I were hastily returned to the United States due to our evadee status, but I traveled to Scotland to pay a call on Harold just after the war. He was glad to see me and I him. It was a pleasant visit, and I managed to meet his lovely wife Lucy and his teenage daughter Jeanette, who was a pretty lass, a sweet girl, and I'm sure a dreadful fear to her father as all teenage daughters are. His older daughter, named after her mother, was off on war restoration duty with the Salvation Army. I was so glad that I had returned to see Harold, as he died about ten years later. John remained in correspondence with me, as much as men do. I could always count on a nice Christmas card if nothing else.

"Meanwhile back in our little boat, we were beginning to think that we had indeed drifted into the Atlantic, or maybe in the North Sea, and were becoming seriously alarmed. Then one overcast afternoon we heard the sounds of approaching bombers along with the sound of bombs falling. Most of the bombs missed us by a few yards at best, some exploding and some not, and one fell no more than ten feet from our stern, shooting us forward. These were obviously a flight of bombers that had been forced to scrub their mission and were heading back to their respective bases. We followed the sound and knew which direction to 'sail,' if we lost airmen could use that word. We now knew where England was, and that we were still in the channel.

"Within an hour of that incident we spotted an inbound troopship from America. We yelled and screamed, but she was just out of range. As we screamed for our rescue, a periscope broke the water no more than a foot from our boat. The periscope's back was to us and she was completely unaware of our presence, but she was staring directly at the troop ship.

"On impulse Les grabbed the periscope, and on just as much of an impulse I pulled down my flight suit, ripped off my undershirt, and slammed it down over the scope. Then I tied the shirt off with . . . well, never mind what I secured it with. One can only imagine the surprise on that U-boat skipper's face when he suddenly went blind.

"An English corvette, obviously on the sonar trail of the U-boat, came at us full speed. We hooted and hollered and waved our arms, and I suddenly came to my senses and quickly pulled up my flight suit. Boy, was that embarrassing! It seemed like every sailor on board had a pair of binoculars.

"They hoisted me aboard first, and I thought they were going to forget the others. When we were securely aboard, the corvette filled the channel with depth charges and appeared to sink the U-boat. I've often wondered if some salver later found the wreck and wondered about the ladies unmentionable tied to the periscope.

"In the short time we were on board the corvette, I had several interesting offers. I found the passageways narrower than they appeared when passing a sailor. I didn't mind. I was willing to do my part for these lonely boys and the war effort, and most of the men remained polite. The captain was nice enough to take me through the ship, as I had never been aboard a corvette. I told him of how I had done this on Titanic and Carpathia, and he shared with me that he had been a seaman on Carpathia during the last war.

"On our landing in Portsmouth, we were immediately taken to S.H.A.F.E. headquarters for debriefing, where we were separated and interrogated for hours. On the surface it seemed like we were being treated like criminals, but we knew that the real reasons were to collect as much intelligence as possible about what we had seen in France and to make sure our friends in the Resistance weren't compromised.

"I didn't think I had much to tell, except maybe where they could find a few cans of good tomatoes. A major part of the exercise, of course, was to pound into our heads that we must never tell of our experience so that we would not be putting the Resistance into danger. We had to sign a document that swore us to secrecy for the rest of our lives, but I don't suppose it matters this many years after the war.

"One thing I did notice was that nobody questioned my being on the bomber in the first place. Obviously someone very high up had arranged my being on that plane, and no one wanted to press the point.

"Just before I was released, I was asked to follow a stern-faced lieutenant and was told not to note or tell about anything I might see along the way. I was taken to a large room and told to wait. The lieutenant left the room, and a few minutes later General Eisenhower surprised the heck out of me by walking in and sitting next to me on the couch.

"General Eisenhower told me that he had heard about how I had rescued Les and told me that he wished he could give me a medal for my heroic actions, but under the unusual circumstances of my 'assignment' it would be too difficult. I told him that I understood, and that meeting him was better than any medal I could receive.

"He put aside that adulation with some comment about just being an ordinary fellow from Kansas. I asked him where and he said 'Abilene.' I told him that we had done an air show in Abilene, and he lit up. 'I remember, something flying circus. My brother Edgar wanted so badly to go up for a flight, but Dad wouldn't let him. So you are that Angel girl?' I told him that I was one and the same. The fact that he remembered me was quite a compliment. Then he gave me an even better one when he told me that he wished he could have me as one of his fighter pilots. I told him I'd like that better than anything, but he just shook his head and said, 'Sorry, lieutenant, but you're headed home.'

"Before we parted I asked Ike, 'Soldier boy, is there anything you want me to take back to your mom?' Ike turned back to me with a smile and said, 'Yes, there is,' and he gave me a big hug. I said, 'I sure will,' and I kissed him on the cheek, 'That will be from your mom."

"I'll bet you've never kissed a five star general have you Great Nephew?"

"Next I was taken to a room where I rejoined the other fellows so we could say our goodbyes. They were nice enough to let Les and me visit with the crew, who were brought into S.H.A.F.E. for security where our conversation could be monitored by some very serious looking officers who stayed with us in the room.

"The pilot had managed to get the plane back to the emergency field at Dover, but the structurally weakened bomber broke apart on landing. The already injured waist gunner was killed, and the tail gunner was badly injured but was expected to recover. The others had a few bumps and bruises. Despite their ordeal they had flown two missions since the crash. One of those was in the plane where I had struck that pose for the nose art.

"An hour later we were in a C-47 headed home by way of Greenland. When we arrived at Greenland, I stopped in at the Ops shack to look up Doc Scea and Childers. The first guy I saw when I walked in was the sergeant who had given me so much trouble at the English air base. He was now a private and didn't seem at all pleased to see me.

"Les and I parted company in New York. After the war Les wrote to tell me that he was going back to look up his French girl. Several months later he dropped me a sad note to say that she had been killed in the war. I never heard from him again.

"I was discharged, but I wasn't ready to settle down, so I did some traveling. While I was still in New York I visited with Ethel and Richard for a week, and then I took the train to Florida. I had to use the train for a while, as aviation gas was still severely rationed.

"In Florida I filled a jar with Cocoa Beach sand, and then I shipped it with a crate of oranges and a large bottle of suntan lotion to Childers. A few months later I received a note that said simply, 'Thanks, Miss Angel. Childers.'

"In October I did rev up the Spartan and flew to Abilene to deliver Ike's hug to his mother. We had a nice visit. Before I left I asked her if she wanted to go for a flight over Abilene. At first she hesitated, and then she said, 'Well, why not?' She got a real kick out of seeing her home from the air, but it was a bigger thrill for her to visit with someone who had talked with her boy.

"This had been a war that had truly encompassed almost the entire world. Everyone was either in service, or knew somebody who was. Those who did not fight rationed their lives, worked in the factories, bought war stamps and bonds, saved scrap, and hung their service stars in their windows. Many mothers lost their sons, and thousands of young brides became widows.

"As I said earlier, George was killed at Pearl Harbor. Eileen's Bob was shot down and was a P.O.W. for two years. He was injured when his B-17 was hit and walked with a pronounced limp the rest of his life. Bud Fox was killed on Peleliu.

"Frenchy Miller flew C-46 cargo flights over the Hump in Burma. One day his plane disappeared over Aluminum Alley, and he was never heard from again.

"My old friend Gusty was the strange case. He flew cargo in the same Air Transport Squadron with Frenchy. He made it all the way through the war without a scratch. Then he was shot dead a month after he came home when he walked in on some kid who was robbing the corner drugstore.

"Tommy Jr. was like so many soldiers. Physically his wounds had healed completely, but mentally he was a mess. On the surface he appeared a whole man, but he was unnaturally quiet now. There were times when he would snap and lash out, not so much in public, but in the private times when he could no longer keep up the pretense. One night he nearly killed his mother before his father could pull him off and bring him back to reality.

"Tommy and his high school sweetheart Betty got back together, and she helped him a great deal. She was patient with him and somewhat understood his demons, if not what he was seeing when they took possession of his soul.

"For the first two years of their marriage I would see Betty now and then with a nasty bruise. He wasn't intentionally mean, and he wouldn't have laid a finger on Betty if in his right mind. Tommy just had his spells like Roscoe's boys. In fact, Tommy Jr. reminded me a lot of Felix in his moods and the expression in his eyes.

"Love and time, and some regular sessions at the American Legion hall on John Street, brought Tommy back to a more normal state. Still Betty could never sneak up behind him or drop a pan. Tommy hated fireworks.

"Every December 23rd he traveled to Arlington Cemetery. He always traveled there alone. Whose grave he visited will always be a mystery, but there was something he saw 'over there' that will never leave his mind."

Chapter 27
Ethel

The house was finished, and it was now too late in the year to start the barn. I told Great Aunt Alice that I thought I should be moving on. I had imposed too long on her hospitality.

She would have none of my self-imposed exile and insisted that she needed help with a "higher calling." She was passing into her later eighties and could no longer comfortably do the heavy maintenance on her beloved airplanes. Great Aunt Alice wanted me to become her aircraft mechanic. I pointed out to her that I had just barely learned how to hold a paint brush and scraper. The thought of working on an engine was far beyond my calling.

"You like to diagram sentences, don't you?" she asked. I told her that it was my favorite pastime and that I had once diagramed the whole *Martyrdom of the Saint Shushanik*.

"That's nice, Great Nephew. I'm proud of you."

From the tone of her voice, I don't think she was really that impressed. Well, anyway she went on to explain that an aircraft engine is like a sentence diagram. It has the propeller shaft and then the main parts that are related to the propeller shaft, and all of the sub-parts of each major component.

She had an old Pratt & Whitney in the barn. We took it apart and laid it on the shop floor of the barn. With Great Aunt Alice's instruction, I began to diagram each part and its relationship to its sub-parts, as well as the preventative maintenance and the tools and fluids related to each part. Looking at it that way made splendid sense to me. We drove to Yoder's Party Store, where we purchased one of those rolls of paper one uses to cover tables at a church pitch-in. I transcribed my notes onto the roll and hung it on one wall of the barn. By the time we were finished, I had a sentence diagram of an entire Curtis Jenny JN-4 to which I could refer for any maintenance I needed to perform on the plane.

In time, I could maintain the Jenny almost as well as Great Aunt Alice could. The only task that I did poorly was the doping of the wings and fuselage. This didn't have to be done very often, but it had been several years and Great Aunt Alice thought it would be a good idea to replace the old fabric and apply fresh doping and paint. We decided to hire one of the Yoder boys, who had a flair for such things. The end result was a Curtis Jenny JN-4 that was practically just off the production line. She was beautiful -- the most splendid "man" thing I had ever done.

We did this through the fall and winter months, and we finished in mid-spring. It was cold in that old barn, so we had to heat it up first with a salamander. I was always leery of setting fire to the old wood and the solvents in the workshop, but we never had any trouble and were cautious to shut it off while we were working. That being the case, we had to work in short bursts on the really cold days, so that left us with more time for Great Aunt Alice's stories.

She told me that there was only one major piece of her story that we hadn't recorded, or that I didn't already know from my own personal knowledge of her later years. That piece was her time with Ethel Roosevelt Derby. This is a compilation of those last tellings of her story.

"Ethel and I were made for each other. From the time I met her, I could see in Ethel the feelings and changes that I would soon see in my own life. In some ways I gave her a chance to stay close to the triumphs of her life as she watched me mark those same milestones in my life.

"I did so admire her achievements in her service and her family life. How many Presidents' daughters would put themselves in the mud and danger of a field hospital in war? How many 'blue bloods' would press for civil rights reform in their own neighborhoods?

"Our exchange of letters was a great sounding board as I was growing. Her adventures in the war gave me inspiration, and my exploits probably gave her a heart condition.

"Those years in the orphanage when we were separated from corresponding with each other were terribly traumatic for both of us. Ethel was the only hope I had for escaping my situation. For two years I dreamed of the day I could slip a letter to her, and she would come to rescue me, but I was foiled at every attempt and beaten for my 'sins.' She in turn was certain that I had perished on Titanic. My last letter to her had been composed at Aunt Molly's home and was sent from Queenstown on the day we boarded the great ship.

"In some ways we were starkly similar. We were both adventuresome women pioneers. We both married amazingly wonderful husbands. We both had dynamic fathers, and loving beautiful mothers. We were both well heeled with many influential friends. We were both great looking babes well into our later years."

Great Aunt Alice gave me a wink. I winked back and said, "You still are."

"Likewise, our lives were starkly different. Roscoe and I were married not quite five years when I lost him. Richard and Ethel managed to get in fifty years before he died. Ethel had the blessings and heartaches of three wonderful children. I would never hold one of my own or feel it stir in my womb, nor would I see any daughters of mine married or suffer the awful task of burying an eight-year-old son.

"Ours was a relationship of correspondence. We saw each other rarely, but we wrote once a week if we could for most of our time 'together.' Ethel had a way of giving me sisterly advice without making it sound like a lecture. A good example would be my feelings for Jean Louis during our winter in Southern France. I would write of how he made me tingle and how I wished he would kiss me. She would write of her Richard, whom she was seeing at the time. She would tell me of why he was so wonderful and how she was conserving her affections for the day when they might be wed. Then she would pour them upon Richard to make their marriage wonderful. 'A girl has only so many "special kisses,"' she would write. This of course led me to save my 'special' affections lest I waste them.

"Her letters gave me the taste of the domestic life I was missing. She would write of baby teeth and first words, school work and bouquets of dandelions, the considerate things her husband had done, and laments about male bathroom etiquette.

"I would write of the boys and barnstorming, Rowe and movie stars, Dr. Jones and battles in Haiti, men who didn't think that women should fly, and men who found out the hard way that we could.

"I couldn't tell her right away about my World War II escape from France, but I did share it with her during one of our private walks some thirty years later. By then all of the officers who swore us to secrecy were likely dead, and it would do our rescuers no harm. I was her adventuress. She was my hearth and home.

"Ethel and Richard celebrated their golden wedding anniversary on April 4, 1963. On July 21st of that same year Richard died. I went to her in August and stayed till the end of September. It was the longest time we had spent together. We talked of old times. We hugged and cried. She gave passionate lectures on civil rights and how we must do what we can to right the wrongs of the past.

"We stayed up late like girls at a slumber party and slept in just as late. She gave me a beautiful society party to introduce me to her Oyster Bay friends. I had never dressed so formally. Ethel told me that I looked ravishing. I told her she was right -- but not since 1935.

"Her grandson Billy took us sailing one afternoon. Often we would relax in the sun room after lunch. Invariably one of us would drift off to sleep, but we were both older by then and understood the need. The one who was awake said nothing about it later. We would instead take advantage of the situation and fall asleep in our own chair.

"I enjoyed most the early morning walks Ethel and I would take. We would drink in the quiet of the newborn day and the beauty around us. It was a natural path for us to walk to the graves of Richard, their son, her beautiful mother Edith, who passed in 1948, and of course the great man himself. For some reason I had never told Ethel of the first time I met her father as he and my father burst into our home in Saugerties. She laughed and said, 'That's father all right.' Ethel laid her head on my shoulder without saying a word. I held her and said that I missed him too.

"Ethel told me that she had tried to find my mother's grave. Her people had narrowed it to half-a-dozen possibilities, but they were unmarked, and there was no way to confirm the right plot. I thanked her for trying and thought of the contrast. Here before us lay her father's remains. My father was somewhere in the cold Atlantic near a ship that would probably never be found. Ethel could visit her mother's grave. I would never be able to decorate my mother's pauper's plot. The dirt was still freshly mounded on Richard's grave, but long after it blended with the cemetery it would still be there and clearly marked for Ethel and all who knew Richard.

"The site of my Roscoe's ashes was bulldozed along with the two markers during the war. His 'grave,' and the bluebonnets that had soaked up the blood of Slim, were under miles of concrete. The terrain was now unrecognizable. Of all of the graves of my loved ones, there remain Rowe's, Carl's, Midge's, and Kinsey's.

"Kinsey passed in 1954. Mr. Vought had a heart attack while shoveling snow the previous winter and either froze to death, or died from the heart attack. The coroner wasn't sure of which. Kinsey tried her best to get on with life, but her heart just wasn't in it. No matter how hard she tried to be cranky, she just couldn't 'crank.' She died a sad and kindly old woman, which must have galled her to no end. We buried her in Yonkers next to her husband, who had died around 1907 from 'consumption.' Nobody but Kinsey knew for sure what he had consumed, and that may be why she had been so hard on Stanley.

"Midge died in 1960, still working at the orphanage. All during her funeral I just looked at the stained glass windows and wept. The church was filled with people of all races and all walks of life. There were firemen, mothers, businessmen, soldiers, nurses, teachers, policemen, coaches, factory workers, professors, nuns, lawyers, and priests, all of whom had been orphans under Midge's care. The funeral was led by Cardinal Spellman, the same one who had officiated at Bishop Collier's funeral. It was the only time that I know of that a Cardinal had led a funeral mass for a nun.

"I was torn about where to bury Midge. As you can imagine, it was a heartbreaking time for me, and my senses were numb. I knew how much she had loved Carl, and it seemed logical to bury her next to him. I also knew how much she loved 'her children.' With Cardinal Spellman's help I decided to build a grotto at the orphanage, which included a tomb for Midge that the children were encouraged climb and play on. It featured a statue of 'Mother Midge' sitting on the head of the slab, with an understanding smile on her face and arms held out to hug. The grave itself was a flat slab with three terraced steps that came up from the slab on the four sides like an amphitheatre. The children were encouraged to play on her grave, and the nuns would often hold classes or read stories to the children gathered on the terrace steps. The children would come to her for a little one-on-one time to show her some music they had mastered or the latest dance recital routine, or how they had learned their alphabet. Each visit would be very personal with greetings and hugs as if she were still alive. One could usually find wildflowers on her statue, and any child who needed some special love was welcome to curl up in her lap.

"I always brought flowers on the date that she had come to take me home from the orphanage, and a special mass was said. It was the morning children's mass. The priest would ask me to tell the story of that day when Midge first became a mother, which I always did, but never without stopping several times for tears.

"In time those who knew Midge moved on, and the special mass was forgotten. Still children placed flowers on the grave and crawled up in her arms, but only because of a tradition whose origins were by then unknown.

"On one of my visits I arrived to see a man in his fifties with a grown daughter. He was lying in the arms of the statue and crying like a baby. His daughter must have thought him mad, but I understood the why, if not the details."

Great Aunt Alice walked over to the sofa and climbed into my arms and I held her like a parent would a small child. She continued with her story as she remained in my hug.

"Your poor mother died in 1975, leaving me with you, my last relative, and Ethel my only remaining true friend.

"I called Ethel just to chat on December 9th in 1977. I had been worried for her, as she had been in poor health for several weeks. For those last several days she spoke of how Richard needed this or that, and of some impending trip they had planned. Not wanting to make her think she had gone into dementia, I went along with her and asked how Richard was. Ethel said that Richard was doing fine, and that he looked so handsome in his new white suit. She told me that Roscoe had come to visit and was looking forward to seeing me again. In every other aspect of her conversation she seemed quite lucid. I believe that she was.

"Then Ethel said to me in the most sincere tone, 'I love you, Alice. I love you so very much. Please call me tomorrow, if you can.' I promised her that I would call between 11:00 and noon.

"That night I had the oddest dream. I was swept into a strange place, as if by a strong current or wind. When I 'landed' I didn't recognize the place at all, but I began to see people I had known. I saw George in his Navy whites. I saw Frenchy. I saw Carl and Mr. Vought. I saw Bishop Collier, Kinsey, Gusty, and Will and Betty Rogers. I saw Slim, Felix, Midge, and my mother, and my father, and Roscoe. I ran to them as hard as I could, but I could get no closer.

"Suddenly they disappeared in a great light that overpowered everything. In the center of the light I saw Flood, for just a moment, and then he vanished behind a hill, leaving behind a disappearing glow.

"A spirit with a woman's voice swept upon me and she took hold of me and we danced two turns. Then she slipped away from me as if being pulled by the wind, while the same wind held me back.

"The next morning I called Ethel. Her daughter Sarah answered. When she understood who I was, she broke down 'Oh, Mrs. Burke, mama's dead.'"

"She was my last and best friend, Great Nephew. All of them are gone, and I've cheated death all of these years. I should have died in my mother's fragile womb. I should have died when the raft broke apart in the river, or when the riptide carried Günter out to sea, or when Titanic took my father and my mother. I should have died with my husband. I do so wish I had died with Roscoe. Living too long is a curse, Great Nephew. It steals from you everything."

Great Aunt Alice shook and cried as I had never seen her. The heartaches of her entire life seemed to pour out of her at once till she was utterly spent. In a weak voice she said "I love you, Great Nephew. I have nothing left to tell." Then she closed her eyes and fought no more.

I kissed Great Aunt Alice and laid her down on the sofa. Her body was limp, heavy, and cold. I covered her with two blankets. She uttered not a sound of thanks or protest.

All night long I sat in the chair across from her and watched for the slightest movement of limb or breath. I was terribly afraid of something dreadful and unknown. Something told me to keep watch, keep watch, keep watch, keep watch, but my eyes grew heavy with the night.

Chapter 28
The Enchanted Amish

I am now much older than what Great Aunt Alice was when I took the summer job. Years have passed, and I have experienced life as I never dreamed. My life cannot be compared to hers in adventure, but I have ventured out beyond the bounds of pre-Georgian literature.

Thanks to Great Aunt Alice I developed a career in restoring ancient aircraft. I've met the rich and famous from around the world, many of whom inherited these planes from their fathers or mothers, who in turn had known Great Aunt Alice and through her learned of our operation. Some have brought me pictures of Great Aunt Alice with their parents and their plane. Great Aunt Alice's Spartan "Ethel" can be seen in the background of some of the photos.

I still have the Jenny and have had several lucrative offers for it, but I can't bring myself to let her go.

When I turned ninety I gave up my full interest in the operation. The Yoder "boy" who first helped me dope the planes is now in his late seventies and runs the business with his grandson. The world headquarters for the company is still located in my barn. This is pleasant to me as it allows me to look in on their progress, and it gives me some company on a regular basis.

I still paint the house and barn every three or four years, at least as far as I can reach. I have an excuse now, as I was in a car-train accident last winter.

I slid on the ice near Yoder's crossing and found myself hung up on the tracks as an Amtrak freight train was barreling down on the crossing. I ran the wheels every which way, but the ice gave me no traction at all. I might have been there all day if that train hadn't pushed me off that spot.

I was driving my old 2012 CGM Solar hybrid, or "the egg" as we called it back then. I remember two things about the accident. I recall thinking that I was glad I wasn't driving Great Aunt Alice's old '33 Flatbed Ford, and I was impressed at how large the numbers are on a locomotive when it gets that close.

The next thing I knew, I was in Chicago's St. Richard's Medical Center with two cuts through my spinal cord. Thank God for modern medicine and the skillful care of Dr. Luksus. In my younger days such an injury would have meant total paralysis. Today it's almost an outpatient operation. I still have some numbness in my left index finger and my left knee, but I'm sure they will perfect the procedure some day.

The car was a total wreck. They found it a mile down the track, and smashed to pieces with me trapped in it like a bent hotdog in a bun. I suppose it's just as well that the car was a total loss. Nobody drives hybrids these days, as they take too much carbon out of the atmosphere.

My granddaughter came to stay with me for a few weeks while I recovered from the accident. She's the one we call Little Angel. She looks so much like her grandmother, my mother, and has none of my phobias. She also likes to fly like her Great-Great Aunt Alice. I think the only reason she comes to visit is to take Great Aunt Alice's JN-4 for a spin. Little Angel has learned to fly a pretty good inside loop, and she loves to buzz the Rosenberg cows.

I suppose I should explain the granddaughter connection. In the years that followed my "summer job," I remained a lonesome George. It was not uncommon to walk into the kitchen in the morning and find a note from Great Aunt Alice that said something to the effect of, "I'm flying to Stockholm -- I'll send a postcard as soon as I can," and sure enough a few days later the card would arrive with a "wish you were here" note.

Great Aunt Alice lived well past the century mark and continued to fly until the day she died. On her hundredth birthday she got into some trouble when she mentioned to the press that she was still flying.

A few days later some bureaucrat from the F.A.A. came to the farm to take away her license, as she was far too old for the regulations. With help from Senator Pence's office, a test was arranged to assess whether she still had the skills required to fly. On hand for the test was a corps of newsmen from around the world, about a thousand spectators, several groups of age discrimination protesters, and officials from various senior associations, the American Legion, the V.F.W., and the Confederate Air Force.

Senator Pence was there as well. He had flown with Great Aunt Alice on a few campaign sweeps, and he wasn't about to let some bureaucrat force her out of something she lived for, and was still capable of continuing.

The protesting bureaucrat was assigned to conduct the test. I knew the man was in trouble when she chose her JN-4 for the challenge. Great Aunt Alice taxied to the end of the runway and said, "Fasten your seatbelt!" Thirty minutes later there was a Kelly green grass stain smudge on the top of the tail, and an alabaster white F.A.A. official who had to be carried from the plane. Rumor had it that he never flew again.

In addition it was the last great barnstorming demonstration the world will ever see. People who were children then still write to me and I can expect several visitors a year to drop in to see her Jenny that she had used for the show. It's fun to hear them tell their children wide-eyed tales of that day as they point to the JN-4 and to Great Aunt Alice's picture which I keep next to the plane when it is on display.

After her triumph over old age and the government, Great Aunt Alice went on to visit every country and continent that she could, and she even flew to Antarctica and landed on skis, just to say that she had.

The reason for part of her travels was for her wanderlust, and some of the rest was to visit with old friends at air shows and mingle with the younger pilots who thought she and her Spartan were really something. It would not be a stretch to say that she had groupies. Much of her travel contacts eventually led to the clientele for my aircraft restoration business.

She was known universally as "Angel" in about every native language, except for the Russian pilots, who called her "Сумасшедшая Птица," which translates into something like "Crazy Bird." I won't go into details, but the Russian nickname has something to do with a Moscow bureaucrat and an open hangar.

While it was fun to share in Great Aunt Alice's adventures, it was also kind of sad to realize that I had nothing to compare. The restoration business had not yet taken off, and I was still just an excruciatingly socially available unemployed professor of pre-Georgian literature. I was almost thirty-five and had never dated more than once in my entire life, and that one experience ended shortly after we ordered our food. The girl excused herself to go to the ladies room, but she proved to be no lady. I didn't even like the food she had ordered.

I don't mean to sound like a complainer. I had a good life. It was peaceful on the farm. The flora and fauna, the change of the seasons, the quiet neighbors -- everything was good about the place. It was a safe place for a literary nerd to exist.

In time the people of the area started to think of me less as a stranger and more an expected part of the landscape. Some of them became quite friendly. When I went to town I would meet someone and say, "Hello," and some of them would respond with things like, "Hello."

I once had a woman walk up to me and ask if I was married. I said, "No." She said, "I didn't think so," and I never heard from her again.

My favorite haunt to visit was the library. I read every book in the place and was on the waiting list for anything that came in. I even read the phone book, which was pretty light reading in a county that was 90% Amish. Sometimes I would read the books right there in the Yoder room. Other times I would take a stack home and read till all hours.

Life was good in Bauerhoff, but as with all things it too had to change. In the years that followed the summer job, Bauerhoff added a chain hardware store that had a paint section with most of the heathen colors. It also featured tools that required electricity. Only a few years before, a place like that couldn't have opened its doors in Freeland County, but our little world had moved on.

We had been "discovered," and the county was beginning to fill with foreign names like Smith and Jones, Brown and McAllister. Saturdays were crowded with tourists seeking to assuage their hectic corporate lives with what they thought was some kind of Amish tonic.

With the bulk purchasing powers of the chain stores, Yoder's Hardware was nudged out of business. Actually Mr. Yoder didn't mind that much. He was getting old and was tired of the fast pace of city life.

Ten years after the summer job, I found myself sitting in Yoder's Amish Kettle Restaurant. The name had been changed to the less inviting moniker "Restaurant" to allow the locals an inconspicuous place to eat in peace, while the weekend farmers and the tourists gorged themselves in the chain restaurants at the edge of town.

Most of the stores that began with "Yoder" had been replaced with chain stores or something with the name "Amish" something. My favorite was "The Enchanted Amish." I'm still trying to figure out what might "enchant" an Amish.

Yes sir, the "Restaurant," or Yoder's as the locals quietly called it, as if it were some secret hiding place, was the only true respite in town. It was now run by a fellow we knew only as "Bill." It didn't seem useful to learn the rest of his name.

The Enchanted Amish

Although a foreigner, Bill understood the value of the place, and he tried to keep it as true as possible. The buns were no longer fresh baked on site, but the breaded tenderloins remained pretty much the same. The milk for the milkshakes still came from Yoder's Dairy, but it had been taken over by some conglomerate called "Midwest Prairie Dairy."

The blessing of the place was that there were still only five tables, and anyone walking in would sit where there was a seat, even if the table was occupied. Since most of the patrons were either old friends or relatives, this made perfect social sense. As a rule I was left to sit by myself as long as there was any room at the other tables. After all I was still a foreigner myself, and my Great Aunt had not been good for the cows. The locals were not intolerant and would speak to me some, but they were also not unnecessarily overly tolerant.

As a rule I liked the Amish, especially the Yoder family, but I would never be one of them. I could honestly say, but not proudly, that there was no one else like me in the entire county. I had grown to actually like myself, and I was proud of the things I had learned and accomplished under Great Aunt Alice's care. Still my social life was a deep and lonely chasm that I longed to fill.

Into this void walked the fulfillment of my dreams. It was August, my favorite month. It's always too hot to do anything in Indiana on most August days, so I managed to do more play than work in the month of August. I decided to drive the Ford to Yoder's for lunch. As I sat there waiting my turn to be served -- she walked in. She was standing at the counter waiting to be seated, not knowing the local custom.

She was medium height, and on the thin side. Her hips were a little broad, but her chest was almost as flat as a pre-teen's. She had mousy brown hair just to her white Peter Pan collar, and clear plastic glasses with those white and silver speckles. Her eyes were . . . well she had two. The dress she wore was plain and straight, and the hemline appeared to be deciding whether it wanted to be shorter or longer. She carried on her shoulder a small white purse, and in her right hand she had a business suitcase big enough to carry an anvil. There was a delicate trail of sweat creeping at a sultry pace down her temple.

She was the most beautiful woman I had ever seen.

I walked up to her and, explaining the local custom, invited her to my table. I offered to carry her case, letting her walk in front of me so I could watch her walk -- and so she could not see me grimace in pain as I tried to scoot the beastly sample case behind her.

She sat across from me and told me her name was Marion, AND that she was an encyclopedia salesman, AND that nobody seemed to want sets of encyclopedias anymore, AND that she had been a school librarian before the cutbacks, AND that her feet really hurt, AND that she didn't know what to order in this place.

Her voice was as sweet as a sousaphone. I've always loved the sousaphone.

I could have listened to her all day. I told her how much I loved encyclopedias, and as her eyes met mine -- I made my move.

"Have you ever had a tenderloin as big as a plate?"